FRIENDZONED

Friendzoned

RACHEL BLAUFELD

HeartEyes
Press

This book was inspired by the True North Series written by Sarina Bowen. It is an original work that is published by Heart Eyes Press LLC.

This book is dedicated to all the hard-working baristas out there, making sure we reach our daily caffeine intake, preparing skinny-one-pump-this and two-pump-that espresso drinks with smiles on their faces. Thank you.

MURPHY

"Excuse me, but I wanted an iced nonfat latte with one sweetener. This is . . . well, it's not that. It's sweeter than anything I've ever had. Either way, this isn't what I ordered and I'm in a hurry. . . so, here."

Taking a deep breath, I tried to suppress an eye roll as a twenty-something, fairly skinny, long-lashed woman waved the coffee I'd just prepared for her in my face. It was no surprise to see she was wearing a pair of cutoff jean shorts and cutesy hiking boots, her curled brown hair splayed perfectly over the collar of her red-and-navy flannel shirt. It was the exact outfit I could imagine myself wearing if I were on the other side of the counter, living my best life in Vermont rather than slinging coffees for tips.

At that moment, I didn't have time to wonder about what-ifs as she shouted at me over the noise of the steamer.

Blowing a frizzy strand of my own tangled red hair out of my eye, I said evenly, "That's what I made. An iced latte with sweetener. Skinny, of course."

Needing to fill the next order, I grabbed the next mug on the counter—a reusable dark blue Yeti, heavy as a brick, one of those fancy yet crunchy stainless-steel ones.

No surprise. We're in Vermont, Murphy. A sticker marked AMERI-

CANO, EXTRA HOT was stuck to its side, and I rolled my eyes for the second time in mere seconds. *What's wrong with one of our paper cups if you recycle it later?*

"No, this has two sweeteners," Little Miss Perfect Nature Lover said, narrowing her eyes. "I can tell the difference. By the way, no need to roll your eyes at me."

Isn't everyone in Vermont supposed to be nice?

"That's not what I meant. I mean, I'm not," I said as my coworker Roderick hurried behind me, carrying a tray of fresh-baked scones for the pastry display case.

Resisting the urge to snatch a sugary calorie-laden pastry for myself, I tried to catch my breath. Lowering my voice to a whisper, I said, "What I mean is . . . the eye rolling wasn't for you." Unable to calm my nerves, I fluttered my hand in front of my face. It was an odd thing to do, and I had no clue why I did it. With Roderick finally gone, I said, "I was thinking about something I had to do later. Here, give me your drink."

I tried to cover my tracks, hoping that one of my bosses, Zara Rossi, was too busy at the register to hear what was going on. I liked Zara, and I didn't want to jeopardize this job or her good feelings toward me. She and her business partner, Audrey Shipley, had taken a chance on hiring me with no barista experience.

Little Miss Perfect raised a brow at me. "Well, maybe a little less energy on what you have to do later and more focusing on my drink. How about that?"

Who was this chick? And where did she think she was? Back in Manhattan, I'd expect this type of behavior—sadly, from my old friends or perhaps even myself—but this was the friendly Upper Valley of Vermont.

Reaching across the counter with my coffee-stained hand, I said, "I'll remake it."

Back when I'd visited the Busy Bean as a customer, I never acted this way. I'd been taught to always smile like a pretty socialite when meeting new people, to be polite and demure like a woman should be. Most importantly, I was expected to never, ever let my emotions get the best of me. Even when my world had been falling apart, I'd flashed my pearly whites and forged ahead, despite everyone's best efforts to disparage me.

After a while, the effort to keep up the facade was too much—even for me.

The thing is, I'd been a little sassy in my former life, but I would have never handed the cup over like this girl did. I would have complained to the manager before buying myself a new drink, but the money didn't used to mean much to me.

Taking the plastic cup from Little Miss Perfect Nature Lover, who obviously wasn't concerned with the environment like the Yeti drinker downstream, I blew the same errant out-of-control strand of hair out of my face. I'd thought my two weeks of training with Kirk were hard, but manning the coffee bar by myself was a lot harder than I'd imagined. In the meantime, he was probably having a grand time in Costa Rica, while I was sweating it out in front of the mammoth espresso machine.

Without a lot of time to dwell on it, I was mentally going through the steps to make an iced nonfat latte when Zara called my name from across the counter.

"Murphy? Do you have the Americano? We have a doc who needs to get back to patients. I don't mean to rush you, but hurry this one order." Her dark hair in a glossy ponytail, tamed and in way more control than my own, drew my attention. I really needed to start putting myself together better for this job.

Looking up for a second, I took in the scene at the Bean. For four o'clock in the afternoon, it was packed. All the tables were filled with smiling, happy-go-lucky Vermonters and tourists. If this were New York, orders would have been shouted over noisy patrons barking for someone or anyone to hurry up. And no doctor would grab coffee on their own in the city. Here in idyllic Colebury, there was a short line at the register, and a guy walking toward the end of the bar.

"Shit." I snatched my hand away from the steamer, blinking

back tears to see a small blister forming. Looking up again, I checked to make sure I wasn't seeing things.

Nope.

It wasn't just any guy. Standing before me was Ben Rooney, although a more filled-out (if that were possible), and obviously more mature and grown-up version of the Ben I knew. It had been close to—I counted in my head—fourteen years since I saw him last, but I'd recognize him anywhere. His jet-black hair was still a wild mess, but the dusty scruff along his jaw and the tiniest crow's feet at the corners of his eyes were new and way, way sexy.

Still, I'd know the guy I'd crushed on for four years anywhere. I'd only recently realized that he'd liked me too back then, but it wouldn't have mattered. My parents would have never allowed it.

Who am I kidding? I didn't allow it either.

Anyway, I swooned over the small creases that appeared as Ben smiled back at Little Miss Perfect.

Quickly pouring nonfat milk over the contents of a yellow packet sprinkled at the bottom of a new plastic cup full of ice, I poured in two espresso shots and pushed the drink across the counter. "Here you go. A brand-spanking-new iced latte."

"Well, the first one wasn't what I wanted, so you can't say that." She cocked her head to the side, mocking me.

I'd never felt smaller, and somewhere deep in my gut, hoped I'd never made anyone feel that way. But I couldn't bother to argue with her because now I'd gone and foolishly made eye contact with Ben.

The last time I saw him was after a graduation party. It had been one of those fancy catered events with purple-and-gold tablecloths representing our school colors, and hired help in tuxedos running to and fro. Exactly the type of party that always sent up Ben's hackles. He used to moan and groan about having to attend them when we studied in my room, sitting on the floor with our thighs almost touching and our backs against the side of my bed. I'd kept my friendship with Ben hidden behind closed doors because he wasn't part of my family's social circle, and I was never quite sure whether he minded or not.

At that final party, I was eighteen and he was nineteen, both of us bright-eyed about the future in front of us. Ben had been ready to leave for Harvard to play football, and I hadn't kept up with where he went from there. Truthfully, it later became clear to me what a bitch I'd been, hiding our friendship. He was the only real person I knew back then. As much as it pained me to think of how selfish I'd been when it came to Ben Rooney, that was the old me, and now I was trying to be different.

I am different.

Being thirty-two years old was a world apart from being eighteen, and I was desperately trying to be nicer, kinder, softer. Basically, more in touch with the real world around me rather than the fake high-society world I'd been raised in.

As Ben stood in front of me wearing rumpled scrubs, looking like he needed a few hours of sleep (yet still amazing), I swallowed a bitter cocktail of regret at how my life was currently in the toilet. Ben and I were nothing but missed connections. I hadn't followed his career, and we weren't Facebook friends like the rest of the phonies I knew from prep school. But it was good to see he'd obviously shed his poor-boy image.

Then there was me, the fallen socialite. I stood behind the counter, gaping at him like a fish, wearing a pinstriped apron over my white Busy Bean T-shirt, my hair pulled up in a bad excuse for a ponytail. And to top it all off, I was pretty sure my eye makeup was smeared like crazy.

"Murphy?" His brow furrowed as he said my name with confusion, and perhaps a touch of disdain.

Forcing my mind out of its current tailspin, I looked up. "Hi," I said, raising my recently burned hand in a slight wave.

"Do you have my Americano?" His voice was stern and gravelly, which contradicted with the smile on his face. He was trying to be all business—I'd give him an A for effort. Pointing toward the stainless mug, Ben dismissed my wave and greeting, but at least he'd let the pretty Vermonter go her own way.

"Oh yes, I'll get it now. I didn't realize it was for you. Or that you live here . . . I mean, it makes sense. You're from here." Despite telling myself to *just shut up, Murphy,* I kept rambling. "But I always thought you'd stay in the city after college."

He'd been so kind and thoughtful back then, and always a little too willing to accept the crumbs I gave him.

Ben was a scholarship kid at Pressman Prep outside Boston, a semi-local kid from Vermont who had been given a chance at greatness. A few students were plucked every year from neighboring middle-class communities and dropped into the elite New England preparatory school. Of course, the scholarship kids never quite fit in, but achieving something greater was more their end game rather than being part of the in-crowd.

Wow, Ben Rooney. He'd been a lost puppy when he arrived at Pressman, and I'd used him while at the same time being mesmerized with him. He was so self-assured and smart, cocky in a non-arrogant way.

I'd talked Ben into helping me with biology and calculus, all the while not-so-secretly crushing on him. He never really responded to my crush, so I left prep school feeling like a fool. Only recently did I understand that he'd liked me back then, but pride kept him from acting on his feelings.

In those days, I'd been nice, befriending him in private. But outside of that, we were from two different worlds and not meant to associate. Ben had tried to hide his hurt and disappointment, but his feelings were pretty transparent. Except, I thought he liked me like a friend.

The final blow to our non-relationship was when he took me to the prom. Bradley Burnett had dumped me two weeks before the dance, and I was desperate, so Ben had been nice enough to pick up the slack.

Across the counter from me, Ben cleared his throat once, then again, yanking me out of my walk down memory lane.

"Murph—look, it's nice running into you. And yeah, I live nearby. I work at the hospital over in Montpelier and have an office in town. In fact, I have to get to the office to see a few patients right now. That doesn't mean I don't wish I had time for your theories on why I didn't stay in the city. I certainly have my own as to why you're slumming it in a coffee shop in the middle of nowhere. But, really, I have to get back to the hospital."

"Sure. Sorry, it was just so nice to see you."

My head felt congested like when spring allergies first come on. A dull ache throbbed in my forehead and ears, the kind of ache that lingered. I wondered why Ben was here in Colebury—at least a half hour from Montpelier—while his blue eyes urgently bore into me, trying to tell me something telepathically. Maybe he simply wanted me to leave him alone.

"Um, my Americano?"

My cheeks burst into flames. "Right. I'm on it."

Forcing myself to look down at the counter, I made the drink. At least this wasn't an order I could mess up. My thoughts, typically a jumbled mess of espresso drink recipes, was now swirling with memories of Ben then compared to the reality of Ben now . . . this new version of him.

When I handed him the reusable mug, he tightened the cap and said, "Thanks. You didn't try to poison me, did you?"

Swallowing my pride, I shook my head. "Of course not. I would never. Plus, Zara wouldn't be too happy with that. She's a good one," I said, the last part a whisper. She'd given me a chance, after all.

"At one time, you did try." He raised a brow, alluding to the badly spiked punch at Burnett's after-prom party.

I'd felt compelled to go to that stupid party, determined to show my ex what a good time I was having with Ben. Except, poor Ben got sick and spent the evening puking, and I was at a loss about what to do with him. I'd never been very good at putting anyone else first. After all, I'd never had to.

Ben took a long sip of his coffee, mesmerizing me with the bob of his Adam's apple. He cleared his throat, drawing my attention away from his corded neck. "Not bad."

Take that, Little Miss Perfect.

"Wow. Murphy Landon. In the Busy Bean. On the opposite side of the counter than I bet you're used to being, huh? Tell you the truth, I'd never thought I'd see the day. You doing this," he waved his hand at the counter, "right here in Vermont."

He stared at me with equal parts fascination and contempt, probably because I let him get rip-roaring drunk and make a fool of himself way back when.

"It's an honest job," I said, "and I happen to need it. Anyway, I thought you were in a hurry, but now you have time to make fun of me?"

I frowned at him, feeling the need to defend myself when I didn't owe Ben a single thing. After all, I'd come to believe that he hadn't always been honest with me. Not to mention, Ben was just as guilty about lumping me into stereotypes as I had done with him. Right?

"Oh, I'm sure you need this gig. Like you needed good grades in high school, as if you weren't going to get into the Ivy League from Pressman. Aw, sorry."

He ran his free hand through his hair. It happened to be his left, and I made the mistake of noting he wasn't wearing a wedding band.

"I don't mean to be rude," he said. "This is such a shock, seeing you here, and I'm not handling it well. You look good, Murph. Nice to see you. Honestly. I mean it," he said, holding a hand up as if he were swearing to it.

Mugs were piling up down the counter for me to fill with drinks, but I couldn't take my eyes off Ben. *He thinks I look good? What does "good" mean?*

"Good seeing you too," I said. "Looks like you're doing well."

Ignoring my comment and obvious assumption of his status, he said, "I just have to know one thing. Have you had some of the real maple syrup yet? You always were fascinated with it in school." His lips tipped up into a smile and he chuckled, and he might have sort of winked.

Is he being playful now?

Either way, I couldn't stop the genuine smile spreading across my face. "From your family's farm, actually. I saw a big table of it at the farmers' market when I first got here."

I stopped for a second and tried to think how long it had been, then I remembered fleeing from New York before the semester ended. I'd left my boss in a tizzy, but my sanity was more important at the time.

"It was back at the beginning of April," I said slowly. "I bought a jug, and I still have most of it. A teenage boy was running the table, and he must've thought I was crazy, staring at the bottle like a magic genie was going to pop out. A tidal wave of memories hit me when I saw it, and I thought back to when you gave me a bottle just like it as a Christmas present."

Giving Ben a small smile, I said, "I wanted to ask about you, but I didn't want to bother the kid. He seemed like he didn't want to get personal. I should've, though. I'm sorry about that."

I couldn't stop the words pouring from my mouth to save my life. A bad habit my mom had desperately tried to cure me of with her endless Little Miss Manners sessions.

Ben nodded. "My nephew, Branson. He's a good kid. No worries on not making it personal; it's been a while. A lifetime, practically." Ben kept his answers brief, obviously not having the same rambling issue as me.

"A lifetime, right?" I repeated his words, not wanting the conversation to end. "Branson . . . I forgot you have an older sister. I guess she's married and has kids?"

"Well, thanks for the support of the family business," he said, ignoring my hopeful conversation starter. This was a different Ben, confidently directing the conversation where he wanted it to go. "Listen, I really do have to go. Guess I'll see you sooner than later."

And like that, Ben Rooney walked out of my life again, but this time on his own terms. Sue me, but I risked a glance at his ass in scrubs, and I'd say the years had been good to him.

Wish they'd been as good to me. Yeah, I still looked young and good and all that, but to be honest, I was lost. And it looked like Ben had found . . . everything.

"Murphy, try to speed it up, sweetie, we have a tiny mid-afternoon rush. Everyone wants a coffee with their fresh baked scone, and I need to get home shortly. Audrey is running late to relieve me, and Dave's waiting for me." Zara winked at me, trying to lighten the moment, and then turned to see Ben leave. "Date night, you know?"

No, I didn't know the first thing about date night.

Zara gave me a meaningful smirk, obviously mentally pairing Ben and me together. The old me would try to set her straight, but not this version. I wasn't controlling everything around me anymore.

At least, I was trying not to. Instead, I moved on to the lineup of cups and settled back into my job, doing my best not to obsess about what I'd wear when Ben came in next.

Whenever that would be?

2

MURPHY

The next day, hump day, I was on the early morning shift with Roderick.

I wished I could say my barista skills were going as well as my scone eating was, but that would be a lie. Honestly, I was a mess. My hands were already dry and cracked from washing them so often, and now they were permanently coffee stained. My hair was an absolute mess—frizzy and dry—and I didn't think there was anyone in Colebury who could fix it.

As I cleaned the counter at the end of my shift, I cursed the jackass crunchy granola guy who didn't think I was qualified enough for a marketing position at his kayak company. I'd been sitting right over there . . . I looked toward the corner of the Bean where the leather chairs sat.

That's where I'd been that day a few weeks ago, gripping my almost empty low-fat latte as I had a brief interview with Ricky the Kayak Guru, who said he'd think about my résumé. Then he deserted me, leaving me alone with a set of mismatched chairs and my thoughts.

Why did I even bother? Maybe my parents were right. Maybe I'd never amount to much without their backing me up. When I'd set up the interview, I'd thought a kayak company in Montpelier would be my ticket out of the well I'd figuratively thrown myself down.

To escape my own negative thoughts, I'd wandered over to say hi to my favorite barista, Kirk. Nothing would cheer me up like hearing about his upcoming journey to Costa Rica where he planned to experience the world. Instead, I whined about how I desperately needed to get out of the Kwikshop and find a beefier job to pay the bills. I'd thought the combination of the marketing gig with the kayak company plus a few shifts at the grocery store would set me up nicely.

Kirk stopped short behind the gigantic espresso machine, looking at me wide eyed as he blurted out the solution. "With tips, a barista job would be perfect for you."

To be honest, Kirk made this gig look easy, and we'd become fast friends during my morning visits to the Bean for a hit of caffeine, despite us being total opposites. I was fancy like a vanilla bean crème latte, and Kirk was simple like a plain cup of joe.

My mid-morning pop-ins usually came at a slower time at the Bean, so we would usually chat over my first few sips of coffee or bites of what I considered a well-deserved treat, although it was mostly me chatting and Kirk nodding. In those days, I still got up wicked early to fit in some exercise. My mom would never accept anything less from me, except she didn't accept me at all lately.

Kirk didn't even wait for me to answer that day—instead, he'd walked over to Zara and told her he'd found his replacement. The training that followed was sort of easy, mostly because Kirk did all the heavy lifting. Now, here I was, exhausted, dirty, and daydreaming about Ben Rooney and why I hadn't run into him before, which was probably because he was successful these days and didn't hang with people like me anymore.

"See you tomorrow afternoon," Zara said, knocking me out of my self-pity when she called out to me.

I was untying my apron, a cute blue-and-pink seersucker-patterned number. It was way too fancy for the Bean, but it was a little gift to myself when I got the job. I ordered it from Nordstrom's, and yes, I was likely the first barista at the Busy Bean to wear an apron from an upscale department store.

Nodding absently to Zara, I wondered if Ben came in every afternoon, and maybe that's why I'd never seen him in here. Mid-morning had been my regular time to come in, after my workout at home—you know, because I couldn't afford a membership at a gym, even if there was a decent one—and on my way to work at the local grocery store.

Oh, the irony. Back in the day, I'd been too lazy to make my own coffee at home, and now I made lattes and Americanos for all of New England. Not all, but close enough.

Zara said something more, but I missed it.

"I'm sorry. I didn't hear that, Zar."

"Roddy's making blueberry-lemon scones. Come a little early so you can try them for me."

"Definitely." I made a mental note to do some extra crunches before coming into work and indulging in buttery baked goods. You can take the girl out of the Upper West Side, but you can't take the UWS out of the girl.

As she leaned her hip against the counter, I glanced at Zara's perfect curves and wondered when she did crunches.

"Anyway," she said, "Gigi is still away, so we need to add something until we get more of her Arnie Palmer cupcakes back in. Oh, For Heaven's Cakes can't keep up. It's the most popular bakery around, and I hear Gigi wants to get into shipping nationwide with Goldbelly. Can you believe it? Someone from our little sleepy town working with Goldbelly? It's some big-time New York food-shipping thingie."

I knew what it was, but Zara didn't give me a chance to answer.

"Speaking of which," she said, "about here and all that, I hope it's going okay for you. We get slammed early morning and late afternoon, but each shift has the midday reprieve. Don't think I'm going national any time soon. I like my snoozy coffee shop." Her glossy hair bounced as she spoke, her eyes bright and her smile wide, reaching her eyes.

I wished I could channel that type of perpetual positive energy. It was probably because she was in love, and I wasn't. Zara kept wanting to introduce me to this Gigi, but she was apparently in love too. Did everyone have to be so happy and great? While I was at it, did she really think this level of busyness was "slammed?"

"It's fine," I told her. "Thank you for all of this. I hope I'm keeping up. Roddy's been a godsend when it comes to the grinder. I'm getting the hang of it and hope I'm not disappointing you."

Grateful is exactly what I was. Being caught up in a scandal was one thing, but being cast out by my family, left to fend for myself after a lifetime of luxury, was something entirely different. Shouldn't my parents love me no matter what? So what if I made a mistake? It shouldn't mean that I had to give up designer shoes and my trust fund.

"This gig sure beats working the register at the Kwikshop, with everyone harping about reusable bags and 'where is this,' and 'where is that?'" I said, using air quotes while mocking my former customers.

Zara chuckled. "Hey, small talk and simplicity is important to most people around here. They've spent a lifetime trying to preserve the beauty of the area and promote its resources, while still keeping it small and cozy."

I swallowed my pride and a lump of regret slid down my throat as I mentally berated myself for speaking before thinking. My life was like a bad episode of *Sex in the City* where Charlotte was forced into small-town life, bagging canned goods at the corner grocery store, but they never wrote story lines like that because they knew they would be awful.

"Yes, I know. It's growing on me, you know? All this nature and natural beauty," I said, only half lying.

Vermont was a pretty nice place, and I was becoming a better person, which reminded me of Ben's reusable mug. He'd always been a stickler for the environment, even in prep school. Of course, I'd teased him for it but he took it in stride, trying to explain the importance to me.

"In fact," I told her, "that's why I'm here. In Vermont. I had a friend in high school who bragged about the area. It felt like somewhere I could find peace, and allow my mind some freedom."

Zara took a step closer into my personal space, something I wasn't used to after growing up in New York. Taking my hand in hers, she said, "Look, sweetie, I'm here for you. We've all made mistakes in our past. I know that better than anyone because I've made a few of my own. So, when you're ready and want to chat, let me know. I have years of experience of listening to other people's problems. Ya know?"

"I'm good. I swear."

"I know, honey. Seriously, though, think about it. You should get to know Gigi. That girl went through hell, and I'll bet you two have more in common than you think. Now, go take a shower and put your feet up after a busy shift, and take care of you."

Well, when I went home, I skipped the shower, but I did prop my feet up while doing some online window shopping. I needed a new car, so there were no new shoes in my future, but a girl could browse while she ate her ramen noodles.

If my friends from Pressman could see me now.

That's why when I arrived at the Bean the next day, I was dressed to impress. It was the afternoon shift, and Rita, one of our regulars, eyed me from the peach sofa she called hers. I learned this the hard way when I first started coming in and dared to sit there one day. Rita not so politely kicked me out of "her seat," and I never attempted to sit there again.

All the attention on my little-more-done-up look made me

uncomfortable, but I kind of hoped Ben would come back in, so I'd gone for the kill. I'd lightly curled my hair in soft waves and wore my plaid apron (another splurge purchase during one of my online binges). Even if he didn't come in, maybe my improved look would help fill the tip jar. After all, I had my eye on a used Hyundai.

As I picked at the new blueberry-lemon scone before my shift started, Zara side-eyed me. "You look nice."

"Thanks."

"You going somewhere later?"

Shaking my head, I muttered, "Taking pride in my work," then plastered a smile on my face and took my place behind the bar.

While I struggled with the correct number of pumps for each beverage, my bar was backed up as usual. Closing my eyes for a second, I took a deep breath and reminded myself this was Vermont, not New York. Despite the one uppity customer earlier in the week, I was doing this. On my own. Period.

"Hey, Murph. I don't think you're supposed to sleep on the job."

Ben's gravelly tone, laced with welcome humor, knocked me out of my stupor. Slowly opening my eyes, I shrugged. "I was meditating for a minute."

"Maybe you can do that after you make my drink," he said, pointing to his reusable mug in the middle of the lineup.

"I can't move your drink up. If I do, I'll have half of Vermont after me. They're vicious here. Vermonters make New Yorkers look easygoing."

Smiling big, I grabbed the next mug in line, this one a reusable ceramic Bean-issued mug for a regular customer. A café au lait, thankfully. That drink I could make easily. As I worked, I felt Ben's eyes on me.

"Seemed like your customer the other day was quite the disgruntled iced-coffee drinker," Ben said.

I glanced at him to see a twinkle in his eye, but I couldn't tell if it was snarky or genuine. Willing myself to stay focused, I made the café au lait and moved on to a damn iced latte.

I prayed to any and every god who was listening that the aforementioned customer from hell wasn't back again. Hopefully, she was passing through, staying in one of the expensive inns in a neighboring town. When I called out the latte, I was relieved when someone else came up to claim it. A sweet teenage girl here with her mom. *Whew.*

Ben was still lurking, but I didn't know if he wanted to say something more or be sure I wasn't poisoning his coffee. Deciding not to speculate, I grabbed his stainless Yeti mug, poured in three shots of espresso, and added hot water.

"Here you go." I held Ben's cup over the bar for him, breaking Bean rules.

"Thanks," he said in a hushed tone.

"No prob." I decided it was best not to beat myself up over the past when it came to him, nor to think about a future friendship with him. Both were a waste of energy.

Surprising me, Ben asked, "Do you get a break at all?"

"Um, I do. Usually once during a shift. They treat us very well, if you're wondering."

Wishing I could let down my ponytail and tousle my hair, but then I'd have to wash my raw hands again, I busied myself with wiping down the bar before grabbing another cup.

Score. Another café au lait, this one in a to-go cup.

"No, that's not what I meant," Ben said as he moved closer. "I don't doubt Zara is good to you."

I could smell his aftershave, something woodsy. Very Vermonty—*duh.* I took notice of his cargo-style khakis and somewhat pressed dress shirt today. He'd never been the type of guy who dressed to impress.

"No hospital for you today, Doctor?" I asked, unsure why I was so prickly.

He chuckled. "Ha, as if. I'm there every day, even the days I'm not supposed to be there. No surgery today, so no scrubs."

"Oh." Stumped, I couldn't think of anything else to say.

"I see patients in the office a few mornings a week, so I get to dress up. Notice the sexy outfit?" He laughed, doing a whole Vanna White thing as he gestured to the front of his body.

As if I need any more excuses to notice his fit physique.

I shook my head, pretty sure Ben's rapid change in personality from the other day would lead to a bad case of whiplash. "Well, lucky you. I wear the same thing every day here," I said, but my joke fell flat.

Ben scowled. "That's not what I meant. I wasn't trying to make you feel bad, or lesser than. Lord knows I endured enough of that to last a lifetime. You look fine."

As I snatched up the next cup, Zara called to me.

"Murph, it's your break. Roddy will come and take over the bar. Hit it, girl. Leave that drink right there."

"Guess that's my cue," I said, sliding under the escape hatch at the end of the bar. "Nice seeing you," I told Ben, wondering why he wasn't rushing to leave.

"Maybe we can sit and catch up during your break?" he asked, not moving from where he was standing.

"Why?" I turned toward him. "You didn't seem so excited to see me the other day." I felt my cheeks warm at my forthrightness and my hair frizzing more by the second because of the sweat suddenly beading at the nape of my neck. Half from embarrassment, the other half from shame.

Ben's blue eyes locked on mine. "I'd like to apologize, hear what's been going on with you. You know? Catch up. For old time's sake."

"No, I don't know."

"Come on, Murph. We used to be sort-of friends, right? After all, you saw me during my worst night ever. You know I haven't been able to drink liquor with a mixer since?"

"Really? That's a bit much, don't you think?" I tilted my head slightly so I could really take all of Ben in.

"Maybe a bit much, but the memory lasted for quite a while.

Kind of like the smell did back then. Remember how terrible I reeked? That's what a few hours hanging over the toilet, marinating in your own puke, will do." His eyes twinkled again, and this time his humor seemed genuine.

"Oh, you think it's funny now, do you?" I propped my hands on my hips, narrowing my eyes on him. "I thought you were going to die on me that night. How was I going to call your parents and explain it to them? I'd never even met them. And as for my parents, they would have had a major conniption. Tarnishing the family name with consorting . . . and a death on my watch."

Oh my God. I had to go there, mentioning the family name. It was a bad move in so many ways.

Scraping his fingers through his unruly hair, he said, "Yeah, the family name. Is it still all you thought it was cracked up to be?"

"Not really, but it's all I have now." I cleared my throat, trying to fill the awkward pause hanging between us.

"So, what do you say?" Ben said, giving me that smile that always melted me. "Take your break with me? Let's talk about something else other than that night or your family name. Neither bring back good memories for me."

"Okay," I heard myself say, and for the first time in a while, I really meant it when I agreed to do something.

3

BEN

Yesterday, I'd kind of been relieved when Murphy wasn't at the Bean when I dropped by. Only because it gave me a chance to interrogate Zara as soon as I made it to the register.

When did Murphy start working here? Did Zara know what kind of money Murphy came from? Was she a pain in the ass? I bombarded Zara with questions, and she answered each one like a diplomat.

Murphy had only been at the Bean a few weeks, including training. Zara suspected Murphy came from money, but it seemed like her personal situation had changed and she wasn't forthright in explaining. No, she wasn't a pain in the ass. Maybe a slow learner when it came to the coffee bar, but she was trying hard.

I'd been shocked as hell to see Murphy the other day after I'd stopped there as I rushed to check on Branson in between surgery and heading back to see follow-up patients. My car was racking up miles on the two-lane road between Montpelier and Colebury, but I owed it to Brenna to keep an eye on my nephew.

Years ago, I'd begged my sister to stay with me at my house. Lord only knew, I had the space. But she'd refused, wanting to keep her crap place in quiet Colebury. Not that any part of Vermont was loud or noisy or even bustling, but she thought

Colebury was best for raising Branson. It was her own small slice of happiness, she called it.

Lately, I disagreed with her, but I wasn't Branson's father, as she so often reminded me.

Yeah, where the hell is he?

Now, seated across from Murphy, who had that smile I'd come to know as her armor firmly on her face, I decided not to reveal anything about me or the little I knew about her since she left Pressman. Not because I didn't care. I cared too much. When I left the ritzy prep school behind, I left our awkward friendship and any hope of it being anything more there too.

While I didn't know much about this version of Murphy, it was obvious something dramatic had happened to result in her working in a coffee shop in Vermont. The last I knew she was working in New York City.

"So, tell me . . . why Vermont?" I asked Murphy as she sat in front of me, her hands neatly folded on the table.

"I needed a change, and for some reason, the way you used to talk about it here stuck with me, so I gave it a whirl. It wasn't completely outlandish. We did go to high school near here."

Taking a sip of my Americano, I realized Murphy didn't have anything to drink. "Wait, don't you get something during your break to eat or drink?"

She frowned at me. "Of course. Don't act like this isn't a good place full of decent people."

"That's not what I meant. Do you want something?" I tilted my head toward the counter.

"I'm good. Roddy had me taste-testing scones when I came in today. I washed them down with a yummy latte. If I have any more sugar, I'm going to fly home."

"Where is home?" I asked. This wasn't a huge town, and I wondered why we'd never ran into each other.

Oh, right. I work all the time, and seems this is a new gig for Murphy.

Noting Zara watching us, I waited for Murphy to answer.

"I have a little apartment, part of a duplex cut into four. It's not much, but it's all mine. Plus, I'm used to small spaces after living in New York."

She raised her chin, absolutely refusing to admit any kind of defeat, and I instantly knew this was a bitter pill for her to swallow. Murphy's pride was always larger than her five-foot-seven-inch frame.

"Funny, I always took you to be the one who would stay in the big city. You were never into the small world surrounding Pressman, other than the syrupy sweets you could find."

"Turned out New York wasn't for me. No real maple syrup," she said, joking, but there was a story there. She might look like the same Murphy sitting in front of me, but this was a more complex version. A Murphy who had lived more, experienced life differently from how she was raised.

"Decent syrup is kind of addicting. By the way, I never forgot what a wicked sweet tooth you have. Remember how you used to plow through those Swedish Fish while studying?"

"I loved those. Actually, I ate so many during college, I got sick of them. I've moved on to Sour Patch Kids. Bonus, you can grab a bag of them at the gas station."

Who is this Murphy? She picks up snacks at the gas station?

When I accidentally let out a small chuckle, of course she said, "What?"

"Nothing. It's nothing. I just had no idea you even knew how to pump gas."

"I can do a lot of things you don't know about, Ben. Except marketing." The last part came out on a whisper as sadness swept over her usually lively expression.

"I'm sorry, what do you mean? Marketing?"

"It's nothing."

Murphy stared at her nails, inspecting the red polish, a few shades darker than her hair. A few freckles dotted her hand, and I looked at her face, noting it was still as creamy and unblemished as it had been in school. I remembered her wearing a hat and tons of sunscreen when we hung out on the lawn, saying her mom would kill her if she got freckles on her face.

As I finished off the remainder of my Americano, I wished I'd bought a pastry. Sometime in the last forty-eight hours, I'd gone from being ready to throttle the surprising blast from my past, to wanting to sit here for another hour or two with her.

I tried to push aside any notions about this version being a new and improved version of Murphy. My old feelings were clouding my thoughts. I'd liked her a lot at one time, but quickly learned we weren't meant to be together.

Murphy took my moment of silence as waiting for her to answer, so she started rambling about her degree. "It's just I wanted to work in marketing when I moved here, because that's what my degree is in, but it didn't work out. I don't even know why I'm telling you this."

"What do you mean, it didn't work out?"

"Honestly, I don't want to rehash it. I'm here at the Bean and happy. Maybe the happiest I've ever been."

A sullen Murphy from our past came to mind. She'd always come back to Pressman despondent after breaks. I'd go over and see if I could cheer her up, and she'd shoo me away, saying I didn't understand. It was part of the divide between us, part of the push-pull dance we always did.

By the time we were seniors, I knew what to expect. If Murphy spent significant time with her family or rich friends, she'd pull back from me except for when I tutored her. As the aftershocks of whatever ensued within her wealthy circles wore off, she'd let me in, only to push me out again.

Why did I put up with it? Because I liked her. Too much. Somewhere underneath all her steely armor, I recognized a softer person. A fascinating person that I really liked.

"It's from our biggest disappointments that we grow, Murph," I told her, feeling compelled to make her feel better like I used to do all those years ago.

She scoffed. "Seriously, you're going to give me some cheesy motivational quote? Who said that?"

"Me, that's who. I'm sure someone more profound said something similar at one point, but that's me saying it to you, and meaning it."

We were back in the dance. Murphy with her holier-than-thou, well-groomed, well-bred attitude, and me with my hokey small-town sayings.

Her green eyes stared me down, a cool grassy meadow inviting me to bare it all. "How would you even know about disappointments? Doesn't look like you've had too many."

"Ha. This coming from you, who knows more than most that I was the poor boy at the fancy prep school. The charity case, the farmer's son, the pity party. I know plenty about disappointments."

I didn't mention spending four years being disappointed by her, only to get my one chance on prom night. Or at least that's what I'd believed. But I was wrong, and now here she was, sitting across from me, wondering about what disappointments life had thrown at me.

"You need to let that go, Ben, the charity angle. Seems like it's a long way in the past for you. You're a doctor now, well-liked and clearly happy, doing your thing."

Her words, meant to be approving, were like a salve on a third-degree burn. I'd spent four years wishing she would think more of me, and here she was finally doing it now.

Swallowing regret for how I jumped on her, I took a moment to gather my thoughts. I'd always let Murphy's pity go by the wayside, knowing it was the price I paid for having her as a friend.

"Yes, I am, but it wasn't without a lot of sacrifice. I was still the scholarship kid in college. The long-snapper on the football team—you know what that means? The lowest man on the totem pole. It played well into me not having a social life, which gave me the time to make ends meet . . . otherwise."

"What do you mean?" Her expression softened, and she didn't look ready to unleash her Irish temper at me.

"That's a story for another day."

"Oh. I didn't mean . . ." Her brow formed a tiny furrow, and she almost looked about to cry.

I didn't know what to make of this new dance. She'd lash out at me and then soften toward me, and then I didn't know what the fuck this was.

"I have to go," I said, rising to my feet. "Patients are waiting. I'll see you the next time you're working, I guess."

The last part came off slightly hopeful and partly resentful. Murphy was part of my past, and not one I was sure I wanted in my present.

Needing to keep this relationship contained, I resisted the urge to ask for her number. I'd come too far to let old habits bring me down, and was proud of who I was and what I'd achieved. Murphy was a former obsession, and she needed to stay that way. Nothing more.

"Okay," Murphy said slowly as she rose to her feet as well. "I'm actually off for the next two days, so I'll see you when I see you."

With that, I sensed that Murphy wanted to keep us—whatever us was, or is—in the past too.

A little too late, I realized that the gnawing sensation in my gut was disappointment as I turned to leave, an empty mug in my hand and a hollowness in my chest.

MURPHY

I woke up on Saturday morning to absolutely nothing—no traffic noise outside my windows, and no work or social obligations.

Even though I'd lived in Vermont for a few months, the difference from New York City still rattled me. The utter quiet, the slower pace, the way I could actually hear birds chirping. There were no horns blaring, no ambulances, and no shouting in the streets. It was so different from what I was used to, it was unnerving.

Wishing I had to work, I set about cleaning my tiny apartment before doing a mini facial and giving myself a manicure.

In my past life, I would have spent half the day at a spa, having another person tend to my body while someone else scrubbed and scoured my apartment. I didn't have those luxuries anymore, but no one had to know. The pictures I posted on Instagram these days all featured me enjoying the Vermont landscape, looking as happy and beautified as I once was.

Take that, old life. I wasn't sure who I was proving anything to, but it still felt important to keep up appearances.

As I popped a K-cup in my Keurig, I thought about stopping by the Bean, but I hadn't just popped in since I started working there. It felt awkward to stop in for my own pleasure and have my coworkers wait on me.

I'm sure Roddy would love to see me and wouldn't think twice about my picking up a coffee and a sweet treat. He'd probably try to hand me one of his homemade soft pretzels, telling me it would be on the house, and we'd have our usual sweet versus salty debate. Nine times out of ten, I went with sweet. It was how I was wired, or a subconscious snub at my mom, who was always lecturing me about curbing my sweet tooth.

Instead of treating myself to a real cup of joe, I suffered through a not-very-hot, semi-acceptable cup of coffee while looking for any new marketing job postings on Craigslist. To my surprise, there was a new post for a social media intern for a place called Hunnie's Honey, Home of Vermont's Most Golden Honey Infusions.

Although an intern position was definitely below my Ivy League credentials and age, if this Hunnie gave me a chance, I could easily pivot the opportunity into something else. Plus, it sounded official, as if Hunnie's place had their stuff together.

And beggars can't be choosers.

Who told me that? Oh, right, it was Ben back at Pressman.

We'd been studying biology, and I asked him why he ate in the dining hall on Sunday nights, when most of us ordered Chinese delivery and watched movies over greasy egg rolls and lo mein. Afterward, we'd usually jump in someone's car and grab a few pints of ice cream for dessert, but Ben said it wasn't in his budget. The dining room was included with his scholarship, and *beggars couldn't be choosers.* Of course, I offered to pay for him, but he declined, saying something about the Sunday pasta night being one of his favorites.

Turning back to my internet search, I hunted around Hunnie's site, noticing they sold at the Capital City farmers' market, which happened to be open tomorrow. With nothing better to do, I decided to go walk around the market the next day.

Until then, I would do some self-care at home, since paying for a day spa was way out of my budget. Also, there wasn't anywhere to go nearby, which was probably for the best.

Standing up, I walked to the corner of the room and snagged my Manduka yoga mat, a symbol of another time and place, and set it up under the window.

The next morning, in a sleeveless green blouse tucked into white jean shorts, I checked myself in the mirror.

This month was the first time I'd been able to wear my summer clothes. Even May had been chilly here in Vermont. In the city, we would have already been sweltering. I was hopeful that later this month and July and August would be warmer. Of course, an even layer of sheer zinc was smeared under my makeup to protect my skin from the sun. My mom's voice was still a constant in my head. After pulling my red waves back into a loose ponytail, I put on a wide-brimmed sun hat and my black shades.

When I first arrived in Vermont, my first thought was *you're not in the Big Apple anymore, Toto.* Shaking my head, I freed myself from old memories of Thanksgiving-break movie nights at home in our palatial mansion, a babysitter on the couch and *The Wizard of Oz* on the television.

As I parked my car at the farmers' market, I sighed. Like an idiot, I'd forgotten how muddy the ground was at the market, and scowled at the flip-flops on my feet. Not wanting to waste money on gas to drive home and back on the winding roads to my quarter of a duplex off the highway, I climbed out of my car and took in the market.

Right away, I saw a corner booth with a bumble-bee-decorated flag and decided to see if it was Hunnie's. A woman about my own age with two perfectly plaited brunette braids and a worn-in baseball hat greeted me as I approached.

"Hey there." Her smile was extra wide, her enthusiasm infectious.

"Hi." Clearing my throat, I said, "Love the packaging." The amber-filled glass bottles were shaped like a wide upside-down V, their angular lines showcasing the beautiful color of the honey inside.

"Thanks. We're lucky to have one of the country's best glassblowers in Quechee, and he may or may not be a relative of someone we know," the woman said as she winked at me.

"Oh, that's so cool. I'm not from here."

A small giggle escaped her. "I could tell."

"Oh," I said, hanging my head.

"No, no, I didn't mean it like that. We win everyone over . . . we love newcomers. They typically stay. I meant the white shorts were a dead giveaway. A Vermonter would never wear those to the farmers' market. One brush against a bushel of lavender, and they'd be . . . lilac. Or a taste of farmers' fudge, and they'd have a huge chocolate-peanut-butter streak down the front."

"Thanks for the heads-up. Now I'll know for next time." The warmth of a blush spread across my fair skin, and I hoped my hat shaded my face enough to hide it.

"Want a taste? The orange, ginger, and lemon combination is divine on its own. You can eat it by the spoonful. The citrus cuts the sweetness of the honey in just the right way, and it's full of vitamin C." She pointed to the bottles in front of her and I peered closer, noting that specks of something tangerine-colored speckled the amber honey.

"I'd love one. While stopping at the fudge stand sounds good, I actually came here to see you. I mean, I'm here to see Hunnie from Hunnie's Honey." I couldn't help but let out a nervous laugh at the tongue-twister of a name as it rolled off my tongue.

"Did you now? Someone recommend us?" She handed me a wood taster spoon filled with the golden liquid.

"Um, no. I saw they're—you're, whoever runs Hunnie's—is

looking for a social media intern, and I was curious about the position. Do you know the owner, or who I should speak to?"

"I certainly do. It's me. I'm Hunnie. Well, my real name's Margaret, but I never was a Maggie or a Margo or a Margaret. My grandma nicknamed me Hunnie, and it stuck. Granted, my family's run a honey farm for more generations than I can count, so it wasn't all that creative."

Inside, I wanted to shrivel up and die a very quick death—she was the owner. My age, successful, cute, peppy, and content. All the things I wasn't but should be.

No matter how broken I felt, I kept a smile on my face. "Oh, wow. Well, nice to meet you, Hunnie. I'm Murphy, and obviously not from here, but I bring a good amount of social media experience, and I'd like to share it with you." I couldn't help but wonder why she needed an intern for her farm stand.

"Pardon me for saying," Hunnie said kindly, "but I've been known to blurt out whatever is on my mind. Why would you want to be an intern? It doesn't pay much. In fact, I call it an intern but it's more a glorified helper. If you have experience, you'd do better in a full-time gig. We're just trying to tap into social media, widen our reach, sell more online, get in touch with . . . what do you call them? Role models? No, influencers, that's it. We're expanding our shipping."

"I hear you," I said. "It's just, I'm looking to get involved here in Vermont. I'm not in New York anymore, and I need some experience here. I need to get my feet wet in this world. Like the thing with the white shorts. I don't understand small town rules or whatever."

Scanning the crowd, she said, "Hold that thought for one second."

Still mentally cursing myself, I shut my mouth. Not entirely sure why I had to fully expose myself, I turned to see what Hunnie was doing.

"Hey." Hunnie rounded the table, her short legs carrying her as fast as they possibly could. "Hey, Ben! Wait up."

The person she was chasing turned around, proving that today was obviously my very, very unlucky day. Standing there in jeans and a white T-shirt, his muscular arms making him look more like a professional football player rather than a physician, was Ben Rooney.

Hunnie hurried up to him, talking a mile a minute. "Ben, did you have a chance to talk with your dad about the land? Don't forget I called you, and you said you would. You promised. I'm still very interested, and if your dad wanted, we could go into it together. You know, the petting zoo would bring a lot of traffic to both places in the summer months. Local families looking for something to do on the weekend and tourists. It would be an awesome destination, and they could leave with syrup and cheese, and of course, honey."

Ben shook his head. "Sorry, Hunnie. I haven't seen him. I've been busy with work and Branson, but I'm supposed to have dinner with my parents next week."

I hadn't realized I'd been inching further to hear their conversation, until Ben looked up and I was standing right next to him.

"Oh, this is Murphy." Hunnie grabbed my hand and pulled me next to her. "She's here about being my intern. See? We'd have an intern too for the petting zoo. Think Instagram. And sales. Posts and likes or loves on Facebook." She looked at me, her eyes begging me to agree. "You could help with all this, right? You said you know what you're doing."

Before I could even respond, she turned back to Ben. "Murphy's from the big city but lives here now."

"Is that right?" He cocked an eyebrow and stared me down. "Actually, I know Murphy from the Bean. Are you sure she's not trying to steal trade secrets?"

Hunnie scoffed. "For who, Zara? Never. Audrey uses my honey to drizzle on her cinnamon monkey bread. We support each other. Stop trying to make trouble, Ben. Always up to no good when it comes to regular life in Vermont. We can't all be fancy doctors."

"I wouldn't do that," I said, tugging my hand back as I turned to face Hunnie. "I'd never share secrets. I don't even get involved in the baking other than what I eat. That's Roderick's area. Sorry, I didn't mean to interrupt you two. I was just going to tell you I'd wander around and be back when you were finished."

"Sounds good," she said, believing me.

I chalked up her carefree attitude to Vermont exuberance. It's as if the water had happy pills in it . . . except when it came to Ben. He was chipper, and then not so nice, and then happy again before becoming all-out cunning.

What was it with him? He never used to be this way. Yeah, at Pressman he labeled himself as an outsider and everyone treated him as such, but he was back home now in his beloved Vermont.

"That's a good idea. Let's wander." Ben grabbed my elbow and led me away from Hunnie to walk next to him. Lowering his voice, he said sharply, "What in the world are you doing, walking around the farmers' market like you belong here? Shopping for . . . what are you shopping for?" He stopped in his tracks and stared me down.

"What are *you* doing?" I hissed out the words but yet forced a smile, never one to make a scene.

"Tell me something. What are *you* doing?" He tossed my question back at me. "Working as a barista, then moonlighting as an intern for Hunnie? You graduated from an Ivy League college in Manhattan and your family has more connections than God. Are you mocking our small-town life here? Is that what you're doing, making fun of us? Getting some sick revenge?"

His mouth tightened as he spoke, and he looked like he was gasping for air. He faced me, his feet planted and his eyes staring me down, daring me to cop to his accusation.

I pulled in a calming breath. "No, I'm not mocking a thing. I meant it when I told you how you spoke so highly of it here, I decided to give it a try. I needed a fresh perspective. I swear. My family wasn't happy with that choice either, so they're keeping their distance from my life," I said, giving him the same story I'd been telling anyone who asked.

"That's stupid. They're disappointed over you being in Vermont? No one would ever feel that way. That's not even normal. Then again, I forgot how abnormal the world was that you grew up in. So abnormal, I was barely allowed to participate in it."

Swallowing my pride, I shoved one hand in my pocket and stood my ground, which wasn't easy with an angry, smoking-hot Ben looming over me.

"Is that what this is about?" I said. "Pressman? And you and me? Seriously, we're all grown up now." How I'd treated him still haunted me, so he had to remember what a little bitch I'd been.

"That has to be a joke." He glared at me. "Who cares about Pressman? This is about you being here, now. Vermont is a modern-day state, I'll have you know. Right here, where I'm standing, is an everyday city. It may not have the glitz and glamour of New York City, but it's home. We even have running water."

Agitated, he ran his hand through his hair, and I took all of him in. It was unsettling how gorgeous he was, how smart and extremely wise. My mind rambled. *It's crazy how he sees through my excuses.*

"Whatever," I said with a shrug. "I'm here and I'm trying, okay? I'm not mocking anyone, and I happen to like it here. This place is speaking to my soul. Think of this as a rebirth."

Ben scowled at me. "You're joking."

Pulling my hand out of my pocket, I mentally chastised myself for nervously wringing my hands. "I. Am. Not. Joking. I'm here to buy some things for my apartment," I said, defending my right to be at the farmers' market. Which was absurd.

Ben's stiff posture seemed to relax. "If so, did you hit up my family's booth? Get your syrup fix yet?"

I shook my head. "No, I just got here. I was talking to Hunnie, taking care of that first."

"Come on. I came to see if my mom was here. I need to drop off a prescription from a colleague for her migraines." He took my hand again, this time less roughly but still firmly. This Ben—adult Ben—was in charge.

All of a sudden, I wanted to cut and run. "No, I don't think that's a good idea. I'm wearing white shorts, and Hunnie says that's a bad thing around here." I scanned around us, desperately looking for someone else daring to wear white.

"Who is Hunnie, the fashion police? Last time I checked, she ran a hippie-dippie honey-infusion bullshit business and wants to do goat yoga on the side, taking my dad along for the ride." Ben spoke while taking two or three big strides and then stopped to look at me again. His gaze burned through me, searching for the truth.

"Goat yoga? She didn't mention that, but it would make for amazing publicity." A million images spun through my head, mostly of Hunnie in her braids, leaning over and kissing a goat.

"It doesn't matter what Hunnie mentioned," Ben said. "I know how her head works. She'll jump from one crazy thing to another. She's another one who's never happy with the status quo and has to constantly be trying out something new. Not that it's bad, but my family has a good thing going on here, and it doesn't need to change."

"Do you have a thing with her?" I asked. "Is that why you're making fun of her? I don't think I've ever heard you talk so poorly about someone, Ben Rooney. Other than me." My mouth snapped shut as soon as I heard the words spilling out of me.

"Hunnie?" Ben gave me a confused look. "Uh, no. We grew up together. You know, like splashing in the kiddie pool naked kind of way. I most definitely do not have a thing for her, and I wasn't being mean. I was just saying she's not the fashion authority, telling you what you can and can't wear to the farmers' market. And no, I won't support her petting zoo with my dad. He has enough on his hands. I help when I can, and I'm not shoveling goat shit."

Ben ignored the comment about me, obviously refusing to admit to liking me back in the day. Of course, I was too stuck up to realize it then.

"Speaking of, shouldn't you be at work?" I asked.

My attitude seemed to have a mind of its own when it came to Ben. Gone were my manners, and I was left with only snark and sass. Embarrassed and needing something to do, I shoved a strand of hair behind my ear and caught my fingernail on my hoop earring like a clumsy idiot.

"Ouch," I muttered, trying to get my finger loose without tearing my earlobe.

"Here." Ben reached over with his gentle surgeon hands and freed my nail. "There you go," he said, his voice the perfect combination of softness and gruff. Happy-go-lucky Ben was back.

"Now, let's go see my mom." Grabbing my elbow, he started walking again, giving me no choice in the matter.

"By the way, what kind of doctor are you?" I asked, trying to keep up with his pace.

"Orthopedic surgeon. All the skiing is good business for me up here. Knees, hips, broken legs. Summer is a windfall of biking incidents. Kind of funny, all things I don't have much time to do myself."

"Oh." I had to stop saying *oh.* My mom's voice rang in my head, chastising me for one-word answers. She'd told me a million times that one-word answers didn't make me sound interesting. "I'm sure it's more than that. It always was with you. Nothing was as it seemed on the surface. You always tried too hard to come off as on the surface, but you were way deeper."

Glancing at me, he grumbled, "Something like that, for sure."

5

BEN

What am I doing, taking Murphy to meet my mom?

"Speaking of deep," I said, searching for the words. "Murphy isn't an everyday name like Sarah or Rebecca."

"So? It's my name and I can't change it. Being here is change enough. I'm doing the best I can." Murphy stopped short, planting her feet, her green eyes blazing. If possible, they were even greener in the sunlight than her blouse.

"Roll with me here. My mom is smart—she's going to put two and two together when I introduce you. She's going to remember we went to prom. She's going to ask about where you've been all these years, and while I don't like to use Google, my mom is a sleuth without it."

This got Murphy's attention, and not in a good way, judging by her squinty eyes and the crease in her brow.

"She'll want to know whether we've reunited," I said to distract her.

Murphy twisted her hands together, looking desperate to run away. "Reunited? We were never together."

"It's no secret I liked you, Murph. Come on, you're smarter than that. We're all grown up now, but my mom still thinks of me as the baby. She's going to press deep, and she isn't going to give up until she gets the answers she's searching for, like a bloodhound chasing a scent."

Finally addressing the elephant in the room—or the field or whatever—I left it out there. It was high time we discussed the unrequited crush I had on Murphy all those years ago, and her complete and total rejection of me. I had a hard time believing she was the only one who didn't know my feelings for her ran deeper than as friends.

Looking up at the sky as a dark rain cloud passed over, Murphy was quiet, deep in thought, looking like my never-ending crush was news to her. "I don't have to go meet your mom. In fact, I need to get back to Hunnie before the rain comes. I really need that internship. You know, I can't work in a coffee place forever. There's nothing wrong with it, though. It's a good place, run by great people, and I actually like it, but I have to do something with my degree, you know?"

My hand grabbed hold of her shoulder of its own volition. "Why? Why do you need all that? Why do you act all clueless, like there isn't something bigger going on here? Are you truly okay? Something's going on with you, and I'm here if you need me."

Questions and declarations rolled off my tongue before I could stop myself. It was just like old times, my true feelings ignored or forgotten, and I was back to wanting to care for Murphy.

"Like you said," she said as she placed her small palm on my shoulder, mimicking my move, "we're all grown up now. I'm a grown woman, Ben. I know we were friends, and maybe you wanted more for us back then. Maybe I did too, but it was more than I could give. More than I was allowed to give."

"According to who?" I demanded, challenging her.

"I don't even know. My parents, my so-called friends, all the social expectations I'd been raised to abide by. But it doesn't matter now because I've been taking care of myself for a while. Maybe I'm still trying to figure life out, but I will."

"You don't have to be that way. I can help you. We are old friends, like you said."

It wasn't the time to delve into her bullshit about society's expectations. Clearly, she was on some sort of soul-searching mission, and I tried not to feel happy to have found myself a part of it. But I was.

Murphy shook her head. "You don't owe me that. You helped me enough at Pressman, and I was never as grateful as I should have been. Look, I get it. I didn't reciprocate when it came to anything with you, and for that I'm sorry." The wind picked up, lifting strands of her coppery hair. "Go see your mom. I'm going to talk to Hunnie. See you at the Bean."

The heat of her hand on my shoulder, singeing my skin through my shirt, quickly faded as she turned and walked away, leaving me confused.

With rain coming quickly, I didn't have time to dwell on what Murphy's end game was. Or mine. I had enough to deal with when it came to work, Vermont, my family, and my life. Murphy was definitely a complication I didn't need right now.

As I hurried over to my family's booth, I decided to quickly give my mom her migraine medicine and get out of there before the real storm—the one that Murphy's presence here seemed to put into motion—rolled in.

Thankfully, my mom was slammed with customers at her booth and didn't have time to draw me into a long chat. Relief swept over me at Murphy bowing out of meeting my mom. If she hadn't, Mom would have dug in, sinking her teeth into this discovery.

Oh, you're Murphy, the girl he pined over every single summer and winter break.

I wasn't sure what came over me to even consider taking

Murphy to our booth. That's what she did to me—she made me forget all common sense.

My dad told me when I left for school, *"Get a good education, son. Do something with it. Be better than me, but don't become one of them. The rich people. They may have money and all the fancy things, but they don't have happiness. Watch and you'll see."*

When I first arrived at Pressman, I thought he was wrong, but a few months in, I noticed most of my classmates were indeed not happy, no matter how much credit they had on their American Express card. I could barely afford a hamburger and fries with a shake on the rare occasion Murphy and I sneaked out together, but when I thought about my family, I smiled. Thinking of home, and the good times we had, always made me long to ditch Pressman, go back home, and just be happy.

Then again, I wouldn't be where I was today had it not been for Pressman.

Which was why I felt so compelled to help Branson. My nephew didn't have a dad to advise him or show him shit. Sometimes I worried he wasn't happy or content. Maybe he was holding all his true feelings inside?

These were the type of thoughts that plagued me, which was why when my mom was busy, I decided to head over to Colebury and surprise him. Maybe he'd want to come spend the night with me, order in a pizza and watch baseball together.

Deep in thought as I drove, I almost missed the compact hunk-of-junk car parked at the curb in front of a duplex with a woman pacing next to it. Who the hell drove something like that in Vermont?

"Shit," I mumbled, unable to drive by, the doctor inside me needing to make sure everyone was okay.

Pulling up in front of the older Toyota coupe, I shook my head. It was hardly the kind of car anyone would want during a Vermont rainstorm like this one, let alone in the winter.

I jumped out of my Jeep into the rain and was approaching the woman when I registered the flash of red hair. *Murphy?*

She hadn't even noticed my car pulling up. She continued to pace, occasionally stomping her foot as she muttered to herself. I couldn't imagine what could be that bad or distracting.

Not wanting to scare her, I cleared my throat to get her attention. Murphy finally looked up, startled, but her expression was fierce. Rain pelted down on her already sopping-wet clothes and began soaking through mine.

Glaring at me, she waved me off. "Ben, go away."

"I can't do that," I said as I walked a step or two closer. "What's wrong?"

"I just wanted to stand out here in the pouring rain, in my white shorts, and get drenched." She spoke through gritted teeth, flailing her wet noodle of a sun hat in her hand. "It seemed like something super fun to do on a Saturday night. Now, seriously, just go because I'm getting soaked and the fun has worn off."

"Are you serious? I'm not going anywhere until you tell me what the hell is going on. You show up out of the blue in Colebury, working at the Bean, and now you're standing outside this run-down duplex getting rained on."

At my words, her eyes caught fire, their bright emerald green a contrast to the rainy gray sky. "I'll have you know this run-down duplex is where I live. I told you it's not much, remember?"

Ashamed of myself, I swallowed the slightest bit of regret. I'd made her feel bad, and who was I to judge?

But I couldn't help myself. This wasn't how I pictured Murphy living her life. It was part of the reason I never allowed myself to think about having or keeping her. I'd always envisioned her living in a penthouse apartment, dressed in the finest clothes, dripping with expensive jewelry—something I firmly believed she wanted. It was a future I never imagined I'd be able to provide for her. Who knew I'd end up like I did?

I didn't have time to wallow in all that past shit because Murphy whirled and stomped back toward the duplex, slamming her fist into one of the doors, the sound echoing all around us.

As she banged on the door again, I waited for her to look up at me. "Stop avoiding me," I yelled through the rain, my hair soaked and my shirt dripping.

"What?" she barked as she turned toward me.

"What in God's green earth are you doing?" I sounded like my mom, but I didn't care. Some caveman instinct had taken over my body, and I needed to take care of this woman.

"Ben, listen. I know you think I'm fragile and spoiled, but I'm not. At least, not anymore. I can handle this myself. I locked my keys in the car, and I just need to get a hanger from my neighbor so I can open the car door."

"What?"

"My neighbor, she's a nursing student. She's probably asleep, but I need a hanger to open the car door."

"This is the craziest thing I ever heard."

Murphy crossed her arms in front of her, tightening her soaked blouse against her more than hard nipples. My eyes did their own thing as they scanned her body, landing right there.

"My eyes are up here, Ben," Murphy spat at me.

"Yes, yes, I know. I'm trying to figure out how you know how to break into a locked car while stuck outside in a summer storm. I couldn't even dream up something this crazy."

She turned and knocked again on the door I'd come to know was her neighbor's, then whirled back around. "I'll let you in on another secret. The car is old, and it locks with the keys inside it. My key to the apartment is on the ring too, and it's pouring down rain and I'm on a lonely, winding road in Vermont. Who the hell is going to help me?"

"Me?" I asked foolishly.

Murphy rolled her eyes. "Ben, this isn't the first time my idiot self has done this. So, yeah, I know how to open the door. A trucker taught me at a rest stop on my drive up here."

"Wait. You let a stranger help you, but you won't let me. A trucker?"

"Yes, a trucker. Now go away." Without another word, she

spun around. The rain continued to pelt us as she banged her fist against her neighbor's door.

This woman was so fucking stubborn, not to mention confusing the hell out of me. She went from debutante to downright independent *I am woman, hear me roar* in the blink of an eye. At least, in my mind.

Knowing she wouldn't let me help, I went back to my car and decided to wait. I was on call, but my phone was quiet. I glanced at the radar and saw this storm should be passing quickly.

For the first time in my life, my fingers itched to google someone. Obviously, the internet held some of Murphy's secrets, judging by her earlier reaction to my mentioning Google, but I didn't want to invade her privacy. I hated when patients or other doctors googled me and came in with preconceived notions about me and what else I did with my time.

It was actually somewhat reassuring that Murphy didn't want much to do with me. Maybe it meant she hadn't googled me. If she had, surely I'd be more acceptable to her—and her family—with my small windfall. Another reason that I hated Google.

I hadn't set out to make big money. In the beginning, I was coding apps while I was in college for chump change, but then I realized how I could help my parents.

Deep in thought, it wasn't until I heard a clanking noise that I realized the storm had let up and Murphy was outside her car, scraping the shit out of her door with a coat hanger.

"Murphy, please, let me do it," I yelled, hopping out of my Jeep.

"No, Ben. Go away. I told you to go away."

"You're infuriating."

At that moment, I couldn't even stand myself. I despised Murphy for what she did to my emotions at Pressman after I carried a torch for her for years. And I was intrigued by this new version of her, yet my heart wouldn't let go of how the old version had broken my heart.

"Please, go," she said while trying to maneuver the hanger to open the door. Her hand slipped and the hanger fell.

Before she could get to it, I'd snatched it up. "Murph, move over. Let me get it, so we can both go home and get dry."

Christ, even my sister calls me to help her with these types of crazy things.

Frustrated, Murphy crossed her arms in front of her, looking formidable.

I forced myself not to look at her tits, but I couldn't help the smile spreading across my face. The new Murphy was a live wire . . . a challenge in all the best ways. And she didn't know I was independently wealthy (that's what my advisor told me, anyhow). At least, I didn't think so. The door to the car popped open, and she rushed in front of me to grab the keys from the ignition.

"Listen," she said, standing next to the car. "I know you think you know me, but you don't. Maybe you knew me back then, at school, but I'm different now."

I'll say.

"Stop smirking," she said, looking like she really wanted to stomp her foot.

"Why are you different? What happened? Tell me."

I stood to meet her eye-to-eye, although at six-foot-three, I had about eight inches on her and still had to dip my head to meet her eyes. With her red hair darkened and curled by the rain, her damp shirt sticking to her skin and her makeup mostly wiped off, she looked gorgeous.

"You want to do this now?" she said, glaring at me. "On the side of a country road with another storm about to roll in?"

"I checked the radar. We're good."

"Ugh." She turned her back on me, taking deep breaths while facing the other way. Then as quickly as she'd turned, she whirled back around.

We were so close I could feel her tiny huffs of breath. I wanted to gather her close in my arms, but I didn't think that would go over well. And I was still holding that stupid hanger.

"Look," she said harshly, "I know I wasn't nice or fair to you at Pressman. I used you to help me, to tutor me, you know that, right? Not just in science, but in life too. Later, when I was sure you liked me and would take me to prom, I used you then too. I wanted to make my jerky ex, Burnett, jealous. It wasn't a kind thing for me to do. If I'm honest, I saw you as expendable. You should hate me. So, why are you standing here?"

I took one small step forward, and then another. Braving Murphy's wrath, I brought my hand to her cheek and smoothed a wet ringlet of hair behind her ear before dropping my hand.

"Murph, I'm standing here because you're you. Every now and then back at school, I'd see something real, get a quick peek at the true you. Inside this debutante who'd been groomed to act like a robot was a real person. A sweet soul. And as long as we're being honest, I thought of myself as expendable back then too. I should've stayed home and graduated from the local high school. Pressman didn't make me feel good about myself, but you did. I liked helping you."

"But I used you," she said, emotion choking her words as I stared into her eyes. She let out a long breath but didn't move.

"And I used you," I said softly. "I had no one at Pressman. At least you let me hang around sometimes."

Blinking hard, she said, "I'm not that way anymore. I'm not a mean girl. At least, I try not to be."

Although the rain had stopped, mist hung in the air, causing Murphy's hair to curl and her eyelashes to hold tiny droplets. I wanted to pull her close, but resisted.

"I can tell you're not, although you never really were a mean girl. I always thought that was more of an act. But really, Murph, what happened to you?"

The last question was a whisper. This Murphy was like an injured animal, cowering in a corner, but if I got too close, her claws would come out.

Not meeting my eyes, she huffed out a breath. "Let's just move on. We solved the problem, and I need to get inside and change out of these wet clothes, and so do you. We don't need to catch a cold. By the way, don't you have patients who need you?"

I took another step closer until we were almost nose to nose. She smelled like huckleberry, maybe her lotion or shampoo, I wasn't sure which. "I'm going to let you off the hook so you can change, but then we're going to get some dinner."

Leaning closer, I pressed a chaste kiss on her mouth. It wasn't long or sensual, but full of promise on my part, and her eyes widened.

"I've wanted to do that since prom night," I said low, "but I'm pretty certain I didn't have a chance before I started barfing, let alone after."

"Ben, please. Not now." She stole the hanger from me and stepped back. Rubbing the moisture off her hand on her shorts, she tried to walk away, but I reached out for her arm to keep her close.

Despite her best efforts to twist out of my grasp, I held tight. "Dinner?"

She nodded, and I let her go. I wasn't really holding her against her will. The keys fell from her hand and she bent to get them, her ass in the air. I swallowed as I took a quick peek, and then bent down to snag the keys for her.

Handing them over, I said, "One sec."

She could tell me over dinner how she went from riches to rags, but right now I wanted to get Murphy inside and dry. And that wasn't the doctor in me wanting to take care of her.

When it came to Murphy Landon, I turned into a raging caveman.

6

MURPHY

"What in the actual freakity-freak is happening?" I asked myself, risking a quick peek in front of me.

Yep, Ben was walking toward his late-model Jeep, clearly decked out with all the state-of-the-art bells and whistles, while I stood next to my very used Toyota. My car was on its last breath, and without a second job, I couldn't afford anything else. Not to mention this was the second time I'd locked my keys inside it.

If I hadn't been so desperate for help on my journey here to Vermont, I would have been worried about Ralph-the-trucker raping or kidnapping me. Luckily, he turned out to be a good guy with a wife and kids at home, and had driven for the last ten years for King Arthur Flour. He'd seen me pacing next to my car like Ben had and asked if he could help. Showing me a picture of his kids, he swore he was a good guy. After demonstrating how to open the door with a hanger, he gave me his number in case I needed somewhere to go for Christmas.

"Shit," I muttered to myself as Ben approached me again, shaking his head, presumably at my self-chatter.

He'd kissed me. On a wet Vermont road. Something I never thought I'd do, but strangely wanted to do a lot more of.

Watching Ben really take in the run-down house in front of

him, I could have lied to myself and said he was checking for storms, but he wasn't. My place left a lot to be desired. A long time ago, it must have been nicer, but now it was home to some nursing students who didn't earn much, a sanitation worker and his girlfriend who lived above me, a truck driver for a local meat company, and me. It was just an old duplex chopped up into small rental units, but it was comfortable and cozy . . . and cheap.

Ben had snagged a backpack from the back of his Jeep and joined me. "I'll change at your place, if that's okay?"

I nodded. "Prepared for overnights, I see?" My comment came out a bit snarky, but he just shrugged.

"Always. My cases tend to run long, or I get stuck with an emergency. This way, I can be ready to do anything at a moment's notice."

I nodded again as we walked toward my entrance in the back. Unlocking the dead bolt, I couldn't help but see my place through Ben's eyes, and wondered if this was how he'd felt in high school. Did he feel uncomfortable seeing us looking at his life with pity?

He scanned the dated kitchen with its nicked cabinets, a dishwasher so old it was easier to wash my dishes by hand, and a faded lime-green Formica countertop. The ratty brown couch I'd found in a secondhand shop sat in the living area across from the open kitchen, along with a television set on an old nightstand from the same secondhand store, sitting catty-corner across from it. At least my one houseplant wasn't dead. It thrived in a way I wished I could.

"Why don't I wait for you to get dried off in the bathroom?" Ben said, still taking in my place, which made me feel naked and exposed.

"And cleaned off." I held my greasy palm in the air as evidence.

"That too. Go, I'll wait."

"Sure, thanks. I can leave a dry towel for you when I'm done. Okay?"

The conversation had me off-kilter. Shame burning through

my veins, I escaped to the bathroom, where I stripped off my clothes and splashed warm water on my face, then quickly dried off and wrapped a towel around myself.

Taking deep breaths, I stared at myself in the mirror. *I shouldn't be ashamed. This place may not be much . . .* and then the door opened and I whipped around as I spoke the last thought aloud. "This is all me."

Ben stood there, confusion all over his face, as if he were the one surprised inside the bathroom rather than the one barging in.

"Really? You don't knock?" I gripped the towel a bit tighter.

He stood on the threshold, one palm clamped over his forehead. "I couldn't wait. I'm sorry. Truly. I realized I was out there judging you, and I don't know where that comes from. That's not me. It never was, and I don't want it to be."

My eyes watered, and I sniffed back any self-loathing.

"I'm sure you worked hard for this," he said, a little more calmly now. "And I know you came from big money, but for whatever reason, your life's not all about that anymore. I respect that . . . I respect *you*. When you're ready to tell me what happened, you will. Until then, I didn't mean to do that. It was just so shocking to me to see this, and even more shocking that I did it—judged you, not that you live here."

Blowing out a breath, I said, "It's fine. I get it. This is a surprise, but I'm making things happen on my own now. You know what? I can change in my room now, and you can have the bathroom." I moved past him, waving at the bathroom behind me while still tightly gripping the towel.

I needed a minute to process all this.

Who is he to come walking into my place, serving up judgments and then apologies, causing me pain and then making me feel all warm and gooey?

The toilet flushed and the water ran before the door opened and out came Ben in the same clothes. "I left my backpack out there," he said, walking through my bedroom.

I was sitting on the edge of my bed, having made no progress in changing into actual clothes. My mouth fell open at the way he'd taken over my shabby apartment in a matter of minutes.

"Be out in a sec," he said as he strode confidently back across my room, bag in hand.

"Oh," I said, apparently back to one-word nonsensical answers.

Hurrying to my closet, I grabbed a pair of jean shorts and a white T-shirt, the most casual outfit I owned. It was what I wore when I cleaned the bathroom, but it felt more appropriate for a summer evening in Vermont than what I had on earlier.

I was at the vanity brushing my hair when Ben came out of the bathroom in a clean pair of khaki shorts and a navy polo shirt. My gaze lifted to meet his as I wondered if his pale blue eyes would look great against the darker shade of his shirt. I was right.

"I need a sec to fix my makeup, and then I'll be ready. But, honestly, we don't have to go out for dinner."

"We do," he said with authority, combing his fingers through his hair.

A memory from prep school flashed in my mind. Ben used to do that when we were studying, and I always wanted to run my own fingers through his hair. I knew he liked me, but he wasn't who I was *supposed* to be with. My parents liked Burnett's parents.

"You okay?" Ben came close and ran a hand down my arm. It felt incredibly intimate, more intimate than I'd been with anyone else.

"Yes, why?" Uncomfortable, I shoved my hair behind my ear with unneeded force.

"You were deep in thought."

Rather than answer, I brushed past him to grab a pair of shoes from the cheap shoe rack I'd bought off the clearance shelf at Walmart.

"Well? About what?" he asked.

I sat on the bed, fastening a pair of Cleopatra-style sandals around my ankles. I might be dressing down, but everyone knew shoes made an outfit.

Not meeting his eyes, I shrugged. "I was thinking about Pressman. That's all."

"And?" He plopped down next to me on the bed. It was a cheap mattress on a simple frame, no headboard, but again—it was all mine.

I couldn't worry about my poor excuse for a bed because if I'd thought earlier felt intimate, this was off-the-charts cozy. We were downright homey like a couple, sitting on the bed and chatting about my thoughts.

I wasn't a prude, but this was a level of closeness I didn't look for in relationships. My parents never appeared to have it or want it, so I grew up thinking it wasn't meant to be or didn't exist.

Ben nudged my ribs with his elbow.

"Ow." I faked a yelp. "Why did you do that?"

"What were you thinking about at Pressman? How ticklish you were?"

"Don't you dare." I scowled and inched away from him. In high school, we'd always been in close proximity with ease. He'd tickle me until tears fell. I'd mistaken it for his being goofy, until I knew better.

Giving in, I sheepishly admitted, "Us. I was thinking about us, you know, studying. Studying with you. Hanging with you, pretending to be studying too. I knew you liked me."

Ben smiled, the most natural, gorgeous thing I'd ever seen, with his straight teeth and small laugh lines bracketing his mouth.

Meeting his eyes again, I blurted, "Your patients must all fall in love with you."

"Why?"

"Don't fish for compliments, Ben. Seriously, it's not polite."

"I see now. You can take a girl out of her fancy digs, but she still has manners," he teased, but not in a mean way. It only reminded me further about the way he used to joke with me.

"Hey, that's not nice."

He laughed, his smile widening. "You know I'm kidding. It's okay to not always be so proper. You've got to let loose, Murph."

I nodded. "I know. But it's tough because this is me. I'm wound tight."

"You always were. Even back when I liked you, and of course, I knew that you knew. I was pretty much Captain Obvious."

Looking down at my sandals, I sighed. "I wasn't nice back then."

"You were nice behind closed doors." His hand found mine and he urged me close again. "I always felt like I got to see the real you, the version no one else was privy to. For that, I was lucky."

"My parents wanted me to be a certain way."

"Well, you're a grown-up now. Making your own way," he said, tossing my earlier words back at me.

"That's right."

"Great." He stood, dropping my hand. "What are you hungry for?"

"Anything but scones." I stood to meet him, and seeing myself in the mirror, I held up a finger. "Wait, my makeup."

"Forget it. Let's go to the diner near my office. Best breakfast for dinner and pie you'll ever have. You won't see a soul. Come on," he said, taking my hand again. "They've been around for over a hundred years. You don't need to impress anyone there. Plus, you don't need makeup."

"Ben . . ." I growled out his name, but he had my hand, and I wasn't ready to let go. I didn't even bother asking if they had a decent salad.

BEN

Walking behind the Jeep to the driver's side door, I tossed my backpack full of wet clothes in the back and cursed myself for getting involved in this. Murphy was a bad habit I couldn't shake. I'd never been able to see the bad in her, and there was a lot of it. Then, like an idiot, I'd kissed her, as though I wasn't punishing myself enough already.

"Let's go," I told her.

Ignoring the shitstorm in my head, I slid into my seat and turned the car away from Colebury and back toward Montpelier. I didn't think the Colebury diner was ready for the interest we'd stir up by going there together, and I didn't necessarily need my sister hearing any gossip about me.

To be honest, I should have gone into the office, done some charting, and maybe focused on my latest pet project. I had some major things in the works, and getting distracted by Murphy wasn't in the plan.

"So, you came back here when? After Harvard?" Murphy asked, but continued to look out at the road ahead of us.

"Yeah, I decided to do med school closer to home and be near my parents. I missed the solitude, or maybe just the quiet here. I'm not a recluse, but all that keeping up with the Joneses—where they were going, what they were doing, and how much it cost—it was too much."

It wasn't like I was revealing anything Murphy didn't know. I couldn't stand any of that shit at Pressman either.

"I guess I lucked out and matched for my residency in Burlington, and then landed a job in Montpelier when the orthopedic surgeon there retired. Funny, he was the one to take care of my broken arm before I came to Pressman, and also the one to send me for the second opinion on my ankle at Harvard. He was a good guy, big shoes to fill. Worked by himself for years. It wasn't until his last five years working, they brought a second guy on."

"Must be nice," she said softly.

"What, the quiet? The regular old homebody part? Retiring," I said, joking.

"No. Being near your family." Murphy's face fell, sadness dulling her eyes. Even in profile, I could see wetness pool in them. Her family might be a bag of dicks, but they were still her family.

"Seriously, are you going to tell me what happened with your family? What made you come to Vermont, working as a barista, making it on your own when you come from one of the wealthiest political families in New York?"

Staring straight ahead, she breathed in, sucking back whatever emotion was ravaging her. "You mean you didn't google me?"

"No, why would I do that? I'm not even on Facebook or Insta-whatever-you-call-it. I definitely don't sit around googling people. I prefer to get my information directly from the people I care about. I guess you can add 'old soul' to the list when describing me."

I risked a quick glance at Murphy and noted her neck reddening. I wasn't sure whether fear or shame was causing it, but I didn't want to push.

"I really don't want to talk about it. Is that okay?" When she finally turned toward me, her expression was as fiery as the ambush making its way up her neck and her hair. Her green eyes blazed, daring me to ask for more of an explanation.

Having no desire to pressure her, I didn't bite. We might have run hot and cold in prep school, but I knew Murphy's tics and mannerisms, probably better than anyone, since we spent most of our time behind closed doors with our guards down.

"Of course it's okay," I said gently.

Murphy would tell me when she was ready. She might have thought it would be easier for me to force it out of her, but that wasn't my style. Not to mention, I wasn't even sure if I wanted to be involved in all this.

I still couldn't wrap my head around the contradictions that made up Murphy Landon. We'd done the push-pull thing for four years, and I thought I'd gotten over it. Yet here I was, pulling into the diner parking lot, about to share one of my favorite places with her.

"Cute," she said as I opened the door, not exactly the reaction I expected from the prep school princess. Then again, I didn't think she'd ever eat here.

"This place helped me survive the early days of working." I pointed toward a booth in the back and she made a beeline for it, sliding into the bench seat facing the door.

Taking a menu from in between the salt-and-pepper shakers, Murphy scanned the page. "What's good here?"

I realized this might have been a bad idea. "Well, I typically get the Biggie Breakfast, no matter the time of day."

She nodded, setting her menu down. "Your love of breakfast food is now coming back to me. You never missed it at school."

"Most important meal of the day. Plus, breakfast for dinner is a real delicacy. We used to have it all the time growing up."

"I've never had it." Her words came out hushed, but I was pretty sure I heard her right.

"What? Breakfast? Or breakfast for dinner?"

"For dinner."

"Of course not," I said glibly. "Not all of us can eat Beef Wellington every night of the week, though."

Her head dropped at my dig. "Please, I know that's how the

old us worked. I'd say something embarrassing, and you'd call me out on it. Back then, I'd laugh, but I'm not laughing anymore. Now I realize how horrible I was."

"That's not what I meant, Murph. Shit, look at me. It was more of a dig at myself, you hear me? I was making fun of where I came from, and how I grew up. If anything, I was slipping into old habits, feeling sorry for myself and making jokes to cover it up. It's an old defense mechanism, but not directed at you."

"Let's just not go there. Okay?" she asked, worrying her bottom lip between her teeth. "Please don't go there. The differences, all the poor-boy stuff you used to complain about. Guess what? Now I'm the poor little rich girl. Do you see me throwing that around?"

"No," I said softly, shame washing over me.

Mildred, my favorite server, came over. "Hey there, Ben. Who is this you have with you?"

She eyed Murphy, and I saw her through Mildred's eyes. Wavy red hair, beautiful face and skin—almost angelic, and definitely too good for me. Murphy might have been dressed in jean shorts and a tank, but I was certain they were some designer brand.

"I'm Murphy, an old friend of Ben's." She looked at Mildred and smiled. "I recently moved to Vermont."

"Is that so?"

Murphy nodded. "I work at the Busy Bean over in Colebury. Do you know it?"

"I do. Designer coffee, adorable furnishings, attracts all the young folk. We only do the old-fashioned drip here. No frilly stuff. Our pies and cakes are sweet enough, though." Mildred gave it to Murphy, but I knew she was joking.

"That's good, since drip is the best kind. Don't tell anyone I said it, though," Murphy said, dishing it back.

"Never." Mildred mimed zipping her mouth closed. "You two need a minute?"

I looked at Murphy and then remembered to ask Mildred, "Any specials?"

"Chef's salad with bacon instead of ham, and peanut butter and chocolate chip pancakes. Not together, of course."

"Oh, those sound good. I'll have the pancakes and a coffee. Milk instead of cream?"

Mildred shook her head. "Only have two percent."

"This is New England," Murphy said with a grin. "I figured as much."

I was used to Murphy being sassy in private, but out in public was a whole new experience. I liked it.

Mildred looked at me. "The biggie?"

I gave her a quick nod, and she was off.

"Looks like you're going to have breakfast for dinner, finally." I studied Murphy, trying to figure out where she was on the continuum of being okay with all this to being freaking out.

"It certainly does. My damn sweet tooth gets me into trouble all the time. I'll need to run an extra mile tomorrow."

"You look great, Murph. I know you're not fishing for compliments, but let it stand for the record. You look great."

"Thanks," she said, pushing her hair behind her shoulder. "Old habits die hard. Every time I eat something with actual flavor, my mom is sitting on my shoulder. I really need to shake her off. My shoulder, that is."

"You do."

"Hey, Mister I Wanted To Be Near My Family."

"I know. Guilty. But I make my own rules, do my own thing, and I don't beat myself up for it."

"I'm doing the same. Making my own rules."

Conversation shifted into something a little less serious while we waited for our food. I admitted I was happy for football to be over. "It was a means to an end," I said aloud for the first time.

"You still look like you play," Murphy said in what I assumed was a weak moment, a blush tinting her cheeks.

"I go to the gym."

With that, our food arrived, and Murphy dug into her pancakes. Although she only ended up eating half of them, when she was done, she said seriously, "Pancakes for dinner may be the best dinner ever."

She seemed so sophisticated in high school, and now she was like a little girl experiencing life for the first time.

"Thanks," she whispered as we walked toward my car after I paid. "That was fun."

"Come here." Snagging her hip, I dragged her close.

"I don't know what happened to the old Murphy," I said, running my hand down her cheek. "But I liked that Murphy a lot. I was almost too wishful back then. But this Murphy is almost too perfect for me. Tell me this isn't a dream."

I didn't give her a chance to answer. Pressing my mouth to hers, I gave in to my urge to kiss Murphy. I didn't care that we were in a parking lot, or that Mildred was probably watching from the window. Anyone from the hospital could run over here to pick up a takeout order.

I. Did. Not. Care.

Her lips were soft and a small moan escaped them, giving my tongue entrance. I kept it PG-13, only lightly caressing her tongue before moving back to closed mouth.

I'd waited to do this for so long—almost forgetting over the last few years how much I'd been into Murphy back at prep school. Since then, I'd busied myself in work and other projects, trying to be a deserving man. I'd never wanted a spoiled woman, though. I couldn't afford a high-maintenance woman's wants or demands back then, and had no desire to do it now.

At this moment, though, my mind was in overdrive as I continued to make love to Murphy's mouth. My heart beat at a frantic pace at the possibilities, and then the skies opened up, rain pummeling us for the second time that day.

Quickly pulling away, Murphy ran for the car, trying to cover her hair with her purse. "My hair doesn't get a break here," she mumbled to herself as we slipped into the car, our wet thighs sticking to the leather.

Blinking hard, I froze. Her comment was like a knife to the heart.

I guess she's the same old Murphy. We just kissed like two long-lost lovers, and all she can worry about is frizzy hair?

MURPHY

"Well, thanks," I said as we sat in Ben's Jeep, outside the crappy duplex where I lived. He didn't offer to walk me in. The closeness I'd felt earlier between us was gone.

"It was fun to catch up," he said, his tone a little curt.

I told myself to open the door and get out. Old Murphy would have given him a megawatt smile and thanked Ben profusely, then primly got out of the car. But this was a version of myself I didn't know. Jean shorts, sans makeup, finishing up a date at the diner for pancakes for dinner.

"Is there something wrong? I feel like the air around us has changed. Did I do something?" The words fell from my mouth faster than I could control them.

"Everything's cool," Ben said, refusing to make eye contact.

Glancing at my place, I asked, "Is it where I live?"

Now *that* got his attention.

His head swung my way, and his eyes narrowed on me. "Seriously, that's what you think? I know we haven't seen each other in years, but you knew me when I had nothing. Do you think I've changed that much? That I would judge someone for where they live?"

Taken aback at the rage rolling off him, I said warily, "You did say earlier you were judging how I lived now."

His blue eyes darkened, and his mouth went tight. I recognized that look. Ben was pissed. I remembered back at the after-prom party when Burnett accused him of settling for his sloppy seconds, and Ben lost it. His face had gone tight, and it took Scott Stephens's steely strength to hold Ben back from punching Burnett.

"Because this is not how I knew you," he said sharply. "Jesus, we keep going in circles. You're not how I remember, and when I ask why, you avoid the question. I think there's something there, more than could have been between us in high school. Besides the fact that we were just kids, we were from two different worlds."

He shifted toward me in his seat and stared me down, his sexy five o'clock shadow momentarily distracting me.

"Did you hear me?" he demanded. "I thought maybe you were here in Vermont as a sign, like it was our turn to be together. And then you go and talk about your hair."

"What?" I had no idea what he was talking about.

"The fucking rain."

I glanced out the windshield. The rain had stopped again, but it had really poured when we were kissing. "What about the rain?"

"All you could say was your hair was getting frizzy, Murph. We'd just shared what I thought was an epic kiss, and you were worried about your hair."

"Oh. I guess old habits die hard."

He slammed the steering wheel. "Don't do that. You're better than that. You pulled the same shit at Pressman. *Oh, Miffy will be mad if I don't get dressed up for her birthday party,* or *I can't go to the hockey game with you because I have to go with my friends.* Crazy thing was, I thought we were friends."

He swallowed hard, and I followed the movement of his Adam's apple and watched the rise and fall of his chest.

"You know what?" he said with a scowl. "Let it go. This is on me."

"Ben . . ." I reached out and touched his forearm. It was so strong, and I couldn't help but think of him playing football or working hard at his farm. I'd never seen the latter, but in my imagination, he was shirtless and surrounded by hay bales. "We were friends."

"Whatever. We were, and we weren't. It doesn't matter."

"It does. We were. And I thought the kiss was epic, but I don't think it's the best time for me to get involved with anyone. I'm working through a lot of stuff, and clearly, I have a long way to go. I'm truly sorry I hurt you. You make me want to get involved, make me want things I didn't know existed for people like me." Begrudgingly, I released my grip on his arm.

Ben turned away to stare out the windshield. "Thanks, but let's just forget it all happened. It's been nice reconnecting and all that, but let's keep this at old friends, okay? It's for the best. I have a lot going on too."

In that instant, I suddenly knew exactly what Ben had felt like all those years ago when I put him quietly, and often secretly, in the friendzone at Pressman. He'd just stuck me in the friendzone box, and I wasn't sure there were any passes to get out.

With nothing left to say—I wasn't going to beg for more—I opened the door. He hadn't exactly fought for anything more years ago.

"Thanks again," I whispered. With my head low, I ran to my door and quickly unlocked the dead bolt before the tears fell.

I'd made mistakes before, but this felt like something much larger than what had happened in New York, and that was devastating. But this—this felt like I was tossing away the only good thing I'd ever known, so I did the only thing I knew to do.

I searched for a cheap packet of Sour Patch Kids.

On Sunday, we were slammed at the Bean. With my hair stuck to the back of my damp neck and clenching my knees together because I had to pee so badly, I breathed out a desperate sigh of relief as Zara signaled for me to take a break.

On top of my disastrous date with Ben, if that's what it was—our outing or dinner or whatever—I'd gotten my period. Every time I looked in the mirror, I obsessed over the giant zit on my forehead and how Hunnie had called out my white shorts. I wanted to follow up with her on the internship but was too chickenshit.

After using the bathroom, I sat down in one of the mismatched chairs in the back of the Bean by the patio doors, looking at my phone and willing it to ring. Then I remembered I was in Vermont and not New York. Thinking of the looks I would get for chatting on the phone inside the Bean made me laugh . . . until my phone actually did ring.

Slipping out the patio door, I picked up this call. "Hi, Mom. How are you?"

"Murphy." She said my name grimly as usual.

I imagined her lips pursed as she said it. I could almost see her disdain, so deep that it must be creasing her Botoxed forehead.

"Hiya, Mom," I said, not sure why I tried to add some cheerfulness.

"Please don't *hiya* me. Your father and I are worried. When will you come back? You know he's supporting the next candidate for governor, and we need you to attend some events with us. It will be good for you. We can clear you of all those rumors and maybe you'll meet someone . . . decent."

Pacing the parking lot, I wished I hadn't answered. It was always the same thing. "Mom, it wasn't a rumor. I lost my job because of something I did."

"You told them you didn't know he was a student there, so you're cleared. It's time to hold your head up and go about the life you're supposed to live."

Of course, I didn't know when I met Preston Parker online that he was a transfer student at Columbia where I was an advisor. He'd said he was twenty-five before I went out with him. It was only for a few casual dates, and I had no idea what I was doing was wrong, but I did it. And then one thing led to another, and the next thing I knew, my reputation was ruined.

"Mom, listen. I'm here in Vermont, so don't tell me what I need to be doing. If I'm right, you and Dad wanted me to leave." Tears pricked painfully behind my eyes, so I thought about mud and rocks, hiking, and getting dirty to shake them off.

"We wanted you to take some space from us. Maybe go to the Bahamas and come back ready to be who we need you to be. Your family name is depending on it."

"I didn't have many choices, Mom. I had no money or job. I'd spent it all in New York on stuff I didn't need because I thought there was more coming. But then you froze my trust fund."

"Only until you did what we wanted."

"Oh my God." I stomped my foot, then quickly glanced around to make sure no one saw. Sure enough, standing twenty feet away was Ben Rooney, wearing his scrubs and looking freshly rumpled.

Closing my eyes, I willed him away. For the fastest second known to man, I worried about my hair, and then I remembered his challenge last night to let it all go. With my mom in my ear, it was even more difficult.

"Listen, Mom, I'm okay. I'm figuring out who I am and what I want in life, and discovering all of this on my own. I even have a lead on a social media position here." *I definitely need to call Hunnie. An internship is better than nothing.*

"It doesn't matter what you want. Don't you get that, Murphy?"

That was my mom, Lyssa Landon, CEO of my destiny and staunch believer in *we don't have a choice in life*.

"It does matter. I have to go," I said, quickly disconnecting the call as Ben approached.

"Hey," he said.

"Hey. I'm on a quick break and have to get back in there. I can even take your mug, if you want." I pointed to the red Yeti in his hand.

"Don't be like that," he said, not making eye contact.

"Like what? Like the help? That's what I am. I make the coffee, and you drink it."

"No, like we didn't have words last night, and you're taking them all personally. It's obvious."

"They *were* personal, Ben. I don't think I could interpret it any other way."

"I know. Shit," he muttered and kicked some gravel with his foot. "I'm sorry. Listen, it was wrong of me. I can't knock the way you were raised if I despised people doing the same to me." Looking up, he said, "By the way, you okay? I saw you having some sort of hissy fit over here."

"Look, I don't mean to be rude, but I just had the usual lovely conversation over the phone with my mom, and I'm not in the mood for this right now. Zara will need me back. If you don't want to give me your mug, I'll see you in there."

I turned on my heel and headed back inside through the patio doors, not waiting to see if Ben followed or used the main entrance.

MURPHY

"Look, I'm sorry," Ben said as I got out of my car at home later that night.

Standing near where I usually park, he was no longer in scrubs. He was freshly showered, his hair wet, wearing another pair of khaki cargo shorts, a white T-shirt, and running shoes. His woodsy scent begged for me to get close, but I resisted the urge.

"Stalk much?" I said while yanking the seat forward to get my bag.

"A little WD-40 may help that."

"Whatever. I know it's probably better off in the junk yard, but it's mine. Let it go," I said, somewhat snippy. "I know how this looks, poor little rich girl who grew up being chauffeured around in Escalades now hits rock bottom."

As I locked the car and slammed the door shut, I caught a good whiff of myself—coffee and grime—and wondered if Zara had ever thought about putting in a shower so we could clean up before we left work. I laughed at the ridiculous thought as I made my way to my door, ignoring Ben trailing behind me.

"Murph, slow down. I'm sorry. Shit, I seem to be saying that a lot. This is new for me. Seeing you, remembering how I really liked you—all of you, even the part who was used to being chauffeured around. It's just, you're different now. I want to believe you're better suited for me, and better for yourself too. God, I know how bad that sounds."

Turning in my doorway, I glared at him. "Better suited? Better for me? What does that mean? I'm still me, a person . . . and I've always been one. I need to try to stop punishing myself for having to live under my parents' rule. And you have to stop holding it against me."

Hadn't I treated him differently at Pressman? He wasn't wrong that I was better now.

Ben caught me off guard, running his palm down my cheek, and I looked up at him. "I see you get it now."

"Am I that obvious? Jeez, I thought I'd been taught better. My poker face is supposed to be perfect." Putting a pin in my thoughts, I spied one of my neighbors parking, and said, "Let's go in."

Ben walked over the threshold, this time with no surprise in his expression.

"Give me a sec, okay?" I said. "I have to put this down and run to the bathroom."

"No problem."

I decided to take a little longer, wiping off my body with a Burt's Bees makeup-remover wipe—a small luxury I still splurged on. It would have to do. Quickly, I changed into a pair of old J. Crew shorts and a loose off-the-shoulder gray T-shirt. Finger-combing my hair and spritzing on some Chanel perfume, a left-over Christmas gift from my mom, I did my best to look and smell somewhat appealing.

"Okay," I said, walking back into the tiny living space of my place.

Ben looked up from a photo of my friend Jordana and me hugging, glassy-eyed and bushy-tailed for lack of a better description. "I remember this. You and," he said, snapping his fingers, "Jordana, that's it. You guys went to a hayride for the other school nearby . . . Wallace Prep . . . and got so drunk.

Jordana spent the night hanging over the garbage can in the custodian's closet."

Although I'd kept the picture, Jordana was a friend from my past life. We occasionally texted or called, sent birthday cards, but she was living the good life in New York and I was here in Vermont. She was one of the ones who didn't turn on me completely, but she still distanced herself a little now that I wasn't *one of them.*

"We did. Bobby Williams asked me, and of course I was dying to go to the Wallace hayride. It was supposedly an epic event. Sadly, one I don't remember much of to this day. I didn't know Bobby was going to slip grain alcohol in my water bottle. Jordana was a mess. Her date talked her into smoking some bad weed."

Ben nodded. "You called me when you got back and needed help."

"I know. You were the only one I trusted not to blow our cover. I'm sorry. It was probably wrong of me to call. I trusted you, though. That had to mean something."

"But not with you," he said. "You didn't trust me with *all of you*. You only gave me parts of you, little bits—your fiascos, bad grades, and anxieties. Which is why I'm here to say I'm sorry. Again. I didn't mean to end things so abruptly last night. I'm not excusing your behavior from back then, but I don't want to act that way too. Seeing the way people acted at Pressman, holier-than-thou and shit, I vowed to never be that way."

Not wanting Ben to belittle himself on my behalf, I said, "It's okay. I get that we're from different worlds, and always have been. Look, I know I was a bitch then, but I'm trying not to be one now. It's just I've been thrust into some strange limbo between your world and mine. It's hard to shake some of the old thinking, but I'm trying to be better. That's the truth."

I fell on my sword because this was Ben, and although it had been well over a decade since we'd seen each other, it was like we were lost in time. With his hair as messy as it was back then, his perfectly scruffy jaw, his feelings out in the open, all I wanted to do was reach out and run my hand over his cheek and put my lips on his.

It was a force I didn't recognize. A desire that had always been there, but was absolutely burning right now.

"That's why I'm standing here. You deserve a second chance, Murph. It's no secret that my heart belonged to you in high school, which is kind of crazy because nothing ever happened. But here we are, all these years later, grown adults, and I'm still carrying a torch for you."

"Ben, please, listen to me. I was wrong back then. I know it. But I am who I am, and there are things I've done, things you don't seem to know about, that you shouldn't be a part of."

"Stop. Like I said, I'm not concerned with all of that. Unless you have an exotic communicable disease." He leaned in and ran his lips across my cheek.

"Ben." I tried to escape his hold, but he kept me close. "I'm not used to this. Silly Ben, Confident Ben, Doctor Ben, all these Bens wrapped up in one package. And a very fit one at that."

"Get used to it. I'm coming after you, Murphy. I'm dropping all the bullshit, the past and where we came from, because I want to know this you." He planted a quick closed-mouth kiss on me. "Forgive me?"

I nodded, not wanting to lose contact with his lips. For as much as Ben gave me a headache from the hot-then-cold vibes, I was sure I did the same.

Oh well, I wasn't going to turn down kisses from Absolutely Delectable Ben.

"Dinner?" Ben asked later, leaning against my hideous green kitchen counter after our kissing and not-enough-making-out session.

It didn't get much further than our tongues tangling and Ben's palm grazing my side cleavage before he'd said, "Let's slow things down." When I groaned, embarrassing myself, he added, "It's not like I don't want more."

I suggested a drink before remembering all I had was crappy wine, but he took me up on it.

"So, you had to work today?" I asked, pulling down two wine-glasses.

"Yep. Low man on the totem pole in my practice, so I get the crappy weekend calls. Broken hip, return offender. Poor guy lives alone, won't listen about getting help, keeps getting up on a ladder to change his light bulbs. Second time this year I've fixed him up. I'm hoping his family steps in this time."

"Aw, poor guy."

"Yep. I was out on an early morning hike with a buddy and stopover at my mom's, but work called."

"Wait? Can you drink that?" I motioned toward the second-hand-store wineglass I'd just handed him.

"Yes. We switch off at five o'clock. Someone else is on for the next twenty-four hours. I do have to go in and do rounds in the morning, but right now, I'm hungry and grateful for the vino."

I took him in, his blue eyes bright, his hair an unruly mess.

"What?" he asked, giving me a curious look.

"Just looking at you," I said boldly.

"Oh yeah?"

"I would've recognized you anywhere."

"I'm pretty sure I knew who you were right away. You look pretty damn good yourself." He slipped his arm around me and pulled me close, whispering the last part in my ear. "But before anything else, I have to eat."

"Oh," I said, disappointed. I wasn't sure when I'd turned into such a vixen. Even when I'd supposedly seduced a student, it was a slow-burn thing. We'd texted through a dating app, then met for coffee a few times.

"It's been fourteen years. I think that classifies as slow burn." My eyes grew wide. "Wait, did I say that out loud?"

"You did, but you don't have to go into any details until you're ready, Murph. I'm serious, I don't know what the hell went on with you, but I want you to tell me yourself." His stomach rumbled through the last part. "How about Chinese takeout? I know you like it. Remember you guys used to order it all the time in the dorms on Sunday nights?"

Ben switched gears, steering away from my transgressions, and I didn't know if that was for my benefit or simply the way he was. An unfamiliar emotion swept through me at the thought of what a decent guy he was.

Sensing myself being taken over by feelings, I said quickly, "They have that here? Good Chinese food?"

This earned me a laugh and a wink. "We may not be the Big Apple, but we've got everything you need right here in sleepy little Vermont."

As Ben pulled up a menu on his phone, I wondered why I'd been such a loser and hadn't given him a chance back then.

Then I remembered. I'd been a snobby bitch, for lack of a better word.

"I'm sorry," I whispered as he handed me the phone with the menu.

"For what? Doubting we have good Chinese here?"

I swallowed, feeling a lump of regret the size of a peach pit slide down my throat, and decided to put myself out there. "I'm sorry for how I acted back at Pressman. We keep circling around it —the past, what happened, how sorry I am, how you did the best you could. Honestly, Ben, you have nothing to be sorry about or to regret. You came there with the best of intentions, and most people treated you crappy. Maybe me the most."

He frowned at me. "Don't say that. You were nice to me . . . in private."

"Just don't. Please don't make excuses. Shoot," I said, picking at a loose cuticle.

Damn. I'm going to make a mess of my home manicure, but it's too late to worry about that.

"I don't know what's gotten into me." I waved at my cracked, faded countertop. "You're starving, and we're stuck in this tiny excuse of a kitchen. Maybe it's talking about Chinese food, reminding me of when we used to order, and you never joined in."

I'd just had this memory the other day, but I didn't mention it.

"Or maybe it's just the day I've had. My mom, she's a piece of work. She taught me to always be this nice person, but that only applied to people in my same social bracket. Everyone else got a fake smile. I tried to be somewhere in the middle with you, but I couldn't make it happen outside of our dorm rooms or the library."

"You tried," he said, rushing to my defense again.

"No, I didn't try hard enough. And for that, I'm sorry."

"You know what? I wasn't always easy back then either. My home life, my lack of what everyone else had, was like a nasty chip I carried on my shoulder. But I don't want to keep circling on the issue either. Let's put an end to this. I'm an adult now, all grown up with my own money and career, and you're doing your thing, making your way in the world. Let's eat takeout as the people we are now, and leave those two in our past."

My shoulders dropped. "Okay." I didn't know how Ben did it, but he seemed to render me speechless often.

"Go on," he said, pointing to his phone in my hand. "See what you might like."

Swiping at his screen, I scanned the menu. "Oh, this place is even better. More Thai than Chinese. It's Thai, you knew that, right? Pho house . . . mmm, looks delicious. I love pad Thai."

Ben grinned. "We're very advanced here. I usually get the fried rice, so I think of it as Chinese takeout. Fried rice is my weakness. You need to try it. Give me the phone, and I'll call." He took the phone back, saying he also loved the ginger chicken. "Should we get a few things and share?"

"Great."

And just like that, it was so easy. Ben ordered the food, told them he'd be there in twenty minutes, and ordered me to relax with a glass of wine before he was out the door.

"Are you sure?" I asked.

"Yep. The owner is a patient of mine, and I like to say hi. I'll have wine when I get back. It's a bit of a drive from here, but I need to support them."

As I poured myself a cheap glass of vino, I couldn't help but wonder, *Is this a date?* It was my second night eating with Ben, which was more than I'd done with a man since fleeing New York.

Shit. I swore silently, another transgression my mom would lecture me about.

I could hear her now. *Ladies don't swear. Especially those in the public eye.*

Good thing I'm not in the public eye anymore.

Although, if she had her way, I'd be back before I knew it. I needed something to hold me here more firmly. My mom would have no problem steamrolling into the Bean and berating Zara—with a smile on her face—and have her begging for me to pack up and leave.

Double shit. I needed to call Hunnie. If she hired me, I could tell my mom it was an actual job. She didn't have to know it was an internship.

Finding my phone tucked into the side of the couch where I'd been planted since Ben left, I looked up where I noted Hunnie's number and dialed.

"Hello?"

"Um, Hunnie, hi. It's Murphy Landon. We met at the farmers' market."

"Oh, Murph, whatcha up to? You lonely on a Sunday night? What are you calling me for? Some company?"

"Uh, no. Shoot, I forgot it was Sunday night and you're probably relaxing. I worked at the Bean today."

"Ha. Well, this is Vermont. Things aren't as fancy here. It's fine to call me on a Sunday night. How's the Bean?"

"I don't mind it. Actually, I'm liking it quite a bit, and thanks for the tip on the white shorts." One thing my mom had taught me that stuck and was worthwhile—always lead with a genuine compliment.

"It's nothing. So, are you up for the internship?"

"Yes, that's why I was calling. I wasn't sure if you'd made up your mind."

"I'm not an idiot. If I can have some big-city chick help me, I'm taking it. That's what I need to get some of those fancy pants in Manhattan and Boston to buy my honey."

Butterflies swarmed my belly. "I can't make any guarantees—"

"Look, Murphy. You know Ben, and that's good enough for me. If he likes someone, and I can tell he likes you, they're good people."

"Oh." Good thing I was on the phone. My cheeks were burning like crazy.

"Listen," Hunnie said, "I gotta run. I'm heading out. Call me tomorrow around two? Does that work? I'm usually at my desk then, and we can set up a time to meet and go over a few projects."

"Sure. Wait—is it okay that I keep my job at the Bean? I know you advertised this as a paid internship, and I don't want to break any rules."

"Definitely stay at the Bean. Zara pays better than I do—unless I can get the Rooneys to jump on board with my petting-zoo idea. Ha. Talk to you Monday. Now, go find that surgeon hottie, hear me?"

Hunnie hung up before I could respond to what she just said, and Ben was knocking on my door.

My head swam with what this all meant in sleepy, small-town Vermont.

BEN

"Wait," I said, empty containers of Thai—not Chinese—food spread across the weathered table in front of us.

"It's true," Murphy said, trying to scowl. "So what? I'm learning."

"Murph, you work in a coffee shop, a fancy-pants craft-coffee joint, and all you have is a Keurig at home. How is this possible?"

"It makes fine coffee," she said defensively. "I used to go out for coffee a few times a day in New York because I didn't have a coffeemaker back then. And then I moved here, and it was a while before I found the Bean. Even so, I still use the Keurig sometimes in the morning. I can't spend ten bucks every time I want a cup of coffee." She pulled her feet underneath her, her back against the armrest, her gaze pinging around the room as she desperately avoided my eyes.

I couldn't help the laugh rolling out of me.

We'd had a great dinner, devouring everything in front of us, and finished a cheap bottle of wine. I wasn't sure what the protocol was now. *Should I leave? Could I stay?*

Then Murphy asked if I wanted coffee and pie. Apparently, she had a pie in the freezer from one of her earlier jaunts to the farmers' market. Cherry. Then she'd said, "I think I have decaf pods for the Keurig," and I lost it.

"This Keurig thing, it's new for you? Like breaking and entering into your own car?" I was joking, but sadness washed across Murphy's face. "No, I didn't mean anything by that. Seriously. I was just kidding."

"It's cool. I know I was pampered. Believe me, the first person to admit that is me. Being here, struggling to make it all happen isn't easy. But I'm doing it."

Murphy's makeup had worn off some, and her hair fell loosely over her shoulder. She looked stunning to me . . . and I was desperate to reach out and touch her.

"You're definitely doing it, but you need a fancy espresso maker or something for home. So you can practice your art."

"If I could afford one, I'd get one. Now I rely on a little extra time at Zara's. Plus, she feeds me sweets when I come in early."

"The attack of the sweet tooth . . ."

"What is it tonight with you pointing out all my shortcomings?" She leaned over and pinched my thigh, and a zing of attraction flew between us.

"Never. I have a lot of them too. We already know I don't want to leave my family, and I work too much."

"Hold that thought," Murphy said, jumping up from the ratty couch. "I'm going to put the pie in the oven."

My mind wandered when she crossed the room, wondering what she would think of my house. It was bigger than I ever dreamed of having, spacious, and way more modern than the farmhouse I grew up in. A pretty palatial buy for a guy like me, it was a split-level craftsman with space to grow. Brenna, my sister, convinced me I deserved it. Plus, Branson used to spend a lot of time at my place. Without a father in the picture, he needed me, and I was hell-bent on being there for him.

"Tell me, why do you work so much? Clearly, you could lighten up a bit," Murphy said as she plopped down on the couch.

Her question made me think of the ski house I'd put an offer on near Mad River, another luxury buy with Branson in mind. But even with all this thinking of him, I wasn't ready to tell Murphy everything. I wanted Branson to know some of the finer things. I'd learned to ski on an unmarked hill, dangerous as fuck but fun as hell . . . but he deserved better. I didn't want him to be the kid who was pitied.

"Hey, where'd you go?" Murphy reached out to tap my thigh. "You were in la-la land for a minute."

Running my hand through my hair, I decided to come clean, not wanting to let my pride get in the way. "Honestly, it's a bad habit. Sometimes I feel guilty for doing well and having nice things. I was thinking about the things I've acquired over the past several years, and things I've wanted. I can't seem to let go of always wanting to do better, get ahead, prepare for some unknown disaster. My parents don't have much of a safety net. I don't want to be that way, but I also want to live a nice life. I just can't seem to balance the two."

She nodded, but I didn't know how or why she would get that. She'd never really wanted for anything, except for now.

"My parents were in a bad place when I went to Pressman. Technology was improving in terms of getting sap, and they had to borrow and scrimp to be able to afford the newest equipment. Thank God, it started to pay off, and they've been able to get ahead these last few years."

Murphy's head tilted to the side, and for a moment, I thought she was trying to read me better, to gauge if I was being truthful. Sadly, I wasn't. I'd helped my parents pay off some of the loans, but protecting their pride kept me from saying anything about it.

"I get the wanting to do better," Murphy said. "It was—*is*—how I am. Just switching gears. I'm sure it doesn't make sense, but it had to be done. Look, I'm not going to be a barista forever. I'll get back into some marketing. On my terms," she said, focusing on herself. It was a welcome reprieve.

"That's good, Murph. But whatever you are—barista,

marketer, whatever—as long as it makes you happy and proud, that's all that matters."

"Okay, Doc Rooney," she said, waving off my advice.

How could I argue when she threw my title back at me?

"I hear you, but listen," I said. "What you do, what you have, none of that matters. It doesn't make you who you are."

Her head dropped forward as she said softly, "But that's just it. I don't really know who I am. For all my life, I was told to be one way. A little too proud, way too rich, the perfect entertainer, a politician's daughter, an heiress, and then I find out it's a shitty way to live. Pardon my French."

She looked up as she said the last part, a small smile on her face.

"Also, I'm not supposed to swear. The media could pick up on it. That's why I needed to be with the *in* crowd at school. Actually, I didn't have to, but part of me needed to be. Why? Because they understood. They got it. I guess what I really misunderstood is that they liked being that way."

I leaned a little closer. "Hey, you need to let go of all of this."

Sweeping her hair back, she said, "It's not only that. I made mistakes. Some that are unforgivable. Like with you . . . and others."

"You can tell me," I said, but left it at that. I wasn't going to press.

Murphy shook her head. "I feel bad we never really went there with our friendship. We were close in private, and not until prom did we really step out into public. There were a few times, I guess, but always under the guise of you tutoring me."

I took her hand and ran my thumb over hers. "It's okay. I wasn't easy to be close to with that big chip on my shoulder."

She dropped her gaze, focusing on our joined hands. "I don't want to talk about this anymore."

"That's fine, but it's not good to keep everything inside, Murph. You'll explode. Trust me."

She didn't know how I walked around pretending to be an

average doctor, living a quiet life in Vermont, when my bank account said otherwise. I was the one on the verge of exploding. Honestly, all the money I'd earned didn't mean much because I had no one to share it with.

"You seem to be the master of keeping stuff hidden." She looked up at me, and it felt like she was trying to see into my soul.

"Well, I learned how to keep my feelings to myself at Pressman. I was the odd man out, and it's not easy to get over that. So, you know what? When you feel up to it . . . let them out. Maybe you can chat with Zara. I know her a little. Her daughter, Nicole, broke her arm, swinging on the trees behind the Bean, and the Shipleys are good friends of my family. Anyway, Audrey called me to take a look at it. With Dave's hockey experience, he's brought some business my way."

"She's my boss, so I'll see. In fact, it's better I don't. Plus, I don't know Dave well. When he comes in, Zara dotes on him, and then he leaves. I wish I could see myself like that one day with someone, but . . ."

"But what? You'll have that if you want it," I said without thinking, then caught myself. Who in the ever-loving fuck was I to give dating advice? "Either way, Zara doesn't care if she's your boss. She's a good person and will shoot straight with whatever you tell her. Used to be a bartender, so she knows how to listen and give it to you straight."

The timer on her old microwave beeped, pulling us out of the serious moment, and in some sort of Pavlovian response, Murphy popped up to get the pie.

"What's all this serving me about?" I said, jumping up too. "I can get it."

"No, no, let me," she said, shooing me away so she could pull the pie from the oven. "The need to entertain well dies hard. Except my mom would be barking orders at the staff to get the pie."

She waved her hand in a bossy way as she said in a haughty voice, "Maurice, get this. Eleanor, bring me a hot tea." Smirking at me, Murphy stood on tiptoe to grab supplies from the cabinet. "Oh well, time to make those delicious K-cups."

"Here, let me." I shot up behind her, using my height to easily pull down the box of decaf K-cups, savoring the heat of her back to my front.

We bantered back and forth as we enjoyed the pie and coffee, and it felt good. Really good.

I wasn't sure if this version of Murphy was here for good, but I knew I wanted to enjoy her as much as possible. I'd been infatuated with her at Pressman, then fantasized about her for years, and now here she was.

On that thought, my phone rang. I pulled it from my pocket to see it was my real estate agent calling, probably about the property I was interested in.

Not wanting to share this side of me, I answered the call and said, "One sec," into the phone, and to Murphy, I whispered, "I have to take this. Be right back."

Murphy probably thought the call was patient related. I couldn't deny my being a doctor, but I would keep how deep my pockets were to myself. I didn't want my wealth to be a deciding factor when it came to whether Murphy gave me a chance or not.

When I came back inside, she was curled up on the couch, reading on a Kindle.

"You look comfy," I said, taking in her smooth legs and her long red hair falling over her shoulder.

She looked up with a smile. "Sorry. I didn't know how long you would be, and I only have a few chapters left in this book."

"No worries." I slid in next to her, noticing the pie plates and coffee cups were gone. Despite it not being much, it was clear Murphy took a lot of pride in her place.

Running my palm over Murphy's bare thigh, I asked what she was reading.

"Oh, this is a great book, but not for you," she said with a devilish smile.

"Why is that? Is it a sappy romance?"

"Not sappy. Super fun," she said, and I glanced at her Kindle to see she was reading something titled *Brooklynaire* by Sarina Bowen. "It's steamy in the best way, and I love the attraction between the hero and the heroine. It does make me kind of sad with all the New York parts, because I can't go back there. Ever."

My heart sank when she said this. The city she'd been raised in was no longer hers, for a variety of reasons that twisted my gut.

"I'm sure you can. Whatever happened, happened. It's in the past," I said, not wanting to push, but feeling the need to give comfort. "Don't get me wrong, I want to know, but on your terms. We all have our reasons for keeping stuff to ourselves," I said before stopping abruptly. Selfishly, I was enjoying this close time with her, and I didn't want to ruin it with serious talk.

Murphy shrugged, not meeting my eyes. "Anyway, Bowen is a great writer, and I almost finished the book in one night. I love the way she writes a love story, especially since who knows if I'll ever have my own to tell," she said, changing the subject but then veering into awkward waters. That was Murphy.

"Oh, come on." I was joking, but did she really not believe she would fall in love with someone incredible? Someone like me, maybe?

The thought floated in one side of my mind and out the other, especially after all her declarations about where she would live and what she would do.

"Yeah, never mind," she said quickly. "That was silly for me to say."

Letting it slide because this felt so comfortable, I said, "Come here." I took her Kindle and set it aside before pulling her onto my lap. "I don't know what to make of all this. Is it serendipitous? Is it a curse?"

The last part earned me a giggle.

"I mean it, Murph, you tortured my thoughts for years. That doesn't mean I've been a monk since high school," I said, and she let out another giggle just for me. "It means you're here, and you're way better than I could have ever dreamed."

Murphy swallowed and licked her lips, presumably thinking of what to say. Not wanting to wait, I swooped in to kiss her.

Pressing my lips to hers, I took my time. Slow and patient, I explored her lips, so much softer than mine. When she moaned, my tongue found its way inside her mouth. Another moan brought me the touch of her tongue against mine.

Murphy shifted, moving to straddle my lap, never breaking the kiss.

I pulled her in tight, and she ground down on my hardness. It was better than I'd imagined and torturous at the same time. My hands wanted to rip her shirt off, and my body told me to toss her onto the couch and climb on top of her. My mind, the spoilsport, said to slow down. Running my hand through her hair, I continued to make love to her mouth, catching her soft whimpers, committing them to memory.

"Murph," I whispered, and she stroked her tongue along mine before pulling back to see me. "This feels so good. *You* feel so good."

"I want more, but it's been a while . . . and I've never been very good at all this." Burrowing her forehead in my shoulder, she said, "I don't mean the actual act. I meant getting involved."

"You don't have to worry with me. I'm patient. Cautious. I want to be careful with your heart because I need you to be careful with mine. You've only been back in my life for a few days, and I want you so much."

"Then have me," she said, leaning in for another kiss.

I devoured her, drinking in this new Murphy, one kiss at a time. Pulling back again, I nibbled on her ear. "I will have you, but not now. I'm in this for the long haul. There's no rush, trust me," I said low, filling her head with promises.

She nodded, but with a far-off look in her eyes that I couldn't read. Didn't she believe me? Or was it something else?

Weaving my fingers through hers, I kissed her one more time, a closed-mouthed kiss full of promise and wishful thinking, before standing and tugging her up with me. I gathered her close, running my lips along her forehead.

"Go back to your book, Murph, and don't think so hard. I'll see you soon." With that, I let myself out, only realizing when I got to my car that I'd made promises to Murphy without even getting her cell phone number.

This was what she did to me. You'd think she'd have less of an effect after all these years, but nope.

MURPHY

I will have you, but not now. I'm in this for the long haul. There's no rush.

That's what Ben had said, leaving me breathless with those simple words. Of course, part of me couldn't believe it because he didn't even have my phone number, but I still hoped.

"Earth to Murphy," Zara sang into my ear on Monday.

"Oh, sorry. I was spaced out. But we aren't busy."

Zara grinned. "No worries. Anything going on you want to chat about?"

Figuring now was as good a time as any to let her know about Hunnie, I said, "If it's cool with you, I'm going to help Hunnie out with her honey. I don't think it will take away from my time or work here because it's only an internship. At least, that's what Hunnie is calling it."

Blowing out a big breath, I felt the stray hair sticking to my cheek flutter across my skin. My hair really needed a deep conditioning. Mentally, I made a note to look into home remedies.

Zara gave me a confused look. "Murphy, no offense, but I know you graduated from college a while ago. You've had real-life work experience, so why an internship?"

Shrugging, I said, "It just works for me now. Getting my feet wet again."

"Look, it's not my business, but if you want to talk, I'm here. Also, Gigi's back this week, so you should pop over and meet her. I know you like her cupcakes, but she could be a good friend to you."

Glancing at the wall clock, I said, "Look at that, time for me to go. So, you're cool with me working with Hunnie? She's waiting for me to call."

I didn't want to blow Zara off, but I wasn't in the mood for a heart-to-heart. Learning about my past only made people pity me, and truthfully, I didn't deserve it. After all, I was the one who'd been blind to how out of it I was. It took me forever to understand Ben actually liked me, and I didn't want anyone to know how clueless I was.

"It's cool," Zara said, waving me off. "Hunnie's a good one. Love what she's doing with the infusions."

I nodded. "Okay, see you tomorrow afternoon." Walking out from behind the bar, I untied my apron.

"Maybe the doc will be in?" Zara called after me. "And don't forget to take a coffee with you."

Ignoring her first question, I kept going but gave Zara a genuine smile. "No need to twist my arm."

A few minutes later, I walked past a few mismatched high-backed chairs and out the patio door to my car. Funny how chaos like this brought me comfort these days. It was such a dramatic departure from my whitewashed perfect world in New York. Kicking my tire, I called Hunnie.

She answered, saying, "Yo, Murphy, want to come by my place?"

"Um, sure. Want to send me the address?"

Just like that, I was driving along a winding two-lane road, dust kicking up in my wake, holding my breath I would make it to Hunnie's apiary without my car breaking down. Her family had owned the place for three generations, she'd told me when I went back to see her at the farmers' market, and she was looking to take it to the next level.

Finally, when I saw a signed marked HUNNIE'S SWEETEST HONEY INFUSIONS , I took a left down the driveway. Tall trees lined the gravel road, and again I feared for my poor car. Doing as Hunnie told me, I drove around the main house and parked in front of what she called her she-shed.

Her shed was exactly how I would have pictured it . . . worn-in ivory-painted wood, an adorable small porch complete with a rocking chair, and the windows wide open. I couldn't see Hunnie living anywhere else.

A tiny wave of melancholy swept over me. Would I ever be so perfectly content?

As I swung open my car door, a reminder of what I'd asked Ben flashed in my mind. *Does he have a thing for Hunnie?*

Maybe I'm just a "friend" to him like when I friendzoned him back at Pressman. After all, when I sort of begged for him to have me last night, he told me to wait.

"Oh, great. You're here."

The door swung open and there stood Hunnie, wearing jean shorts and a red tank, her hair in a messy bun on top of her head, her feet bare.

"If your white shorts didn't give you away as a newbie back at the market, that car would have. Jesus, you are not prepared for Vermont winters, girl," she said, pointing at my beater.

"I know. Sadly, this is the best I can do for the moment."

"Well, we're going to have to deal with that later." Hunnie waved me in, her bun bouncing on top of her head.

Not bothering to lock my car, I walked up the one step to her shed and entered what looked like a magical emporium. Glass bottles of all shapes and sizes filled with golden liquids lined the far wall of shelves opposite a log-burning fireplace. The other wall served as a small kitchen, housing a farmer's sink, a stove, and a fridge. The fourth wall, faced with exposed brick, held picture frames of every shape and size.

"Most of them are my grandma Christine." Hunnie pointed at the wall and then turned her attention back to me. "So, here's the thing, Murphy. When I put in the ad, I thought I'd get a student from Burlington University, home for the summer and willing to do my bidding on the cheap. But now I have you, a city slicker wise beyond what I need. To be honest, I can't pay much, but I'm going to pay you more than I would a student."

"Believe me, I'd like nothing more than to do this gratis for you, but . . . but you saw my car," I said, stumbling over my own words, a stranger to this kind of brutal honesty. I ducked my head, letting my hair curtain my burning cheeks.

"I would never let you do this for free," she said, "but I need this to work. Yeah, my parents have given me a lot of leash with this infusion stuff, and I need it to fly. Also, the petting zoo . . . it's what all these moms with disposable cash are looking for when they come for these hiking and ski weekends."

Hunnie plopped onto a purple velour couch and motioned for me to sit in a red velour chair. This place was like Alice in Wonderland's secret hideout.

"You see, they want an authentic experience," she said. "Know what I mean?"

I nodded, not fully getting it, *but fake it until you make it.*

"I don't want to take advantage of them. That's not me. But they want to feel like they really did Vermont. And of course, goat yoga will be on the menu."

I couldn't help it, but my mind went right to Ben and what he said. He knew she would want that, because he really knew her and she really knew him. It wasn't like how things were with us.

Standing, I walked toward the wall of photos. My mind spun with a few ideas, something else I couldn't help. My mind liked to work, and it needed the exercise. After years of Pressman and college, taking the courses my parents told me to, then working as a student advisor after getting a marketing degree, I needed a chance to do something I actually liked.

"I'm not from Vermont," I said as thoughts pinged in my

brain, "but what strikes me about this place is the connections, the roots you all have planted here, more firmly planted than the ancient trees. You're firmly entrenched in the area . . . in the soil."

Wandering over to the window, I placed my hand on the glass, taking in the beauty outside—tall bright green trees, lush grass, wide-open fields, and a few dogs roaming about. It was straight out of a picture book.

"Must be pretty in the fall, when the leaves are changing," I said. "What color do those turn to be?"

Hunnie patiently granted me this change of subject, a complete one-eighty from the internship or her honey, but a necessary diversion for me. "Red, burnt orange, yellow. Those sugar maples line the road all the way to Ben's family's place. Most turn to be a deep red. The Rooneys have red for miles in the fall. With all that new equipment Ben helped them buy, they get sap for days. I think the biggest thing is keeping all the lines clean. That's what can ruin syrup."

I was stuck on the name Ben. He could be over there now. What would he think of me in comparison to Hunnie? She was making her dreams come true with the support of her family, and I was trying to find mine in spite of my family.

Heading back to the photos, I reached out to trace one of presumably Hunnie and her grandma. "I think we should add hints of red to your profile. Can we change up the color of your logo? I like the yellow, but it's the obvious choice for honey, and I think we can do something more vibrant like jewel tones. Red, purple, navy . . . like this room. It will make the honey stand out. Especially in your pretty jars."

Up until now, I was talking to the wall, but I turned and caught Hunnie taking notes. Her appearance might be all hippie-dippie, her personality a hundred percent Vermont-friendly, but the woman was a boss.

Turning back to the framed photos, I said, "We need to add your authenticity to the marketing, like you want to add that to the overall flavor of the experience. Something like *this blend is dedicated to my grandma, who not only gave me my nickname but my business stickiness.* As for the goats, I need time to think on that, but the honey is obvious. You've put all of yourself into these blends."

Hunnie ran up from behind me and threw her arms around me from behind.

"Sorry, sorry. Yeah, we're supposed to be professional women, but that's just what I was thinking. I knew I'd like your big-city thinking. Thank you." She stepped back and really looked at me, as if trying to see deep inside me. "What are you doing making coffee, Murphy Landon? You know what? Don't tell me. We all have our shit. Just figure out your next step while helping me, okay?"

"Okay."

Pulling her hair out of the bun, she shook her head left and right, her long brown locks falling loosely.

"That reminds me," I said, frowning. "I've got to get back home and deal with my hair. I need a deep conditioning."

Hunnie scoffed. "You don't need a thing. You're gorgeous."

"Thanks, but some days . . . never mind. Tell me, should I mock up some social media posts for you?"

"That would be great, and for payment, the going rate is . . ." She leaned close to whisper the rate so only I could hear it.

"No one else is here," I said with a laugh, "but yes, that's great. I'm actually really excited about this. If it's okay with you, I'll snap a few pics on my phone that we could use on Instagram."

Hunnie waved me off. "Go right ahead. I actually have to call a guy about the goats. Is it okay if I go do that on the porch?"

"Sure. So, Ben's family has agreed to the petting zoo?"

"Actually, I don't know," Hunnie said, a smile in her tone. "But I'm going to bet on you helping change Ben's mind about convincing his parents."

I'd been looking at my phone, but I whipped my head up at that. "Me? I don't know about that."

"Oh yeah. There's never been more of a sure thing than you two. The energy between you is like a roaring fire pit in the fall."

Waving my hand, I said, "Go make your call." I'd agreed to her payment terms and was jazzed about the work, but I didn't need to subscribe to Hunnie's ridiculous romantic notions.

I took a moment to absorb the vibes of Hunnie's place and then stepped outside quietly, careful not to interrupt her call.

As I slid into the driver's seat of my car, Hunnie shouted, "Wednesday is Fourth of July. You have plans?"

Closing my eyes for a second, I huffed at my own stupidity. "You know, I forgot," I said across the roof of my car.

"Zara's closed. Did you know that?"

I shook my head, more at myself than anything else. "I'm off, but I didn't give it much thought."

Hunnie grinned at me. "I bet you're used to fancy barbeques and fireworks."

"More like catered parties on the beach in the Hamptons, and private fireworks displays," I said, feeling the need to be honest.

"Well, you're not going to get that here. Maybe a couple of sparklers in someone's yard, although no one wants to scare the animals."

Swallowing my pride, I asked, "What do you plan to do?"

Hunnie gave me a huge smile. "I thought you'd never ask. My family usually builds a bonfire right over there." She pointed her thumb over her shoulder toward a grassy clearing as she spoke. "We make hot dogs and s'mores, and usually drink some moonshine or boxed wine. My brother and his kids always come. His wife skipped town, so it's mostly for the kids. Nothing fancy."

I nodded, chuckling softly to myself.

"What's so funny?" Hunnie asked. The woman didn't miss a thing.

"I was just thinking that probably no one wears white shorts."

"Definitely not, but you should come. We usually start around six. Come whenever."

"I don't want to intrude."

"Come. Maybe Ben will see the fire and stop by. His parents usually have something over at their place with Branson and Brenna."

"Thanks, I'll stop by. Not because Ben might show up, but because I don't want to be alone on the Fourth. So, thanks."

"Great. See you then."

I jumped into my car before I could say anything else, afraid I might cry.

I'm a long way from home, Toto.

12

BEN

As I drove over to my parents' place on the Fourth of July, my phone rang. For a second, I wished it was Murphy, but we hadn't exchanged numbers, and I was taking it slow as promised. It had also slipped my mind that the Bean would be closed today, and I couldn't sneak in to get a peek at Murphy and maybe get her number.

"Hey, Hunnie," I grumbled into the Bluetooth. The woman was like a dog with a bone when she wanted something.

"Ben. Sorry to bug you on the Fourth, but . . ."

I rolled the window up all the way so I could hear. "I'm on my way to my parents'. I'll talk to them about the goats and reindeer and whatever else you want to have out there for the kids to pet."

"Thanks, but that's not totally why I was calling. But yeah, I was going to remind you. Ha."

Typical Hunnie.

"You okay?" I asked. Typically, people called me when they needed to see a doctor. Whether it be an ortho they needed or just a referral, they called. I was the doctor, not the person they called just to chat. Even though I'd lived here most of my life, having an MD after my name made me an outsider.

"Yeah, I'm fine. Nothing like that. We're doing our usual

bonfire with my brother and the kids, and I invited Murphy. I was going to see if you wanted to stop by."

I sighed. "Hunnie, you aren't playing matchmaker, are you?"

"Who, me?" she said innocently, and I could practically hear her blushing across the line.

"Yeah, you. I'm doing you a favor by talking with my dad. Leave it alone."

"Okay, okay," she grumbled. "But stop by for one of my s'mores. You can't say no to a little chocolate, marshmallow, and graham cracker with a real honey drizzle."

"I'll see how my timing works," I said, noting the increase in my pulse rate. Of course I wanted to go. "And you know it's not the honey drizzle drawing me," I said without thinking.

Her tone knowing, she sang, "Oh, I know."

"Good-bye, Hunnie," I said and then disconnected the call.

Rolling the window all the way back down, I let the fresh air wash over my heated body.

I always did July Fourth at my folks' house, even when I was a teen. Every year, the town had a small parade down the main street in the morning for little kids, but otherwise, there wasn't much unless you wanted to head toward Burlington. If the Fourth happened to fall on the same day as the farmers' market, there was live music and more hot food, but this year would be quiet.

I suspected Branson was upset with me because he'd hoped I would take him to Burlington, but this was a busier day for me. The start of a holiday weekend meant a lot of accidents. The next few days would be worse. Between all the biking, hiking, skateboarding, and swimming, coupled with drinking and a few days off, this was usually one of my busiest weeks of the year.

Now I was torn between being a good uncle and spending time with my parents, and leaving early to go see Murphy.

"Ben, tell Mom it's okay for me to head out to the river and light sparklers with my friends," Branson said to me after we ate. "We're not going to drink, and Phil's dad can drive me home later."

My stomach was full and my head preoccupied, so I didn't bother asking questions. "I think it's fine, Bren," I told my sister.

She frowned at me. "Yeah, because you go home to your house and work, and you don't have to sit up and worry about him."

"That's not fair. I worry plenty," I said, thinking she was also making a point about my lonely existence with no one to care about. Standing, I said, "I'm actually going to head out. I'll drop him off and make sure it looks kosher."

"What?" Branson asked me.

"Make sure everyone is behaving. I'll be discreet," I said.

As he shoved his hair off his forehead, I thought how I did the same thing. At least Brenna didn't bother him about getting a haircut. She'd learned that lesson from my mom and me a long time ago.

After dropping off Branson with his friends, I made a quick U-turn and headed toward Hunnie's place. I parked by the main house and waited a minute before heading toward the bonfire.

"Hey, look who made it," Hunnie said, announcing my approach before I could clear my throat.

"Hey, Ben." Her brother, Josh, stood to shake my hand.

He was close to ten years older than Hunnie and me, and I didn't know him well growing up. Now he lived in town and worked for a trucking company. He married someone who was here hiking the Appalachian Trail and fell for him during a crunchy phase. Two kids later, she decided she wasn't meant for this life and hightailed it back out west, leaving him with a couple of toddlers. Of course, everyone knew the story.

"Hey, man," I said, shaking his hand. "Happy Fourth."

"Holiday takes on a new meaning when you have a couple of kids you want to get home and get to bed," he said, cocking his head toward the bonfire.

"I'm sure," I said, but really had no idea. I'd just dropped Branson off with friends so I could see Hunnie.

"Hi." Murphy looked up at me from the fire, the flames reflecting off her red hair as she stood and walked over.

"Hi," I said back, really wanting to pull her in for a hug. To Josh, I said, "Where are your folks?"

"Oh, they went in to watch a movie. Mom's been nagging Dad for weeks to watch some movie about a kid abandoned on a train platform in India."

"*Lion*," Murphy said. "It's called *Lion*. I cried like a baby watching that movie while crossing the Atlantic on a plane to Europe. It won several awards."

"Wow," Josh said, staring at Murphy. "Not that it won several awards, that you remember watching it on a plane to Europe. I don't remember what I had for breakfast."

"Give it a rest, Josh," Hunnie said, stepping in. "Go make sure your spawn don't set their faces on fire roasting their marshmallows."

"Happy Fourth," Murphy whispered. "Hunnie dragged me into this, but it's been nice. Her parents are sweet," she said, standing next to me.

Hunnie made her way over to the kids, squeezing honey on a graham cracker for one.

"It's not big-city standards, but it's a pretty family-focused day around here. Friends and family, I guess."

Smiling, she said, "I'm liking it. Fireworks always give me a headache, or maybe it's all the specialty cocktails served with them at parties. Either way, this has been nice."

"I'm glad. You know what's making my holiday?"

Murphy stared at me, and if I thought I wanted to kiss her earlier, I was wrong. I really wanted to kiss her now, so much so, I wasn't sure how I managed to resist. Reaching for her hand, I held her soft fingers in mine.

"You," I told her. "It's really nice seeing you."

"Back at you, Doc," she teased, but her eyes told me she meant it. It was almost as if a flash of relief passed over her features as her brow smoothed out and her eyes brightened.

We stood there for a while, taking each other in until my phone rang, breaking the moment.

"Shit," I mumbled as I glanced at the screen. "It's the hospital."

Taking the call and walking away from the fire a bit, I learned a group of kids—thank God, not including Branson—were in an ATV accident. Two broken legs needed to be set, and a potential broken clavicle. It was going to be a long night.

"I have to go," I said, rejoining the group at the fire. "It's always this way on the Fourth, lots of kids jerking around and accidents. Thanks, Hunnie."

Pulling Murphy into my arms, I whispered in her ear, "Thanks for being my big-city fireworks," before kissing her cheek, letting my lips linger for a beat. And then I was out of there and headed toward the hospital in Montpelier.

13

BEN

"Hey, dude, what's up?" I said as I answered my phone the following Tuesday while walking out of the hospital. It had been a long holiday weekend of surgeries and follow-ups and running interference between doting parents, nurses trying to do their jobs, and cocky teenagers.

I'd stopped into the Bean twice for coffee since the Fourth, and both times I'd missed Murphy. Yesterday, I had a meeting in Boston, so I'd been gone most of the day between the drive and the traffic.

This morning I'd had a surgery, and I couldn't say I was disappointed when the second surgery was canceled because the patient was running a fever. It meant I could stop by the Bean and see if Murphy was working. Of course, I could call and ask Zara if Murphy was in, but what fun is that? I still didn't have Murphy's number, but I liked seeing this side of her—a little frazzled, more real, less robotic.

My nephew's voice came over the line. "Mom wanted me to ask if you could take me to dinner. I'm fine staying home alone, but she worries. She'll check to make sure I called you, but it's okay if you're busy."

"I'm never too busy for you, Bran. Of course I'll take you to dinner. I'm actually heading that way now, but I need to stop off and run a quick errand in Colebury first."

Clicking the locks on my Jeep, I popped the door open and slid inside.

"Why?" he asked. "Are you stopping by Oh, For Heaven's Cakes?"

I decided it was easier to agree rather than start explaining Murphy to Branson. He already had enough to deal with when it came to relationships. Lord knows when Brenna got upset, she blew a gasket.

"Yeah, I was thinking of getting some goodies for my office staff for when I go in tomorrow. And the Bean for a coffee for me. How about you? Want something for later?"

"Nah. I don't like all that sweet icing, but Mom does."

"You're right. I'm going to grab some treats for her too. So, I'll be by in a while to get you. Want to go to Wayside?"

"Yeah."

"See you in a bit," I said and disconnected the call.

On my way to Colebury, I thought about Branson not having a father in the picture. Sometimes he resisted spending a lot of time with me, so I wondered why he gave in so easily this time. Maybe girl trouble? After all, he was sixteen.

I needed to see my parents too, and I'd thought about asking them to join us for dinner but decided against it. Poor Hunnie was going to harass me until the cows came home if I didn't talk to them again about the petting zoo.

I spent the rest of the drive on a call with my nurse, telling me about an emergency appointment she'd scheduled for me tomorrow, a friend of hers with severe knee pain who she promised I'd see. It would be doing her a big favor.

Hey, that's the life of a small-town doc.

Pulling into the Bean, I spotted Murphy's beat-up Toyota in the lot and smiled to myself.

I snatched my Yeti and ran to the front door. Trying to contain my excitement, I took a deep breath before yanking the door open. For a second, I'd wondered if Murphy would want to go to the bakery with me.

"Earth to Ben," Zara said, pulling me from my thoughts.

"Sorry, was thinking of a patient," I lied.

Zara smirked. "Yeah, right. Americano, extra hot? Murphy can make it for you."

"I guess you don't miss a thing."

Shaking her head, Zara rang up my order before sending my mug down the bar. "Your secret's safe with me," she whispered, "but give Murph a minute. These New Yorkers have her working on some type of rainbow drink their kid must have, and of course they're walking her through the steps."

"Rainbow?" My voice was also hushed as I took in Murphy, concentrating as she squeezed multiple syrups into frothy white milk.

"As luck would have it, Gigi had dropped off some syrup samples that were sent to her bakery a while back. Thank heaven," Zara dead-panned.

"Here you go, the Unicorn as you call it." Murphy handed the drink over to a teenager, and the girl's dad looked at her with a smile.

"Just an Americano," I told Murphy, making my way to her across from the mammoth espresso machine.

"Thank God. That one's easy." With her hair slicked back into a low ponytail and a floral apron cinched at her waist, Murphy looked the part, but I didn't think being a barista was her calling.

"Murph, why are you working here?"

"Shh," she said, frowning at me. "I need the job. It's a good job."

"Are you doing the internship for Hunnie?" I asked, and she nodded. "Good."

When she brought my Americano to the pickup area, I noted there wasn't anyone behind me.

"Do I have to call Hunnie for your number? Or are you going to give it to me?"

Murphy playfully flipped her ponytail to the side, and I had to hide my surprise. This was the most youthful, carefree side of her I'd ever seen. She used to be so in control.

Before she could respond, I explained. "Well, I wanted to call you ever since it occurred to me that being from the big city, you've probably never been to a drive-in."

"I've had food from a drive-through before, Ben. Don't be silly."

"Not drive-through, Murph. Drive-in." I wanted to reach across the bar and kiss her silly, but I resisted the urge.

Realization dawned on her face. "Oh, I've never been to one. You mean where you watch the movies? From your car?"

Feeling a win, I pulled my phone out of my cargo shorts pocket and said, "Go ahead, give me your digits. I have to go grab some snacks for my staff and pick up my nephew, but I'll call you later with the drive-in info."

She mock-glared at me. "So, you're going to tell me what to do? That's how you do it?"

"Murphy, hurry up and give me the number before you get another rainbow drink to make," I said, glancing at the father begin his approach toward the coffee bar. "And for the record, I'm going to take you to the drive-in and kiss you like I did the other night. This time, under the moonlight. Maybe a little more if you're well behaved."

I tossed in a wink, trying to be playful when the tightness in my pants was anything but. Christ, I was a doctor. I should know how to play things calmer, cooler, and more collected.

She faux growled. "I'm at work, Ben. Don't tease me."

"I know. So, hand over your number and an Americano, and I'm out of here."

Murphy didn't protest anymore but started rattling off digits while making my espresso shot, and I punched them into my phone like a drowning person gasps for air.

The next day, driving home from work, I couldn't stop thinking about the talk I'd had with Branson over dinner the night before. The poor kid felt like none of the girls liked him because he wasn't "rich enough."

When he divulged feeling that way to me, my heart broke. I knew the feeling all too well.

My parents had struggled as I was growing up, trying to keep up with producing, bottling, and selling enough syrup in the spring, plus fermenting cheese year round to keep us afloat. The problem was the new technology—sturdy and hygienic lines that ran from the tree carrying sap—were pricey.

Unlike other farmers in the area, my parents hadn't inherited our property. Instead, they'd scrimped and borrowed to buy the land and add to the existing trees, tapping the lines themselves, cleaning out buckets and tirelessly grading colors, repairing equipment, and then fermenting cheese in the off season. Eventually, they bought a few cows for their own dairy and had done a little better financially year-round, but expenses were always going up. They'd built Toptree Maple and Cheese over the years, but it wasn't without a lot of sacrifice and hard work.

The main difference between my nephew and me was for all those years, I had my dad to lean on, but Branson had no father figure. Only me. I was glad he was turning to me now, and I hoped his getting some more physical activity—like hiking, skiing, and maybe biking—would give him more confidence.

As I made my way home, my phone rang. Answering via Bluetooth, I was elated to learn it was my real estate agent calling to tell me that my offer on the ski house had been accepted. Assuming the inspection turned up no surprises, the land and the small house on it were mine.

After disconnecting the call, my phone seemed to stare at me from the center console. I wanted to call or text Murphy, but I wasn't sure why. I hadn't been up front with her about my finances, but something about this new purchase made me crazy proud.

I pulled my car into a driveway, then turned around and went the other direction toward Colebury and the Bean. When I'd texted Murphy last night to tease her about having her number, she'd replied she was going to bed because she had work to do for Hunnie early in the morning, and then had to work at the Bean in the afternoon. But with this news in my pocket, I realized I wanted to see her more than I wanted to shower and get out of the stiff pants and collared shirt I'd worn all day to see patients.

"Hey, need a coffee?" Murphy said as I got out of my car in front of the Bean.

"No. Actually, I need you."

She must have just finished her shift, her apron gone and probably tucked into her tote. Reaching back for her ponytail holder, she pulled her hair free, shaking it all around her face.

"Stalk much?" she asked as she approached, a worry line creasing her forehead.

"Maybe, but not in a bad way."

She started to bite her bottom lip, and if the worry line had gone away, I'd take it to mean something different.

"I'm just joking," I told her.

"I know," she said, leaning against my Jeep, looking pensive.

"You're gonna ruin your white shorts, and I'm going to have to report you to Hunnie," I said, trying to joke again. "By the way, you look nice. Too nice for having just worked behind the coffee bar."

"Come on, Ben. Be nice. Maybe I treated you badly in high school, but it doesn't warrant this."

"Hey, I'm kidding again." I took her hand in mine. "Obviously, I'm not doing a very good job of it."

She looked down at the ground, refusing to meet my eyes.

"Hey, what's wrong?"

"Nothing. Everything. I'm just trying to do my best and not doing even a little bit good."

"I don't want to take away the way you're feeling, but you need to tell me more." My thumb traced a path over hers—my way of asking her to level with me—and it seemed to stop her mood in its tracks.

Her expression relaxing, she sighed. "I'm sorry. My bad mojo got the best of me, but I'm cool now. And look at me, white shorts still white after a shift. I had to put them on because I need to do laundry."

This reminded me of Pressman and the pink socks in the corner of her room. "Are you still as good at it?"

She playfully shoved my chest. "Why yes, I am, Mister Doctorpants."

"Remember how upset you were over those socks?"

Murphy smiled at the memory. "Well, first I had to admit to you, of all people, that I'd never done laundry. Second, I had to call my parents and admit I'd forgotten to send out my laundry on time. And third, I had to borrow Chloe Curtain's socks. Yuck."

This made me laugh out loud. "So?"

"That's gross, Ben. Feet have such germs."

"You could have asked me to show you how to do laundry."

"I know, because you knew how to do everything. Still do. Look at you, showing up and making me laugh. Operating on people and saving lives. Saving the environment too with your Yeti cup that you never forget. Which makes me think, are you really a doctor or just pretending? You seem to pop up all the time."

Grinning, I pulled my hospital ID out of my back pocket and handed it to her.

"Benjamin Jones Rooney. I never knew."

"My mom's maiden name. She wanted to keep it in the family. She was an only child, and when she took my dad's name, that was the end of the line."

Murphy smirked at me as she handed my ID back. "I could call you Jonesy. Who knew?"

"My mom would like that, I'm sure."

"Ha. But would she like me? I'm not doing too much. I'm

nothing like Hunnie or you or Zara. I'm still trying to find my place."

"We all start at a different time. I mean it. You were on one path, and now you're on another."

"We'll see, since you seem to know it all."

I ran a hand through my hair, noting I needed a cut, or a "trim" as my mom liked to say in disdain. She'd prefer I kept it neat and short, but I guessed this was my way of being me, especially in a sea of robots at Pressman. The habit stuck afterward.

With Murphy's volatile mood, it felt like a bad time to tell her about the land. She was in a down place, and throwing my success in her face felt wrong. It's not something I would ever do intentionally, so I skipped that little tidbit.

"I also happen to know of the greatest drive-in theater about an hour from here. So funky, it's a must. We can make an adventure of it. Really experience Vermont on a scenic drive and all that."

"See?" Murphy said with a grin. "There you go again. Perfect suggestion. It's like you always know what to say."

"How about, you look so gorgeous?" I blurted.

She scoffed. "I just worked at a coffee house. I hardly think that's what you really think, and I'm not fishing for compliments, Jonesy."

"Well, you look absolutely radiant, which is why I'm going to do this."

Without hesitation, I leaned in, and my lips met hers for a closed-mouth kiss. Breathing in all that was Murphy, I took my time, savoring, promising . . . until she pulled back.

"I work here, remember?" she said.

Taking her hand in mine, I walked her down a hillside and backed her up against a tree. This was a small town and I was the doctor in the next town over, but I didn't care. Pressing myself into her smaller body, my hardness met her softness, and I couldn't keep from groaning. Our mouths moved together like we'd done this forever, and then she opened for my tongue.

We stayed like that for a while, grinding into each other, doing with our mouths what we'd like to do with the rest of our bodies, until my lips broke free and ghosted across her cheek, sucking on her ear before traveling down her neck. Her head fell back, and I couldn't resist running my tongue down her smooth skin to her clavicle and back up.

"Christ, Murphy. You make me take the Lord's name in vain. My mom wouldn't be happy."

Murphy ran her lips across my forehead. My messy hair must have been tickling her, but she didn't seem to mind.

"You also make me want to drag down those prissy white shorts and see what's underneath. Thong, bikini, whatever, I want to rip it off and devour you."

"Ben!"

I stepped back slightly and placed a quick peck on her lips. "But I won't, not now. Because we're adults. Now, I can't promise what may or may not happen at the drive-in."

This earned me another fake punch.

"Kidding," I said with a chuckle. "Sort of. Now, when are you off next? Since it might be a late night."

"Friday. But what about you?"

"I'm used to little sleep, and I don't operate on Fridays, so that's perfect. I'll pick you up Thursday around six?"

She nodded, straightening her tee shirt and smoothing her hair.

"You still look gorgeous," I said, and led her back to her car, waiting for her to get in and drive away.

As I got into my own car, I glanced toward the Bean and caught Audrey and Roderick ducking away from the window. Knowing they'd been watching, I had to chuckle. It didn't bother me a bit.

14

MURPHY

"See ya on Saturday," I said on Thursday while walking out of the Bean, too jumpy with nerves to even let the *ya* bother me. The old Murphy would have never used such slang. Good old Mom would have been sitting on my shoulder, shaking her head.

With anxiety rattling through every bone in my body, I tried to still my mind. Perhaps the latte in my hand was a bad idea, but Ben was picking me up later, and I couldn't recall being this nervous in a long time. It was hard not to keep thinking about high school, because that was the only reference point I had when it came to him.

During those years, our relationship came easy. But then again, it was mostly behind closed doors.

Sliding into my car, wedging my newly minted, limited-release Busy Bean Yeti into my cracked cup holder, I couldn't stop the smile from spreading across my face. Scolding myself for wasting time, I sped home to work on a few advance posts for Hunnie. She'd loved the family-based slogans I'd been doing, and apparently, her clicks and sales were starting to climb.

After downing my coffee, jumping in the shower, and curling up in my robe on my bed, I wrote three new story lines for

Hunnie's social media, and then made the mistake of spending some time on my own.

Like an idiot, I clicked on a link for an article in the society section of the *New York Post*.

> LANDON FAMILY MOVING ON AND ABOUT THE CITY WITHOUT THEIR DAUGHTER
>
> *Former State Representative Marshall Landon and his wife, Lyssa, were seen last week at the annual Firefighters Benefit sans their daughter.*
>
> *The couple's only child, Murphy Landon, usually attended the event each year with her parents, and was a boon to Landon during his last run for office. Parading Ms. Landon and her undeniable wealth of community service plus her fluff job in the Ivy League around town was a tactic Mr. Landon used for years. The father-daughter duo were photographed more than any other pair. Always smiling, Ms. Landon never let the crowd down.*
>
> *Last year, we reported about her illicit relationship with a twenty-five-year-old graduate student at the Ivy League university where she worked as a student advisor, and we have learned that Ms. Landon has recently left her position. When interviewed last year, Ms. Landon maintained that she didn't know he was a student at the school where she worked, and that the pair only went on a few dates and were not intimate. Her parents have been surprisingly quiet on the issue, stating 'it's nonsense' and 'no comment.'*
>
> *It's rumored that Mr. and Mrs. Landon have sent their daughter away to repair her image.*

I didn't read any more, quickly clicking off the page and sitting up in bed. More than anything, I hated that the media insinuated that it was my parents who sent me away. I left of my own volition, wanting to be someone different, better, a whole person dedicated to a new cause. Shaking my head, I stood to get dressed for my date, wondering what someone wore to a drive-in. I was determined not to let the bad press ruin my evening.

By the time Ben knocked on my door, I was in my third outfit. Skinny jean capris, a lightweight gray off-the-shoulder T-shirt, and a loose pale pink sweater over my arm in case I got cold.

"Hi," I said as I opened the door.

"Hi, there." Ben walked inside, seemingly taking command of an empty room.

Right then, it clicked with me that our roles had reversed. In prep school, I had all the perceived confidence and power, and now Ben did. Was that why he liked me now?

"You look great," he said, pulling me in for a kiss on the cheek, distracting me from my negative thoughts.

"I hate to say it, but I didn't want to look like an outsider like I did at the market."

"Never. You look like you . . . but better. Less makeup, more natural. It's a perfect look on you, Murph."

I ducked my head, my cheeks hot.

"Hey." Ben brought a finger under my chin and tipped my gaze up to his. "Don't hide from me."

Stepping away, letting my sweater fall on the couch and pretending to look through a pile of shoes, I mumbled, "It's so embarrassing, I've never been to one. I've been to Broadway premieres and award shows at Carnegie Hall, but not a drive-in. Isn't that ludicrous?"

"Those," Ben said, changing the subject when my hand rested on an Adidas sneaker.

"Really?" I stood up holding them. "I've never worn these on a date. If that's what this is."

"Murph, it's a date. The shoes are perfect. Look at mine," he said, and I glanced down, relieved to find Ben wearing a pair of running shoes. "And I'm kind of glad you've never been to a drive-in."

"Why is that?" I asked, plopping down onto the worn sofa to slip on and tie my shoes.

"Because back at Pressman, I didn't think there would be anything I could offer you." He sat down next to me. "Something different from what you already had, more exciting than what you'd already done in life. And now I am."

Speechless, I nodded.

"Don't get me wrong, I'd like to take you to a nice dinner, something farm-to-table with a good bottle of wine to share, but this is fun too, I think. New experiences."

I turned on the couch to take all of Ben in, with his flat-front khaki shorts, navy T-shirt, tousled hair, and running shoes. No watch, no jewelry, no airs about him, just pure goodness.

"This is what I thought about after I *stalked* you yesterday." He used air quotes when he said *stalked* and his face lit up. "I hid my feelings for you years ago. I was a stupid teen who didn't know his head from his ass, but I'm a man now. A good one, and I can be with you, share experiences with you, and I deserve to. When I was younger, I didn't think I deserved to do any of that."

With my hand on his knee, rubbing circles, I said, "No. If anyone doesn't deserve something, it's me. I'm the one who stopped anything from happening with us."

Ben stood up and pulled me with him, gathering me close. "But it's happening now, so we can leave that all behind us. Come on, we'll be late."

We walked out my door, leaving the heaviness in my apartment with only something exciting and fun ahead of us. I wished my whole life could be like this moment.

"Comfortable?" Ben asked as we drove down the highway, and I use the term generously. The two-lane road was more like a better-maintained back road.

I nodded. "So, do you do this often?"

He glanced at me, giving me a curious look. "What? Drive?"

Pulling my knee up and leaning it on the passenger door, I looked over to study Ben. "The drive-in."

"Haven't been since summers during college. Although, I'm pretty sure they still show the same movies."

"Ha." I laughed. "It really is beautiful here. I don't think I ever realized how stifling the city air can be."

"It's home for me. I wish I could help more on the farm, but my parents understand. Plus, I like to hang with Branson when I can."

"How is Brenna?" I asked, remembering that the last time I asked, Ben avoided the topic.

"It's a sticky subject. No pun intended. Sorry, the syrup humor just comes out sometimes." He grinned at me. "It's sticky, get it?"

"I get it. I'm not as dumb as you think." My mind drifted back to high school and all the tutoring Ben gave me.

"Oh, you're definitely not dumb." He reached over and squeezed my thigh. "I was always impressed with your attention to detail."

"Hmm." I shifted my gaze back to the road and the green trees lining it.

"Anyway, Brenna lives in Colebury. She has a small house she rents. It's not enough, but she does her best. Got pregnant my first year at Pressman," he said, a sadness darkening his tone.

"That's tough. She knows the dad?"

"She's not like that. Didn't sleep around. Yeah, she knows Branson's dad. He didn't want a baby or a family or any of that. Signed over rights."

I frowned. "I don't get how someone can do that."

"He did. Anyway, I try to be there for Bren. Got her out of bartending at the Mill. It's a great place, but she was only working nights, and that was hard with a toddler. When I started at the hospital, I helped her get a job at the information desk. Pay isn't great, but it has full benefits. Of course, she signs up for every extra shift and works any overtime opportunity that comes her way. So, it's too much."

"You seem pretty involved," I said, quickly adding, "Which is a good thing. It's the type of family I wished for. Caring and concerned."

"I try, at least. You know what? This exit has a fast food joint. Want to grab a quick coffee? It's our last chance."

Just like that, Ben changed the subject. It was clear Brenna and Branson were mostly off-limits. I couldn't help but wonder why, but I let it go.

"Sure. I don't know how good the coffee will be compared to my K-cups," I said, grinning as I gave him the side-eye. "They're pretty gourmet."

"Oh yeah?" Ben said, his tone back to jovial.

"I can't believe how stopping for coffee—not fast-food coffee, but expensive coffee—was part of my daily routine. Not once, but sometimes two or three times a day, at ten bucks a pop. Crazy, when I think about how much my life has changed since leaving New York."

Steering the car into a parking lot, Ben asked, "Do you miss it?"

"Sometimes I think I should miss it more. I almost force myself to miss it. It's crazy, but I don't. Yeah, I know K-cups aren't great, but this independent feeling I have is pretty awesome. My parents don't get it. They want me to go back to how I was. Dependent. Obedient."

"Come on. Let's be independent." Ben hopped out and helped me out of the car, taking my hand as he led us into the restaurant and to the counter. "You know, there's only one of these places within an hour?"

I rolled my eyes. "Oh, I know all about crunchy, healthy, earthy, hippie, farm-to-table Vermont."

"So, you're a big fast-food eater? Should we ditch the picnic I brought and grab some cheeseburgers?"

Ben pulled me closer and I leaned into him, loving the

warmth. My insides melted like the processed cheese on the burgers sold at the Golden Arches.

"Let's keep the picnic, okay?"

"Okay," Ben said, giving my hip a quick squeeze.

We ordered coffees—cream and sugar for him, only cream for me—like we did this all the time. And strangely, it felt like we did.

15

BEN

Back in the car, I gulped my coffee. "Not quite as good as an Americano made by you, hence the cream and sugar," I said while glancing at Murphy.

"Why, thank you," she said, playfully bowing in her seat.

"Do you like it still? Working at the Bean?"

Tucking a loose hair behind her ear, Murphy turned to look at me. "I like it fine. It's good to be here in Vermont. I'm liking Hunnie more than I thought I would. In fact, I have this idea for her. Oh—" Murphy stopped short and bounced in her seat. "I remembered these fancy honey sticks from the city. It's like a straw filled with honey that you snip the top off of and pour into a drink or whatever."

I nodded, not wanting to interrupt.

"It could be cool for syrup too, you know?" she said, her excitement making her words come out fast. "Anyway, it cuts down on all the sticky mess of a big jar, and it's super cool. It could look so funky with her infusions. I'm not sure where she would get them manufactured or the cost, which is why I probably won't tell her about it. It's just an idea."

More than anything, I wanted to pull over and look Murphy in the eye, but we had to make it on time to the movie. With

Vermont roads, you never knew what type of obstacle you could come upon.

"Murph, you should tell her. Listen to you—you love this idea. I'll bet Hunnie will too."

"I don't really know enough to suggest it. I'm not sure I'm equipped to figure it out."

As I cleared the emotion from my throat, my heart beat overtime. "You are more than equipped. You could and should figure it out. And yes, it would work with syrup. I'd love to know more about it."

Running her palms over her thighs, Murphy stared straight ahead. "Well, I'm not sure you're qualified to say what I'm equipped for, Doctor Ben. Ha, I'm just kidding. All of this makes me nervous. It's all new to me, sticking up for what I want. I'm not Hunnie."

Now my heart went into triple time. I knew I should tell Murphy about the apps and the business stuff I handled on the side, but I couldn't stop being cautious. Inside, I was a poor boy looking for approval from the rich girl.

"Of course you're not Hunnie. You're you. Think about it, okay?"

Murphy nodded.

The rest of the drive passed quickly, filled with mindless chatter and music. I learned Murphy loved Ed Sheeran and refused to turn him off when he came on my satellite radio. I pretended to protest, but anything that made Murphy smile was good with me.

"Look at all this green," she said, staring at the trees as we zipped past. "It's so . . . I'm not even sure of the word. I don't think I appreciated the surroundings when we went to Pressman."

"Definitely seemed like most didn't, except when it came time to ski."

"I'm sorry about that," she said, turning as much as she could to focus on me. With her green eyes blazing, she almost looked like she was going to cry.

I reached over to grip her knee. "It's no big deal. I could ski, but I didn't have all that fancy equipment. But enough about that." We were heading into dangerous conversation territory, and I didn't want to spill how I felt the need to provide Branson with more.

"Well," she said, "it's like I'm seeing this part of the country through new glasses this time around. The unfiltered beauty. I'm sure that was a selling point of Pressman to my parents, but it went over my head."

"Lucky for you, you're having a second chance to see it. And lucky for me that I'm getting a second chance with you."

Murphy's eyes widened as she stared at me, looking surprised. Even luckier for me, we pulled into the parking lot for the Fairlee Drive-In.

"So, this is it? A motel?" Murphy asked, cocking an eyebrow at me.

"Just you wait."

I drove us around back of the motel, and when she saw the forest surrounding a huge screen and all the cars lining up in front of it, Murphy breathed out a *wow*.

"Hope it doesn't disappoint," I said as we pulled into the gate to pay.

I spoke jokingly, but I wasn't laughing inside. Here I was, a board-certified surgeon, an app developer, and a self-made man, unsure if I could actually impress a woman.

"Look at all these trees," Murphy said as I found a good spot to park. "I mean, I didn't love working in the Kwikshop because some of those customers could be a pain for not a lot of money, but this is cool." She opened her door and leaned out, turning around to see the screen.

"You worked at the Kwikshop?" I said to her back.

"Yeah, for a little bit, but I didn't like it." Bringing her head back into the Jeep, she asked, "How will we watch?"

Deciding to let the grocery-store gig go, I jumped out and went around the hood. Taking her hand in mine, I led her toward the back of the SUV and popped open the liftgate.

"Oh." Murphy let out a happy sigh. "Fun. And I don't even know what the movie is."

"Me either, but it doesn't really matter." I pulled a blanket from inside and laid it on the floor of the rear of the Jeep and opened the picnic basket. "It's really a cooler, but it works."

She hopped onto the blanket. "I'm sure it's perfect."

My pulse settled to a normal pace with Murphy so happy. Was she always this easily pleased, and I didn't know?

"Wine?" I asked, pulling a glass from the cooler.

"Are you sure we should?" With her head cocked to the side, she took me in, all of me.

Not going to lie, it felt like something I'd never felt before. Golden. Intimidating.

"Not me, you. I'll get you home safely later." I winked and gave her hand a squeeze.

"Okay. Sure, that would be great."

I poured some white wine for Murphy and cracked open a bottle of water for myself. "Cheers."

"Cheers."

Dusk fell around us, and the screen brightened as they played some older commercials before the sky fully darkened.

"This is so nice," Murphy said, leaning against the doorjamb.

"You look relaxed. Have another sip of wine."

"Are you trying to get me drunk, Jonesy?" Murphy said, laughing.

"No, that was your game plan years ago," I said, and this got me more chuckles.

"Hardly," she said, hiding her face behind a curtain of wavy red hair.

"Let's not talk about back then," I said when a screen announcing the movie came on.

Murphy gasped. "*Pretty in Pink*. Did you really not know?

How could we not talk about back then? It pretty much consumes my mind, and this movie is basically us. Reversed, but us."

Swallowing my confusion and pride, I ran a hand through my hair, wishing I'd gotten a haircut. It was always the last priority on my list. "I didn't know. Let's just eat and watch and take it for what it is. A movie."

"For the record, I'm sure you come from a great family. And not the wrong side of the tracks."

Murphy scooted closer and rested her hand on my thigh. Her fingers skimmed along the hem of my shorts, and I forgot all about high school and being the scholarship kid.

"We're here now," I mumbled, pulling her close.

I pressed my lips to hers, inhaling her scent, sweet yet complicated. We stayed like that for a while, wrapped in each other's arms, kissing, exploring, and catching up on what we'd missed over the years.

"Okay," I said with a chuckle as I reluctantly pulled back. "Stop attacking me. The movie's starting."

I was joking, but any more making out and we'd be back on the road on our way home.

"Tell me what you'd like." I pulled over the cooler. "Brie? Apples? There's also a cold pasta salad and mini grilled chicken on something that looks like a pretzel bun. Oh, and a crustless quiche."

"Do you moonlight as a chef somewhere?" Murphy picked up her wine I hadn't realized she'd set down until now. I'd been too focused on kissing her.

"Sadly, no. There are a lot of things I do well, but cooking isn't high on the list. The Wayside prepped everything for me. It was a toss-up between these goodies and a stack of pancakes, but I didn't think they would travel well."

"Apples with brie sounds perfect. And salty pretzel buns are a close second to pancakes."

Murphy slid all the way back toward the doorjamb again, and while I missed her closeness, I wanted her to eat. I set up all the little containers and handed her a fork and a plate. We nibbled and watched a disgruntled Molly Ringwald pout on the screen.

"I had a huge crush on Molly growing up," I said, staring at the screen. "Guess I always had a thing for redheads."

Murphy turned her focus from the movie toward me. "You watched Molly Ringwald?"

"I have an older sister. I didn't watch anything I wanted until I landed at Pressman, and then I didn't have a TV. I watched what you guys all put on in the lounge. God, if I never see *The Bachelor* again, it'll be too soon."

"I always hated that show. I think I was afraid my parents would sign me up for *Millionaire Matchmaker*."

"Is that a thing?" I was pretty glad I didn't have food in my mouth, because I probably would have choked.

"It's a show I used to sneak and watch in college. Didn't you ever just let loose?"

I shook my head. "No. First, I was set to be the tight end, and had a small sliver of hope of playing beyond college. It was a pipe dream, but then I tore up my ankle during a game and ended up playing special teams. It gave me time to focus on my science prereqs and pick up other little odd jobs."

Murphy slid the food to the side, and still watching the movie, moved closer to me. With her head on my shoulder, she mumbled, "You must've never slept. I get that, though. My parents dragged me all over New York during school. I never really had a normal social life. Probably why I'm a mess right now."

Trying not to be a creeper, I took advantage of her head on my shoulder to take a quick whiff of her hair. It smelled like the tropics, all coconut and citrus.

Forcing myself to focus, I said, "I slept some, but I did burn the candle at both ends. Sports gave me a free ride, and my brains got me through a lot of coursework, but I was ready to get out of there. When Geisel admitted me for med school, it was a happy day because I could be near my family. Dartmouth is only about ninety minutes away. Anyway, my point is, and forgive me for saying this, but I don't get your parents using you as a puppet."

Murphy swiped away a tear, and I suddenly felt like a jerk.

"Hey, I didn't mean to make you cry."

She looked up at me, her eyes glistening in the glow from the screen. "It's not that. It's you. You're so strong in your convictions, balancing family and work and life. And I'm a barista, trying to do social media for a hippie making honey infusions."

I brushed a coppery curl from her face. "That's the best part about you, Murph. You're figuring stuff out, making mistakes as you go. You're real now in a way you couldn't be back then, and I like it."

"Really?"

"Really." Taking her small hand in mine, I ran my fingertip over what I assumed was a blister from the espresso machine and pulled Murphy halfway onto my lap.

Our mouths touched again, and we made out while the movie played, until it was Molly's turn to go to the prom in her pink dress.

Murphy and I sat there quietly, snug in each other's arms, waves of unspoken memories flowing between us. It seemed strange to be so unbelievably comfortable and uncomfortable at the same time.

I had to wonder—this time around . . . was it real?

MURPHY

"Thank you," I said, and I meant it.

The movie had just ended and yet Ben and I continued to sit, our thighs touching as our feet dangled off the back of the Jeep.

"I like this," he said, running the back of his hand along my leg. "Being with you."

Ben kissed me, and it felt like the first time all over again. When our lips met, something electric happened. I'd read about it in books—sparks, fireworks, whatever you want to call it—but I'd never considered it a possibility for me.

For years, I'd been resigned to do what my parents wanted when it came to my relationships, and then I met Preston Parker on a dating app. Things felt natural and fun with him, but when I found out he was a graduate student where I worked, I knew the universe was out to get me.

"For years," I mumbled without thinking, lost in the memory, "we'd gossiped about this person and that person and all the elephants in the room, and this time the elephant was me."

"Hey, where'd you go? What was that all about?" Ben gently bumped my shoulder with his.

Ducking my head, I said, "Oh, it was nothing."

"I don't think it was. I wouldn't think anything on your mind was nothing, Murph."

Ben's words were like a balm to my tortured soul. Pulling in a deep breath, I met his eyes.

"I'm not sure where you came from," I blurted helplessly, "but I know I don't deserve you."

"Stop," he said, and his lips met mine again.

A moan traveled up my throat, a reaction I could control even less than my verbal onslaught.

When big lights flicked on all around us, Ben pulled away with a frown. "We've gotta go. But let's continue this at home."

Squeezing my knee, he hopped off the back of the Jeep and helped me down. We quickly tossed the leftovers in the cooler, and of course, Ben walked me around to the passenger door.

"One more, okay?" he asked and swooped in for a toe-curling kiss without waiting for an answer. His tongue collided with mine, and I forgot about the spotlights being on and the cars all around us.

A quick blast from a horn made me jump in Ben's arms, and he pulled me in tighter.

"Let's roll. I'm not finished with you."

Seated in the car, I watched Ben run around the front and hop in, ducking his head to slide his big frame inside the door, and I let a small sigh of happiness.

Ben fiddled with the radio as we pulled out of the lot and onto the road. It was blacker than black out, and for the briefest of seconds, I missed the bright lights and traffic of the city.

"This is so surreal," I said, staring out the window. "Being out here in the darkness, driving along a pitch-black road . . . no taxis, no noise, no high heels clicking on the concrete."

"I'm sure. I had all that noise when I was in Boston. It was energizing when I first arrived, but then I grew tired of it."

"It feels like an extension of the old me. Of course, I miss the pace the most. I find it so hard to slow myself down sometimes."

He nodded toward the classical music streaming from the

radio. "That's why I listen to this, especially when I operate. I may live here, but my job demands my hands and brain being fast. This slows me. It's good for me, and my patients."

"Bach," I whispered.

"Yes, you know him too? Do you like this?"

I'd forgotten how many symphonies I'd attended as a middle schooler, and then again when I returned to New York from Pressman. "Classical tunes . . . I never would have thought. What else do you have up your sleeve? Show tunes?"

"Show tunes are definitely not my jam. This is, though. I guess I'm an old soul when it comes to music. I was wondering if you were too, that's all." His voice faded off in the end, like he was hopeful I was an old soul too. Like he'd found his people.

"It's nice. Bach. I was sort of thrown into knowing it. My mom was, and still is, on the board for the symphony at home. It's been her pet project for decades. We went a lot. Although, we had to go. I'm not even sure my mom likes classical music or would know an oboe from a clarinet, but she likes the prestige that comes with it."

This made Ben laugh. His deep, raspy chuckle filled the car. "Why would she be on the board then? Just for the prestige? That's what I don't understand. I get that she did it for appearances' sake, or your dad or whatever, but why? In the whole scheme of things, why live your life that way?"

Leaning my head back into the headrest, I closed my eyes. "That's what we do. We do what we don't want to because everyone is watching. You know in the movie *Ocean's Eleven*, when Anthony Garcia says something like, 'Someone is always watching in my casino?'"

Ben nodded without interrupting.

"That's my life. Someone is always watching. Was, I guess," I said. The words came flooding out of my mouth faster than women running into a surprise sample sale on Fifth Avenue. "Now that I've been excommunicated and shunned and won't fall on my sword, it probably doesn't matter anymore."

"What happened?" Ben turned his head for a second and then back toward the darkened road. A pair of headlights hovered in the rearview, but nothing came from the other direction.

Disbelieving, I glanced at him. "You really didn't google me?"

"Nah. I don't do that."

"It's amazing to me how genuine you are. And always have been."

"It's called being a real person. I have feelings, emotions, and I live by them."

"That's how I'm trying to be. Better to myself, gentler on my insides, kinder on the outside. Does that make sense?"

He nodded, again not interrupting.

I watched him push his hair out of his eyes and wanted to move the conversation to something lighter, like why doesn't he get his hair cut? But my heart wouldn't let me.

Resigned to finally having this conversation, I said, "You know I worked at Columbia. In student advising."

"Yeah, I think so."

"Well, it was a cushy job in the business school, highly sought after, and I landed it as my first job out of college. Family name, strings pulled, all of it."

I cleared my throat and stared at Ben's profile, trying to gauge his reaction. He appeared to remain nonplussed, keeping his eyes on the road, but his features relaxed.

"I moved into an equally cushy apartment on the Upper West Side, near Columbus Circle. I didn't make many new friends because I was still tied to my parents' world. Their events, their social circles, and their finances. I was able to live and do things many of my peers weren't able to, but I wanted to date. Really date. So I tried a dating app. It was awkward and strange, but felt like I was finally in the real world like a regular person. You know?"

Ben laughed again. "I don't know, but I understand you wanting to do something on your own. Something like the common folk."

I frowned. "When you put it like that, it sounds crass."

He gave me an apologetic look. "That's not how I meant it. I'm only trying to understand the divide between how you lived and how mostly everyone else did or does."

"Yes." My reply was soft, but he'd hit on the truth. "The divide was gigantic. Anyway, I met a guy online. He said he was twenty-five, and I was thirty-one at the time. We went for coffee and hit it off. He was fun and exciting, from New Jersey, and said he was an entrepreneur. I never checked or asked a lot of questions. Then we went for a drink, and he walked me back to my apartment and kissed me good night."

"Sounds pretty normal."

"Well, he must've gotten a load of where I lived or maybe he knew beforehand, I don't know. We went for one more coffee and shared another kiss outside my building before he called the *Post* and outed himself as a Columbia student having relations with an employee."

"What? It was a setup?" Ben looked at me for a second, his blue eyes blazing with fury.

"I don't know. He led them to believe we were more intimate than we were. He also didn't explain he was a graduate transfer student and twenty-five. It didn't matter, though. My name was smeared and my reputation ruined. My parents weren't interested in explanations or rebuttals. They wanted me to do some sort of ridiculous penance like community service, even though what I'd been accused of wasn't against the law, and publicly date someone of their choice. But I couldn't do it."

"So, you came to Vermont? For a do-over? A new life?"

"Well, I tried to stay in my job for a year, but I couldn't stand the curious looks and the cold shoulder people gave me. I thought if I just put my head down and did my job well, people would forget. Truthfully, I don't know if they did or not because my parents certainly didn't forget. I had to escape, and so I did. I guess it was a cowardly move."

"What? No way. It was brave, standing up to generational wealth and all those tired standards."

"I agree. They're tired, but those standards are—*were*—a way of life for me."

"You're moving forward, not backward, Murph. That's all I know."

We'd been so deep in conversation, and my thoughts were so heavy and disturbing, I'd lost track of time. On a long exhale, I realized we were back at my place.

"Sorry the conversation got so down toward the end," I said as Ben parked.

"No reason to be sorry. I'm glad you decided to open up."

"And we had a great time at the drive-in. Can't believe I'd never been. Can we go again sometime?"

Ben turned in his seat. "Definitely," he said, and then his lips were on mine.

Not wanting my neighbors to see me making out, I asked, "Want to come in?"

"Also definitely," he mumbled, his lips tickling mine. Then he jumped out and opened the door for me.

"You don't have to do that every time, you know?"

"I do."

With no further argument, I took Ben's hand and led him to my door. I'd never been so assertive, but something about this felt perfect and right.

"I feel bad that you're still far from home," I said when I locked the door behind us.

"Is that your way of saying I can't stay over?"

I dropped my head in my hands. "Oh God. You must think I'm so naive or spoiled."

Ben shook his head while turning and backing me into the door until my shoulder blades were against the wood, his hardness pressing into mine. "Don't worry, I wasn't going to stay. I'm liking this, taking my time with you, Murph."

Then he kissed me. Not with a sense of urgency, but taking his time just like he'd promised.

"As for my place, it's on the other side of Montpelier, but it's not a big deal. I drive at night to get to emergencies."

Our lips locked again, and Ben's hand slid down my back, eventually grabbing my butt—*my ass?* My former New York socialite self couldn't reconcile with this newer, more casual and hip version of me.

"You feel so good," he murmured, pulling me out of my head as he leaned further into me.

It wasn't forceful and it didn't hurt. In fact, it felt so alpha, or caveman, or in charge. Whatever, it felt great, and I wanted more. As I leaned further into Ben, a low moan or maybe a growl made its way from my mouth.

"Was that me?" I said breathlessly.

"That was you."

Ben broke free from my lips and kissed his way down my neck before running his tongue over my collarbone. Then he knelt lower, lifting my shirt and pressing his mouth to my nipple.

First, he sucked through my silk bra, before pulling the fabric down and blowing warm air on the chilled skin. Goose bumps spread all over my body as he continued to suck on me and then blow warm breaths.

I didn't want to admit I'd never had this type of sensation before. Yeah, I'd been groped or felt up in the past, but it had been a while. And it had always felt so cursory—obligatory and unemotional.

Moaning, I couldn't help the sounds coming from my mouth. My head banged back into the door, and Ben was kneeling on the floor, pulling my jeans down and tugging my panties to the side. It happened so quickly, I couldn't remember if I'd done any maintenance down there. It had been a long time since I'd had the full monty in Manhattan. Now, I was all about quick and down-and-dirty trimming.

A deep rumble came from Ben's chest, and then his mouth was

on me there. All over me, devouring, licking, nipping. With a long swipe, he released my most sensitive spot from his mouth, and said, "I'm sorry if I'm rushing you. I had to taste you. I've been waiting . . . well, years."

He didn't say another word until I came apart, all over his mouth, face, tongue, whatever you want to call it. It had never happened like that for me. This was a rebirth or something. Sometime between Ben spinning my back toward the door and now, I'd become a highly sexual woman.

After sliding my panties back in place and pulling my jeans up, Ben rose to his feet and trailed a long line of kisses over my collarbone and up my neck, finally landing on my mouth. He tasted like me, and it was so intimate, I thought I might combust.

"See?" he said, smiling against my lips. "Not only am I not staying over, but I'm not even seeing your bed."

"What about you?" My head spun with confusion. I'd never been in an intimate situation where sex or intimacy wasn't quid pro quo.

"What about me?"

Running my hand up and down his back, I said softly, "You. Pleasing you."

Ben gave me a quick squeeze. "Next time. This way we don't run out of time. If there's always something left to look forward to, there will never be a last time."

Then he kissed me and said thank you—when it should have been me doing the thank-yous—before he slipped out the door and into the night.

In a haze, I walked toward my bathroom and peed, but refused to wash my face or brush my teeth or shower. I wanted to hold on to everything about that experience for as long as I could.

17

MURPHY

I couldn't believe that Ben had gone down on me. That's what the cool kids called it these days, not the high-society ladies, but I wasn't one of those anymore. Back in New York, prior to the fiasco, I dated guys my mom had picked for me. They gave what I called a smidge of oral to receive a healthy helping of it themselves. It was perfunctory, at best.

And yes, I thought in Ivy League vocabulary, even when I was thinking of oral sex.

Anyway, now that I'd experienced what I'd been searching for when I signed up for online dating—to be utterly devoured—I'd resisted showering as long as possible, but decided one was in order when Hunnie texted me the next morning.

I'm making a new concoction and never had anyone taste test for me. Come over?

A small smile split my face. No one had ever asked me for my honest opinion before. Ever.

Instead of being truthful, I texted back.

How do you know I'm not at the Bean?

Because I just ran (okay, I drove) into Colebury for some cupcakes for later, and I stopped into the Bean. Ben was there.

I told myself not to take the bait. Hunnie was fishing, and I was too easy to lure in.

Sure, I'll come by.

Heard you went to the drive-in. Ben said it was a late night and he needed a pick-me-up before picking up his nephew for an overnight.

I'd already shrugged off my clothes and was jumping in the shower with my hair in a topknot when her last text pinged my phone. After a quick rinse, I threw on capri leggings and a loose tank, shoved my feet into flip-flops, Hunnie and her footwear judginess be damned. Grabbing a sweater for later, I dug into my purse for my lipstick.

Happy that I needed to actually get dressed, I completely ignored Hunnie's prying and decided to head over to her place for an in-person inquisition. Except when I pulled up in front of her she-shed, I wanted to turn around when a realization hit me.

I'd never had a friend I could talk freely with . . . I was taught to always be on guard. Was I supposed to just chat openly? Using crass language? Of course, we did that in high school in the privacy of our dorm rooms, teenage girls trying on new personalities and expressions.

"Get in here," Hunnie called out as she opened her door.

Grabbing my sweater from the passenger seat, I rolled my eyes. As if Hunnie was going to let me escape.

Dressed in cutoffs, a loose black long-sleeved tee falling off her shoulder, and an apron in a cute bee pattern, Hunnie totally looked the part of honey infusionist. Secretly, I wished to be that cool. Although, I wasn't jealous.

"Now that's what I would call sexy country chic, and I mean that in a very good way," I told her as I stepped onto her porch.

"Why, thank you. I see you're done with your white shorts."

"After you put me in my place."

"Whatever. Get in here and spill." She waved me inside and shut the door.

"Do you really need me to taste something?" I dropped onto her couch and watched her flit around the room like a bumblebee herself.

"Yes, I'm not a liar. But I want to hear about the drive-in too," she said while risking her life on a stepstool. She appeared to be climbing the shelves to the right of her kitchen, one toe on the stool, the other on a shelf as she tried to reach something at the top.

"Wait," I yelped, and she nearly fell.

Holding on to the shelf for dear life, she turned to me with huge eyes. "Are you trying to kill me?"

"No . . . sorry. Hold that thought and stay right there. This is such a perfect shot of you. Wearing that outfit and scurrying around—you embody your brand right now."

I ran out the door and grabbed my bag I'd left in the passenger seat to pull out my phone. I snapped ten pictures of Hunnie doing her thing before she climbed back down with a jar of something dark purple in her hands.

"Blackberries," she said, like everyone kept blackberries on the top shelf. "I have one jar left, and I want to make a special limited-edition batch for this weekend."

"Make sure to take some pics when it's finished," I said as I swiped through the pics I'd just taken, "so we can promo it. I can post it super quick. I assume it's going to be local only? No shipping?"

"Yeah, yeah. Hey, want to come with me tomorrow?"

"Where? To the market?"

Hunnie busied herself opening the jar of blackberries. "So it can breathe," she said. Then she grabbed a jar full of a pinkish honey with flecks of green. Dipping a spoon in it, she shoved it my way. "Here, taste."

Knowing better than to argue about calories or anything of the sort, I opened my mouth for the spoon. "Mmm, that's actually amazing. What is it?"

"I took my signature elderberry infusion—which, come fall, will be the most popular honey because it fights colds—and I added a touch of lemon and also mint. I'm calling it Forest."

"Give me another taste," I said, and when she obliged, I studied the jar. "You know, it does look like a forest, and the mint is perfect. I need to think of some great copy for Instagram on this. We could do some super-fab reels set to music."

"Don't forget we start with all raw Vermont honey, and then we source as much locally as we can."

"Never."

As we stood across from each other in Hunnie's open kitchen, I felt her staring at me, questions swirling behind her eyes.

"You know Ben spoke with his dad, and the petting zoo is going to be a go." Hunnie did a small twirl, her hair flopping on top of her head, looking like she didn't have a care in the world. Her attitude was both nauseating and infectious at the same time.

I shook my head. "He didn't tell me. We're not on that level."

Leaning my hip into the counter, I welcomed the biting pinch it created as waves of melancholy washed over me. *Ben is just a hookup. We don't share personal matters on that level.*

"Would you stop it?" Hunnie gently grabbed my chin and forced me to look at her.

"Stop what?"

Releasing my chin, she snapped her fingers in my face. "Snap the hell out of it. He likes you, and you like him. Don't second-guess it. It was my news to tell. Anyway, we're going to look at animals after the market. Do you work tomorrow? I need you to come and take pictures."

"I'm off tomorrow afternoon."

"Great. Now sit down and tell me about the date. Oh, and Ben let it slip you have some fabulous business idea. He was all pimping you out, like you matter to him." This time she winked and struck a pose with her hand on her hip.

"We're old friends, you know? And I guess we're having fun now, but it's not permanent. I'm going to move eventually, and Ben loves it here in Vermont. He has roots here," I said, moving over to settle into the velvet armchair.

"Well, you're growing roots. Now, shoot the shit, Murphy."

She stared me down, sitting with her legs crossed in front of her, her back to the side of the couch. Matching her posture, I swallowed my shame and started to spill my soul.

"We went to the drive-in, he brought a picnic, and we had fun. I'd never been. Then he came back to my place and took care of me, but wouldn't let me take care of him." Although I desperately tried not to do it, the end came out like a question. I didn't want to admit to my lack of experience.

Hunnie nodded knowingly. "A ladies-first man. I always knew it. They're the best kind of guy to catch." Leaning forward with interest, she said, "Was it really good? Divine? Go on."

"Um, that's all I'm going to say because I'm a lady, or at least used to be one. But it wasn't ladylike at all, against the door."

Frowning, she blew out a frustrated breath. "Don't you dare leave me hanging like that."

"Hunnie, you're my boss."

"Hush. I'm your friend too. Speaking of which . . ." She popped up again and picked up a little box. "I got you a cupcake. This one is from Gigi. She heard you loved maple syrup, so it's a maple-glazed vanilla cupcake made just for you."

My mouth dropped open. "But I don't even know Gigi . . ."

"Girl, I've been singing your praises. She's desperate to meet you," Hunnie said, shoving the box toward me.

Gingerly, I opened it up and took in the perfectly crafted cupcake covered in a khaki-colored icing and dusted with gold and pink sugar. "Wow."

"Look how it matches your nail polish," Hunnie said, staring at my hand holding the delicacy housed in a shimmery box before going back to her seat.

"Yes, it does. I put on this shade this morning while finishing the book I'm reading . . . *To See You*. I thought it went well with the cover, especially the pink accent color."

I closed my eyes as an idea came to mind. *Nails, books, cupcakes, coffee . . . was there anything better? No.*

"Earth to Murphy?" Hunnie raised her voice, drawing me out of my musings.

Opening my eyes, I sighed. "Sorry, I just had an idea for Zara. Must be the Vermont air. I'm a creative busy bee here."

Hunnie smiled. "Maybe it's because you're happy. You know, really happy? You look happy."

"Maybe," I said cautiously. "How would you know?"

"I know," she said. "Because for a few years after high school, I was really unhappy. Stuck here in Vermont, wanting to do something like Ben did, or the few others who got out for a while. Then one day, I was sick with the flu and stuck here in my shed. My mom made me soup, and tea with honey. Ben's mom dropped off fresh cinnamon-maple rolls, and other neighbors stopped by to check on me. When I was finally better and able to get up and see the crisp blue sky . . . well, I knew. This was a place to be happy. To be grateful, content, and not want for more."

Hunnie's eyes glistened with emotion but she smiled the whole time she spoke. All I could think was she had her shit together in a way I wasn't sure I ever would.

"I get it," I said, staring at my hands, "but honestly, I don't think I even know what happy is. For most of my life I was told what I needed to do to make everyone else happy, but my own happiness was at the bottom of the list."

"I don't get that," she said with a huff. "At all. It's not that I don't believe you, but I can't wrap my head around it."

I shrugged. "It's impossible to get. It's just the way it is. But I'm here now and trying to break free of it all. It's hard, a lot harder than I thought. I will admit this idea I just had makes me happy-ish."

Hunnie held up her hand. "Then go with it, but don't tell me until you tell Zara."

"Deal," I said with a smile.

Hunnie stared at me. "God, you truly are stunning. I can see why Ben can't let go. You know, I remember his mom going on about you. 'He's hung up on this Murphy girl. Mopes around about her every time he's home.'"

"Oh God," I said, leaning my head back against the chair. "It was a bad time in my life."

"His too. He didn't want to go on that scholarship. His dad nearly forced him out the door. It was good, though, he needed it. Total mama's boy. Now he's all about Branson and work and more work. You know about . . . never mind."

Hunnie looked away for a second. There was a story she wasn't telling me, but since I didn't want to spill all my secrets, I didn't push.

"Anyway," she said, "tell me what Ben was going on about. Your idea?" She stood and went back to her blackberries, lifting the jar to smell them.

Getting up too, I paced. "It's just something I thought of. Back in New York, they had these straws filled with honey. Yes, I know, not environmentally friendly, but so pretty and perfect individual servings. Your infusions would look gorgeous in them. I envisioned them at parties or little gift shops . . . shoot, I'm going to kill Ben for telling you."

Leaving her fruit, Hunnie turned and clapped. "Yes. Girl. Yes. We need some samples. Do you have someone in New York who can send them?"

Not wanting to reach out to anyone from my former life, I said, "I'll call one of the stores who carried them and ask."

"I'll reimburse you. This is part of your intern responsibilities," she said with another wink. "We're back to work now. Can't be all play. After I see the samples, I can think of manufacturers.

Now, go home and eat your cupcake, and please, please, go in and meet Gigi. You're a genius, and she wants to meet you."

"I don't know about genius. Maybe only here in the middle of Vermont."

"You're somebody, Murphy. Here, there, anywhere . . . you're gonna do great things."

I scrunched up my face in thought. "Isn't that Dr. Seuss?"

Hunnie laughed. "I know, but it's also the truth. Now, scat and write a post on my weekend special . . . call it blackberry-pie honey. I love the sound of that. Right? I may have to make it a regular thing."

She blew a kiss at me as I headed out the door. I couldn't help but wonder if I would have as much fun when I decided to try a big city again.

18

MURPHY

Taking off my pink apron on Saturday, I looked down at my Bean tee and skinny jeans, which I was wearing with chunky black patent Doc Martens I bought during my freshman year of college. It was about as Vermont as I got, and the best I had to wear to go look at animals with Hunnie.

"See you tomorrow," I told Audrey, who'd popped in to check on the temperature gauge on the industrial fridge. Apparently, a few years back, the power went out and the big monstrosity occasionally went on the fritz after being reset.

She waved me off. "I don't think I'll stay after I come in to start the baking, but call if you guys need anything. Family day, you know?"

I nodded like I did, but I knew nothing about fun family times that weren't press opportunities.

Grabbing my bag from the back room, I checked my phone. One text from my mom about a party coming up in October, and if I'd be willing to make an appearance. She even offered to buy me a dress and arrange for salon appointments—which meant she was going to style me up however she liked.

Scrolling through, I saw a text had come in from Ben, and decided to respond to my mom later.

Hey there. I hear you're going to look at animals. Beware of poop if you're wearing sandals.

Snapping a picture of my boots while walking to my car, I decided not to reply with words. I simply sent the photo and waited. A few seconds later, my phone rang.

"Hello?" I said, acting surprised.

"Don't hello me," Ben said with a mock growl. "You've been holding back on all of us. Do you have a secret Vermont wardrobe?"

I giggled into the phone, leaning my butt against the trunk of my car. "These are so old. Bought them on a whim for a Halloween party freshman year. For some reason, I thought a barely there negligee paired with clunky boots was sexy back then. Thank God, sorority rules forbid photos at the party, because I'm not sure I ever want to be reminded of the night."

"I don't know if I agree with any of what you just said," Ben said, his sexy voice rumbling over the line.

I can't lie—a shot of something surged through my body, making my cheeks burn. I told myself it was the Vermont sun, but deep down I knew it wasn't.

"Well, you'll have to live without them. Can you imagine my parents' reaction if they saw them?"

As Ben laughed, I could hear someone call his name in the background.

"Branson is hanging with me this weekend. We're watching golf on TV. I don't even know who I am, but he seems to like it. Anyway, wanted to see if you wanted to go walk around the Montpelier farmers' market on Tuesday? They're open. We could bring some dessert back here if you want."

"Oh yeah. I actually work Tuesday morning at the Bean, and I could spy on some other honey vendors while there."

"Great. Can I pick you up around five or a little after?"

"Sure. You want to drive back and forth to Colebury? I can meet you."

"I want to. I'll stop for a coffee. Make sure you tell them to make me a good one."

"I'll see . . ."

"And, Murph?"

"Yes?"

"Wear those boots."

"With knee socks?" I asked, lowering my voice to a husky purr.

I don't know what came over me—I was wanton in a way I'd never imagined. Like a heroine in a historical romance yearning for a man, taking what she wanted or needed. I was no longer the woman I was raised to be, and it felt good.

Ben blew out a frustrated sigh. "Murphy, you're really making me regret having my nephew here."

Snapping out of my decadently sexy moment, I said, "Go. Don't regret being with family. See you Tuesday."

I hung up before the conversation could go any further, and thought about goats as I settled in my car, trying to cool my hormones. Apparently, this was what happened when a young girl was repressed all her life.

Later that night, tucked in bed after a day with Hunnie and her goats, I was reading my latest romance, jotting some notes in the margins. *Not those kinds of notes.* I noted themes, an outfit or two for color schemes, along with a few other ideas.

A plan was coming together in my mind on how to promote a few of my favorite things together, plus make a small name for myself. I was energized in a way I'd never been. Refusing to think about my parents and what they would think of my small town idea, I dove back into the book. This one was about a rake and a woman from the wrong side of society.

I was at the good part when the hero was suckling on particular parts of the heroine's body, her bodice slowly coming off, when my phone dinged. Grabbing it, I noted it was eleven o'clock, and the text was from Ben.

I can't stop thinking about those boots.

Absolutely nothing could stop the broad smile from spreading over my face. I could feel my laugh lines scrunching and knew this moment would lead to a wrinkle. If my mom knew, she'd be pissed.

Before I could dream up a witty response, another text dinged.

Sorry for the sultry text, but I mean it. Looking forward to Tuesday.

Still unable to think of a comeback, I searched through my GIFs. When I found the one I wanted, I sent a small GIF of Nancy Sinatra singing "These Boots Are Made For Walking."

Almost immediately, the little bubble with dots popped up.

That's not helping. You're a shameless flirt.

I'd been called a lot of things, but *shameless flirt* had never been one of them. So I sent back one word.

Me?

Because I didn't even know how to do this texting and flirting thing (we didn't learn it in our decorum class), I followed up with:

A flirt?

Yes. You. I have to behave. My nephew is asleep down the hall. Also, Nancy Sinatra? You know her?

Of course I do. My parents loved her dad.

I didn't feel like talking about my parents anymore. They only dragged my mood down, and I'd already spent most of life living for what they wanted.

All of a sudden, a happy thought shocked me back to reality. *Gosh, what would my mom think of my reading romance novels?* Not much, I expected.

You know Nancy met Elvis when he came back from the Army?

Not expecting that little tidbit, I responded with:

Are we playing trivia now?

Sorry to disturb you. As you know, I'm actually a bit of a closet music aficionado. Elvis is a favorite.

Hey, I'm only reading in bed. You're not disturbing me. I forgot to ask . . . were you always into music?

Yeah. But never those boy bands you listened to at Pressman, or the grunge groups the guys liked. It wasn't until college where I found a crew who liked decent music.

I couldn't stop thinking about how little I knew about Ben, even though we'd been friends for four years in high school. I guessed it was because I'd kept our conversations on the surface.

I wish I knew back then. At Pressman. I wish I knew a lot back then. More about you.

Dots bounced on my screen for a long time as Ben composed his response.

You're going to know now . . . better late than never. Go read,

Murph. I have to operate this Monday, filling in for my partner.
See you Tuesday.

That's it? That was where he was going to leave it?

Like I said, I didn't get this texting and flirting thing. Maybe this was some kind of hard-to-get deal?

Setting my phone down, I tried to get back into my book, but it was useless. My mind was way beyond the sexy rake.

BEN

Blowing out a long exhale as I knocked on Murphy's door on Tuesday, I hoped I hadn't been too assertive when it came to my pressing her against it the other night and having my way with her body. Or when texting her.

I'd been feeling fucking great after our movie night. Despite the shitty circumstances that brought us together, we were finally in the same place at the same time. Emotionally and physically, I thought.

"Hey," Murphy said as she pulled the door open.

Schooling my expression, I managed a smile. Her place was in such disrepair, and I couldn't help but worry. I was certain Murphy had never lived as low before. Would she know what to do if the rickety door broke or her ceiling leaked?

"Hey, yourself," I said instead of letting my thoughts spiral any further. Instead of kissing her like I wanted to, I leaned in to hand her an extra-frothy latte.

"For me?"

I nodded. "Zara said it's your favorite. Although, my Americano wasn't quite as good as usual."

"Did the new kid make it?" Murphy asked quickly, her voice tight as she pushed a lock of hair behind her ear.

As I stepped inside, I took a moment to take all of Murphy in —long red waves cascading over her shoulder and her eyes bright, wearing a flannel shirt knotted at her waist and cutoffs.

Staring at her bare feet, I said, "He did. The new kid, that is."

Frowning, Murphy said, "I wonder if Zara's unhappy with me. Did she say anything to you? Sometimes you two chat when you come in, I noticed."

"I doubt she's unhappy with you. She made you your fave drink, all by herself." I shut the door behind me and thought about skipping the farmers' market. Maybe we could stay in? Like old times when we stayed in her dorm behind closed doors.

"I just wondered because they started Zane pretty soon after me." She bent to grab her boots and a pair of what looked like ankle socks.

Farmers' market, it is. I don't want to hide being with Murphy.

"Murph, look at me," I said firmly.

Trying to ignore her knotted shirt riding up a bit, exposing a flash of creamy skin, I forced myself to look her in the eye. "I don't know Zara well. And for the record, she talks to anyone who comes in regularly. She was a bartender, so talking comes naturally to her."

Murphy rolled her eyes at me, propping her hands on her hips. "Don't stereotype. It's not nice."

"You're right. Either way, I don't know Zara much more than my running in for coffee. There was the one time her daughter, Nicole, fell at school, and Zara asked me to do a favor and take a look at her ankle. Thankfully, it was only a bad sprain. Anyway, Zara is good people. She's not doing anything to spite you."

As Murphy sat down to pull on her socks and boots, I said, "I'll tell you this. The new kid is a friend of Kieran Shipley's—he and Roddy introduced him to Zara. I only know because Zara told me this when I asked if she would consider hiring Branson. She's giving this young kid a chance, so Branson still has to hunt around. No hard feelings about it, since she actually suggested he try at the hardware store."

Standing up, Murphy came over and hugged me tightly. "Thank you. It may not feel like much to you, but knowing that means everything to me. Yesterday, Zara asked me if I wanted to work for Hunnie full time when I was on my break, and I panicked."

"Come here." I pulled her into a hug and kissed the top of her head. "Murph, you've got to understand this isn't New York. Everyone is aboveboard here. Honesty is practically the law in Vermont."

Murphy laughed, and I could feel her giggle vibrating against my chest. "Seriously, I was nervous. I even had a silly idea for the Bean, and was too afraid to share it with Zara after that."

"By the way, Hunnie texted me that she loved your idea for the straws. So if I were you, I wouldn't be scared to share any ideas."

Pinching my side, Murphy broke out into a wide grin. "Yeah, thanks for throwing me under the bus."

"It was a perfect idea, and I could tell you weren't going to share."

"Whatever. Let's go. I can't stare at these walls anymore."

"Anxious to head to my place?" I asked, changing the subject so I wouldn't keep worrying about her apartment. I did make a mental note to find out who her landlord was and see if they planned to update the place.

"You promised me dessert," she said with a little sass.

"I did. I also don't have a Keurig, but I do have the real stuff if you want."

"Ha-ha. I'm going to be caffeinated and sugared up after my latte. I don't think you're going to want to serve me anymore," she said, grabbing her purse. "Maybe a small dessert."

"You're looking very Vermonty, Murph," I told her as we walked out the door.

"I'm channeling my inner Hunnie. I actually hid my white shorts in the back of my closet."

"Did you now?" I joked, opening the Jeep's passenger door for her.

"Also, it's going to freeze soon."

This had me laughing as I got into the driver's seat. "It's the middle of July. Give it at least a month."

"Two, I heard. September."

"Could be. But then we get to have ski season, the most gorgeous time of year around here. Sadly, also my busiest," I said while backing the car into the street.

"That's too bad. You've got to live a little, Ben."

"Do you ski?" I asked, imagining she learned in Aspen.

"I do. Or I did. A long time ago. We took a couple of family trips to Jackson Hole. Actually, I should say they were more work trips for my parents. Networking, fundraising, and all that good stuff while I was stuck in ski school and babysitting night at the hotel."

Blown away, I shook my head. "I can't imagine. I'm sorry to say it, but I can't."

"It's okay. At least I knew how to ski and wasn't scared in college. I went a few times with friends. It was fun."

"I learned. Or I should say I'm self-taught. We used to goof around as kids on borrowed skis and back hills. Then, on one of the breaks from Pressman, I was sick of hearing all the ski stories, so I went over to the Mad River area and rented a cheap pair of skis and jumped on the lift, studying what other people were doing as they hopped off the lift at the top. Then I just jumped off after them, trying to do what they did. Probably not the best idea, and a sure way to get hurt. Thank God my football coach never found out."

I wound my way along the narrow road lined with country homes and tall trees, wondering what Murphy's home looked like when she was growing up.

Glancing at me, she said, "You're pretty cool, you know that?"

"I don't know about cool . . ."

"Back then, you never even told me about how you learned to ski, but I do remember you going on a few ski trips."

"Well, I told everyone my dad taught me, because I'm from Vermont where everyone skis, right? But not everyone can afford it because it's expensive. I didn't even have ski pants. That first time I went, I wore jeans with long underwear underneath, and an old winter coat."

"So, do you ski now?" Murphy asked.

"When I have time. I do like it because it's an odd juxtaposition. You're flying down the hill, seconds away from possible death, and yet it's peaceful. Gives me time to think."

I took a quick peek at Murphy's profile to see she was quiet and listening. "You know, you always did that," I blurted before thinking.

"What are you talking about?" She turned to look at me. I could sense the movement in my veins.

"Jeez," I said, taking one hand off the wheel and running it through my hair. "I didn't mean to say that out loud. What I meant was you were always a good listener. You always seemed to give me your full attention when we were hanging out in your room at Pressman, and now too."

Leaning her head back, she let out a belly laugh.

It was my turn to say, "What?"

"It's all part of the training from my mom on mingling in high society, and being a politician's daughter. *Be a good listener, Murphy. Always act like you're interested, Murphy.*"

Not going to lie, my heart clenched, and I had to resist rubbing it. My fingers tightening around the steering wheel, I said, "So, it's just an act."

"Mostly, but never with you. Truth is, I was always able to be myself with you. I mean, the other night, the intimacy," she said, her cheeks turning pink. "I haven't had that with anyone. Yes, I've been physically intimate before, but never emotionally comfortable while doing it. Oh. Wow. I didn't mean to take the conversation there."

"It's good. I was worried I rushed, took things too fast or far. But," I said, turning into the dusty parking lot, "hold that thought for later. First, all things Vermont."

"Sounds perfect right now."

After parking, I hopped out of the Jeep and rounded the front, but Murphy was already jumping out. "It may be perfect, but let's not forget your idea for Zara or our good time against your front door." I took her hand in mine and walked toward the entry gate.

"Let's do this. Let me tell Zara and then we'll discuss it. I don't want to jinx myself."

I nodded. "Deal. And us," I said, lifting our clasped hands in front of us. "You know what? Don't answer, I'll show you later."

This got me a half smile, enough to create cute crinkles at the sides of her eyes. I'd take it.

"Oh, look. Honey. Let me take a quick look," Murphy said when we started walking the aisles.

"Sure."

She wandered over toward a table, taking my hand and me along with her.

I'd lived in Vermont almost all my life, and I'd never been happier. Problem was, if this thing with Murphy was going to last, I'd have to eventually be honest with her, and I hadn't been totally honest with anyone. Maybe Brenna, but that's about it. I didn't want anyone to think I wasn't "good, decent people" anymore.

"Hi," the woman said with a big smile as we walked up to her table.

"Hi." Murphy smiled back before picking up a small mason jar of honey.

"That's local raw honey," the woman said with pride. "We have a small apiary by Norwich, and we try to come up here once a month."

"Oh, it looks beautiful," Murphy said, then picked up a little brochure on the honey.

"Want a taste?"

Murphy nodded. Taking the spoon, she licked the honey from it with a grin. After telling the lady how good it was, she then bought some.

After all the thank-yous and pleasantries, we walked away.

Keeping my voice low, I leaned in to ask, "Sleeping with the enemy?"

Murphy waggled her brows. "Just a little foreplay. Sampling what's out there, you know."

I couldn't stop the huge laugh barreling from me. "Come on. Let's go check out Vermont's best syrup, Toptree. Although, you know this isn't the season for syrup, right? We sell it all year, but March is the best time to get it."

I tried to calm my nerves as Murphy turned to look at me. My mom was probably working our table, ready to pounce on my sidekick for a quick interrogation at a moment's notice.

"I didn't know that until I started doing this gig for Hunnie," Murphy said, her turn to wink at me. "I've been studying up on all things Vermont."

Making our way through the aisles, we reached my family's setup where a long dark green tablecloth covered the shabby table beneath. Live potted plants lined the center display of our syrups, including the blackberry-flavored one front and center. Waning sunlight reflected off the glass bottles. Pictures of the cheese we offered were arranged in front of the plants. After working many times at farmers' markets on summer breaks and weekends when I was home, I knew there was plenty of inventory in coolers underneath the table.

But rather than finding my mom or dad behind the table, I was surprised to see it being manned by our family farm's bookkeeper.

"Hey, Ben."

"Marley, what are you doing here?"

She shrugged. "Your dad found some humidity getting into the big fridge where he ferments the cheddar, and your mom stayed to keep him company while he fixed it. You know those two . . . everyone dreams of being as close as they are."

I nodded. My mom and dad were somewhat of a legend in the area when it came to long-term romance. Then there was my single-mom sister and me, the eternal bachelor. We didn't even come close to their legacy.

"I'll have to give him a call. He didn't mention it when I talked to him over the phone last week, so it must've just happened."

"This morning. He tasted a bad batch, so he looked into it."

"Well, I'm sure they're grateful you're covering for them. Thank you."

"Who is this?" Marley said, ignoring my appreciation in favor of giving Murphy a curious look.

"Mar, this is Murphy, an old friend who just moved to the area. Murphy, this is Marley. She does the books for the farm and is practically family."

"Murphy, nice to meet you." Marley held out her hand, and Murphy shook it like a pro.

"I love the syrup," Murphy told her. "I'm a sucker for anything sweet."

"Well, let's get you set up with some."

Next thing I knew, I was watching Murphy slowly lick a spoon with blackberry syrup on it, her tongue gliding up and down to get every drop. The way she was making love to that spoon, I couldn't help but wish that spoon was my mouth, or finger, or . . .

Well, you get it. It was the most sensual thing I'd ever seen. I really needed to get a hold of myself and my uncontrollable fantasies when it came to this woman.

Murphy tossed the spoon in the trash, moaning with pleasure. "Mmm, I love that. It's absolutely heavenly." Turning toward me, she said, "Ben, I never had this one."

But what I heard was, *"Ben, take me to bed."*

"I'll take a bottle," she told Marley, pulling out her wallet from her crossbody bag.

"On the house." I gently pushed her wallet back toward her

purse. "Put it on my tab," I told Marley with a wink, and she went along with it.

I didn't have a tab, but Marley knew damn well I'd be picking up the cost of the fridge repair for my dad. She did the books, so she had a good idea who paid a lot of the farm's bills.

We chatted a minute longer before saying our good-byes so Marley could help someone else who was waiting. Strolling the aisles, holding hands, Murphy and I bought a couple of grilled Vermont cheddar sandwiches and hand-cut fries to share for an early dinner.

"I can check out the competition too," I said, taking a bite of the sandwich.

"So, cheese?" Murphy asked before taking a bite of her own.

"Yeah, well, syrup is a winter thing workwise, so the cheese is more like a side gig that ends up taking year-round. I'll tell you this, my parents do make a mean grilled cheese on Saturdays and Sundays in the tasting room. They like to add fresh peppers and onions."

"Wow. I need to go. This sandwich is good, but I'd rather have yours. Or theirs."

Sitting on the picnic bench, we ate and talked about Hunnie making blackberry honey, and Murphy being desperate to get some now. And we also talked about the goats.

"That was the deciding factor for my dad on the animals," I told her. "He figures it'll be great for the gift shop and lead to many grilled cheese sandwiches and syrup sales. Once people have a taste of the product, they seek it out more and more. He's hoping it gets so busy that Brenna will want to work for him, and take off some of the strain of her raising Branson by herself."

"Why doesn't she want to work for them now? It's a family business, right?"

Setting my sandwich down on the bench, I sipped at my water as I took in the beauty in front of me. "She doesn't want handouts or to be stuck doing syrup and cheese because they do. But let's not ruin our evening by talking about her stubbornness. Let's talk about goats."

Not arguing with me, Murphy laughed. "They're very friendly and like humans. Apparently, they're good with kids, and yes, they do stand on your back during yoga. Did you know Hunnie is getting certified to be a yoga instructor?"

"I heard something about it. Online, right?"

"Yes. I love how she chases her dreams. It's inspiring."

"You're inspiring," I said, leaning in and stealing a quick kiss. "Come on. Let's grab some dessert and get out of here."

Grinning, Murphy jumped up from the bench.

With a bag of cider doughnuts between us in the center console and two hot cups of mulled cider in the cup holders, Murphy and I pulled up in front of my place.

I pressed the button to open my garage doors, which were now a faux wood. They matched the trim of the house, a single-story craftsman. It had been updated when I bought it, except for the attic, a large open space reached by a staircase off the kitchen that I'd made into a bedroom for Branson.

Now as I pulled my Jeep into the fairly neat garage, I wondered what Murphy would think of my home.

"I don't know if I will ever get out of this car," she said with a sigh. "It smells so good in here."

"Don't tell me you're the apple-candle type of girl? They're nice and all, but after a few hours, they really stink up a house."

"Sounds like you know a lot about this subject." Murphy pretended to be joking, but I detected a hint of jealousy in her question. I'm not going to pretend I didn't like it.

"Brenna used to burn them when I was living at home. I'd run outside as fast as I could, if you must know."

"Well, if *you* must know, I haven't been a girl in a long time. As for candles, back in New York I used to burn a white-lily scented candle. It was the signature scent from a boutique where my mom and I liked to shop."

After shifting the car into park and turning off the engine, I ran my hand down Murphy's cheek. "Well, we don't need scented candles in Vermont. We open the windows and breathe in all the natural scents."

"Is that so?" She leaned her cheek into my palm, seeking deeper contact.

"Fun time?"

She nodded.

"Sorry my mom wasn't there."

"After all your warnings?" Murphy's head popped up, and she smirked.

"Still."

"Hunnie said your mom used to curse my existence, so I'm definitely holding off on meeting her."

"Don't be silly. Besides, Marley will report every detail about meeting you at the farmers' market. She may be more subtle in her tactics than my mom, but her gossiping is just as deadly."

Murphy playfully growled at me, and my mind went other places than my mom.

"Let's go inside," I said, changing the subject.

Murphy jumped out and walked behind the car while I grabbed the snacks.

"Welcome to my place," I said, opening the door to the house, juggling the cups and the bag and holding my keys in my mouth.

"Here, let me take something." Murphy took the cups and bag, and I let her walk in front of me.

"Wow. This is so cool," she said, wandering into the open kitchen that led to an open floor plan. Setting the food on the dark green granite island, she looked around wide-eyed. "Nice digs, Dr. Rooney. I'm impressed."

"Brenna found it. One of the other doctors at the hospital owned it, and had to put it up for sale when he moved to Alaska to work in an underserved community. When Bren heard it was going on the market, she wouldn't let it go. She dragged me here one night, telling me she needed to pick up something for Branson from one of his friends, and surprised me with the real estate agent waiting for us in the kitchen. Once she dragged me through the house, she pulled out the heavy artillery, insisting that I deserved it."

Murphy smiled at me, tilting her head. "Aw, she sounds unbelievably committed to you. I mean in a family way, something I know nothing about."

"She wants me to make a life. A real life."

Murphy kicked off her now muddy boots by the door leading to the garage and hopped onto one of my kitchen stools. Peeking inside the bag, she plucked out a doughnut and took a bite. With a dusting of sugar on her lips, she looked relaxed and at home, like she belonged here in my kitchen. Seeing her like that gave me a twinge in my chest that I'd never experienced before.

"Looks like you have a pretty good life," she said after chewing a big mouthful. "Mmm, these are good. Have one."

I moved closer, leaning my hip against the island as I stood in front of Murphy. "Brenna wants me to have a life of my own, one where I'm not always taking care of her and Branson. A life with someone who matters to me."

"So, what's stopping you?" Murphy asked the question without a hint of artifice, an honest question between friends.

Leaning down to steal a small bite of doughnut left in her hand, I chewed before running my sugary lips along hers. "Didn't meet the right person."

"Oh." Murphy's eyes widened slightly before she glanced away. "I'm sure she's glad you're helping with her son."

I nodded. "Enough about them. Let's take a tour."

It was enough. Talk about Branson led to confessions I wasn't ready to make yet.

Forgetting the ciders, leaving them to get cold, Murphy put her hand in mine, and we turned the corner so I could show her my home office with a red leather couch and fireplace. I liked to do my charting there on the weekend, I told her, and she listened intently as we made our way back to the living area with a dining table in the far corner.

Murphy spun around. "Another fireplace. So cool."

"I have one in my bedroom too." My voice was low, husky with want. I cleared my throat, trying to tame the desire running through my veins.

"You do?" Murphy's eyes met mine, bright with excitement and sensuality.

"Too bad it's not cold enough tonight to build a fire. Soon. By the time September comes around here, we usually see a frost."

"I'm shivering at just the thought of it."

We walked slowly, something undefined burning slowly between the two of us. When we entered my room, I flicked on the light, but immediately dimmed it.

"A four-poster bed. Hmm, not what I was expecting." She ran her tongue along her lips, now wet and tantalizing.

"It came with the house," I said with a shrug.

"Nice." She moved over to the bed and sat down.

"New mattress," I said for some reason as I sat next to her.

I wasn't sure who leaned in first, but in the next breath we were kissing in a furious frenzy. I worked at loosening the knot on Murphy's flannel shirt, tugging to loosen the buttons, and she shrugged it off.

"Wow," I said, leaning back to take in all of her in a red satin bra.

"Left over from my New York days," she said. "I can't afford this now."

"Everything is going to change for you, Murph."

I leaned over to press my lips to her neck, then worked my way down her clavicle, lingering on the line of smooth skin where her bra met her breast.

A small moan escaped her, and I tugged down the fabric and found her nipple. As her head fell back, I worshiped her other breast before she came up and shoved me down, yanking my shirt over my head and relieving me of my khakis.

Murphy grinned at me. "Commando, Doc?"

"It's comfortable. Surprised you know that expression, little lady," I said without thinking.

I wasn't sure how she would react to that, but she laughed and worked her way down my body, kissing every inch along the way. Taking my length in her hand, she caressed me up and down and back up again.

"Rougher," I grumbled, and she obliged.

It was my turn for my head to fall back, and multiple moans poured from me. I was so enthralled by her small palm working me, it wasn't until her lips ghosted over my tip that I realized she'd leaned over me. She took all of me in her mouth, still using her hand, and I was going to explode. Soon.

"Murph, I'm not going to last."

"Good," she mumbled, refusing to back off.

On a load roar, I emptied myself into Murphy's mouth, something my high school self never believed would happen. But my adult self was embarrassed by how quickly it had all gone down, and worse, before I took care of her.

Flipping her onto her back, I kissed her hard, tasting myself on her lips and not caring. "I believe in ladies first, Murph. Don't test me again."

Not waiting for a response, I crawled down her body, grabbing her cutoffs and practically tearing them off. Remembering her feminine scent from the other night, I couldn't wait to dive in. This time, I took it slow, building her to a crescendo and then bringing her down, not wanting to end this too quickly. I was at my new favorite buffet, and planned to eat as many desserts as I wanted.

"Please," she finally whimpered.

Sliding a finger inside her, I put pressure in the same place that had set her off a few nights ago, and she jolted off the mattress, calling out my name as her body spasmed.

"Ben, what are you doing to me?" she whispered when I made my way up to her, settling next to her on the pillows.

"Just the beginning, Murph."

My hair fell in my eyes and she swept it out of the way, then placed a kiss on my lips. "I see you still refuse to cut your hair. How can you see to operate?"

Turning away from her, I hid a smile. "Promise not to tell?"

She nodded as her fingers drew figure eights on my chest, and I ran my palm up and down her thigh.

"I wear it back in a headband under my cap."

Surprising me, she quickly turned over, yanking me so we were front to front, my hardening length poking her. "Stop. No you don't."

"I do."

"If the guys from Pressman could see you now—fancy doctor, pretty boy, amazing lover."

I scowled. "They'd laugh all the way home to their mansions."

Squeezing my ass, she said, "Stop it. Don't be like that. Own it. As for me, they'd run all the way home to tell their moms and dads how I ruined my life."

"I don't care. I'm the lucky one holding you now." Sliding my hand down her back, I bumped my hips against hers, and we started to grind into each other. "I want you, but also want to take it slow."

"Why don't you have me slowly?" she whispered. "Oh God. Did I just say that out loud?"

Running my tongue along her bottom lip and then the top one, I said, "You did. And I think you were on to something."

I reached behind me into the nightstand drawer to grab a condom from the new box I'd stashed there. "Ready for me, Murph?"

All she had to do was nod, and I was on top of her. Kissing her mouth, I ran my hand down her side as I slid into home.

20

MURPHY

"I should go home," I murmured sleepily, curled into Ben's side.

"You don't have to." He ran his hand down my back, sending shivers up my spine and causing goose bumps to break out all over my skin.

"I know." The words came out a bit melancholy. This felt incredible, glorious, being cuddled with Ben in his big king-size bed with sheets that smelled exactly like his woodsy Vermont scent.

A little chuckle bubbled up my throat.

"What?" he asked, never missing a thing.

"You'll laugh too. I just remembered always thinking you smelled so good at Pressman. When we would sit next to each other, I would sneak a sniff here and there. You always smelled so natural."

He rolled on his side, sliding me the other way so we were face-to-face. "That's because I didn't wear all that expensive cologne like everyone else. Christ, I couldn't stand the locker room after practice."

As he twirled a strand of my hair in his fingers, I wished I could stay. A chill made me shudder, and Ben pulled the blanket over my shoulder.

Burrowing under it, I said, "I can't believe how chilly it gets here at night. Even in the summer."

"No humidity," he said, brushing his lips over my cheek.

"In the city, we would roast no matter the time of day. We'd head home late at night after having dinner or drinks and the lights would be flashing, horns blowing, and the humidity was no joke. But it was okay. The city felt so alive. Electric, almost."

As soon as the words were out of my mouth, I regretted them.

"I'll bet it was," Ben said evenly.

He didn't stop rubbing my back or occasionally kissing my neck, but the air around us changed. I'd tipped my proverbial hat, which was why I had to leave Vermont. Eventually, I was going to move to a big city. Not New York, but somewhere I could make a name and a new life for myself.

"Shhh," Ben whispered into my temple. "I can feel you thinking. Don't do that. Enjoy this moment."

Agreeing, I nodded, scrunching my nose as the ends of his hair tickled my face. "I still need to go. It's a weeknight. Tomorrow, I work noon to five at the Bean, and I still have to finish up some details for Hunnie."

"Okay," he grumbled. "But I'm going to keep you in my bed one of these nights."

"You're pretty confident nowadays." The words spilled out before I could stop them.

"I am."

In the next second, he was thoroughly kissing me. His lips parted and my tongue entered his mouth. We'd already had a perfect evening, and if I wasn't careful, he'd be inside me again and I'd be spending the night.

Ben was the one to finally break the kiss. Slapping my butt, he said, "Let's get you home."

Tucked into his Jeep, the world totally dark around us, I saw the clock flashing a few minutes after eleven on the dash. "I'm sorry you have to drive me all the way back to Colebury. Another difference between here and the city. There I could get an Uber or taxi or town car."

Ben kept his focus on the road, but mumbled, "Whatever your fancy, right at your fingertips, huh."

I wasn't sure what his tone was laced with. Resentment? Jealousy? Or was it envy?

"You know, I've never spent the night at anyone's place. Yours was the first I ever considered . . . staying all night."

Not taking his eyes from the road, he said, "Murphy, you're thirty-two years old. That's not believable."

"My mom would've had a fit if I were spotted coming out of someone's place in the morning or vice versa, so I never did it. The thought of disgracing her was my worst fear for most of my life. And then I did exactly that."

Glancing at me, he asked, "Were you happy then?"

Swallowing my pride, I gave him the truth. "No. I had this dream job and a fabulous apartment and all the salon appointments in the world, but no."

"Are you happy now?"

His words took me by surprise. So blunt and to the point, but exactly what I needed to hear.

"I think so," I said slowly. "Yeah, I think so."

"Well, there you go."

Ben reached over to turn on some music and began humming along to Dave Matthews Band.

"No classical?" I teased.

"Not this time of night. I need to get you home in one piece and myself back home the same way I left."

"Sorry again about this."

"Let's make a deal—no more apologies. I do this drive all the time. Montpelier to Colebury, then back and forth again. Brenna likes the area for her and Branson. I'd like her closer to me, up by my parents' place too, but she's stubborn. It's how I started popping into the Bean. Not like we don't have coffee by me or at the hospital, but I like the vibe at the Bean. Zara's good people. So, how did we get on this? Oh, right. No more apologies."

"Done." I agreed before he was barely finished talking. I'd never been so jumpy, interrupting every few seconds, but I wanted what he promised.

"Maybe I should've gotten one of those industrial lofts over by the Bean," he said, "but Brenna talked me into the house. Now I do the drive."

"I'm lucky I learned how to drive. Most kids in the city don't learn. They don't need to," I told him. "Of course, we spent the summers in the Hamptons, and I learned there. I was so desperate to learn that my parents gave in to me. Don't get the wrong idea, though. They hired someone to teach me. They didn't bother themselves with it."

"I think I recall hearing about this at Pressman. You were asking me about driving in the snow, saying you'd never done that. Did you ever get a chance?"

Heat crept up my cheeks. "No."

"And you're living in Vermont now? You're going to get a chance sooner than you think."

On that, we pulled up in front of my place.

"I guess, but not for long—" I cut myself off before saying anything more.

"Huh? What's that all about?"

"Nothing. Honestly, I'm tired is all." I brushed at my eye, willing the tears to stay put.

Vermont was where people put down roots. Look at Ben with his family loyalty and relationships with all the small business owners. That wasn't me. I knew absolutely nothing about roots or long-term connections.

Ben opened the passenger side door and escorted me to my front door.

"Night, Murph." He pulled me in and pressed his lips to mine. "Hope to see you before it snows," he joked.

"It had better not snow here in July."

I opened my door and slipped inside, watching through a small crack in the door as Ben walked back to his car.

"It will snow a few times before I leave," I whispered to myself as I closed the door.

MURPHY

"Murphy?"

I turned around to find a shorter woman with a blond topknot on top of her head, staring at me from across the coffee bar.

"Never mind," she said without giving me a chance to respond. "Of course you are. I don't know why I asked. I know you are. I'm Gigi, by the way."

It was Wednesday afternoon. My head was somewhat in the clouds, half dreaming of my date the night before, half panicking over what it all meant when it came to Ben. And me. And the future.

"Hunnie's been talking up a storm about you," Gigi said, "and honestly, I was getting jealous. She's got her act together, and it's hard not to be envious, and then she plucks you out of the sky to help her get even better."

I finished making the latte I'd been working on when Gigi first interrupted me and set it on the bar while she rambled away.

"Anyway, I'm sorry to barge in on you here, and I know you're busy. I'm shocked you can do all that without burning yourself or making the wrong drink. Kirk was a master of that, listening and making lattes at the same time."

Wiping my hands down the front of my pink apron—no

longer impressed it was designer since I was all about function these days—I finally spoke. "It's taken me a while, but I think I have it down now. By the way, I am Murphy." I felt the need to clarify her earlier rhetorical question.

Looking to make sure there were no more drink orders coming down the bar, I smiled at the famous Gigi, happy to finally meet her. "Thank you for the cupcake, by the way. It was delicious."

"I hear you're a fan of the Arnie Palmer one, but that maple one was just for you. It was a one-off, but since it passed your taste buds, maybe I'll make it a regular."

Sneaking a peek out of the corner of my eye, I noticed Zara watching us with interest. Refocusing on Gigi, I said, "Well, this is Vermont after all. I would think a maple cupcake would go over well."

"Yes, but you know, I'm on this Goldbelly delivery thing for my Arnies. It's been amazing, but I need more of an online presence. Who would believe little old Colebury represented on Goldbelly?"

I nodded. "It's all the rage. I know from when I lived in New York."

A customer walked in and ordered a regular drip coffee, and Zara poured it for him. Cup in hand, he walked toward the peach sofa just as Rita walked through the door. Her eyes widened and she scurried over to her seat, tossing her bag down and seated on the sofa before the guy even made it there. Not missing a beat, he changed direction and headed over to one of the tables by the window and cracked a book open.

Lost in my thoughts, I tried to think about that happening in the Big Apple. Maybe on a Sunday with the *Times*, but someone would be clamoring for the table after not too long.

"Can you help me?" Gigi said, pulling me out of my fog.

Mentally, I tried to catch up. "Help with what?"

"With social media. Like Hunnie. I'll pay you." Her topknot bounced from side to side with her excitement. "You see, I just got married and need to save some time for my sweetie."

In a flash, I saw an Instagram campaign focused on *falling in love with cupcakes* set for this coming autumn. Before I could even say I didn't have a lot of time to give or ask how much she was going to pay me, I was nodding my head in agreement.

"Great." She clapped her hands with delight and did a little jig. "Hunnie said you usually meet at her place, so maybe I could join in? Isn't it so cool? Her shed?"

"It certainly is, but I need to swing by your shop first to get a feel for it."

"Of course, anytime. It's Oh, For Heaven's Cakes, just down the street from here."

I chuckled. "I know. I've been avoiding it. As if the Arnie cupcakes here aren't bad enough for my waistline."

"Lucky you," Gigi said with a big grin. "Now you get free cupcakes anytime you want. Listen, think about what you want to charge and send me a text. Here." She held out a business card. "That's my information."

Stunned, I reached for the card. "Okay," was all I could say before she whirled around to leave.

"Catch you later," she called out over her shoulder with a wave.

I couldn't help but notice her cute pink high-tops and wondered if Hunnie scolded her for those like she had my white shorts.

As I washed my hands, I didn't hear Zara come up from behind me.

"Pretty soon, you're going to need a business card."

Drying my hands, I tried to stifle a giggle. "I doubt it, but I'm definitely having fun with this."

Zara's hair was pulled back, all shiny, black, and tight. With bright cheeks and a broad smile, she always looked happy. Another one lucky in love, making all their dreams come true.

"Do you still want to work here?" she asked, as up front as always.

Swallowing my pride, I leaned against the counter by the sink. "Yes, I do. I need to."

She gave me a serious look. "I get it's not what you went to school for, and I don't want to hold you back."

Shaking my head, I said, "I want to be here. I like it here. Actually, I had an idea. It may be silly, but I was thinking we could host a book club here."

"Oh yeah? So you're not only dreaming up ideas for Hunnie and Gigi?"

"Making coffee is my number one priority," I said with a smile. The shop was still quiet, but that usually meant any second we would be slammed, so I decided to hurry up and tell her my idea. "Yeah, a book club. I've been reading a lot lately. Chick lit, romance, sometimes steamy, sometimes not . . . I like it all. Even the historicals. Seriously."

"Is that so?" Zara asked with a smirk.

"Yes. It's such a great escape. I'm actually loving it, and I'll bet we have a lot of readers in the area. I was thinking we could choose a book and set a date, maybe a Friday or Sunday, and then have a little discussion here. Everyone would buy coffees, and we could come up with a specialty dessert. Oh, maybe Gigi could help with that."

"I like it." Zara nodded thoughtfully. "It would definitely be so nice for the community."

"And . . ." Before I lost my nerve, I shared the rest of the idea. "I saw this thing on the internet on matching makeup and nail colors to the book cover. The trend started in New York, but it's spreading around. Bloggers are picking it up. It could be fun. Colebury is ready for it," I said, taking a long breath when I was done.

"It's definitely a stretch for here, but I'm willing to give it a try. You're the resident big-city girl. Does this mean you're putting down roots here?"

Swallowing the giant lump in my throat—there was that word again, *roots*—I shook my head. "I'm definitely growing to like it here more and more every day, but eventually I'll take my experience back to a city. Not New York, but somewhere I can make my own name."

Zara raised an eyebrow. "What about Ben? I see the way you two look at each other. And you can't deny you're spending a lot of time together."

Unable to stop a huge smile from forming, I felt my eyes crease. "We go way back, and we're definitely having fun." *Fun like I've never had.* "It's fun now, but it's not a long-term thing."

She gave me a speculative look. "Are you sure that's how Ben sees it? I've never heard about him being this gaga for someone. He may not live in Colebury, but he spends enough time here."

"I'm sure," I said with a certainty I wasn't sure I believed but forced myself to get behind.

Then we were saved by the chimes above the door when a customer arrived, a book tucked under their arm.

Zara nodded toward the book. "I'm liking the book club idea more and more."

With no further discussion of Ben, we went back to selling and making coffees.

22

BEN

"Hi, Mom," I said, picking up the phone as I was leaving the medical center. There was no use ignoring her call. She knew I saw patients on Wednesday afternoons and would be getting out around now—in time for dinner.

"Ben, I'm so glad to get you on the phone. Dad is grilling steaks, and we wanted to see if you wanted to come eat."

Sliding into my car, I said, "Sure, that would be great. I wanted to tell you guys some news anyway."

"About Murphy?"

I stifled a sigh. Of course Marley had already spilled the news about seeing us together at the farmers' market. "Not exactly."

"But I heard you were out with Murphy last night. Is it the same Murphy?"

Pulling out of the parking lot, I said, "Mom, I'll see you in a few, and then you can ask me anything you want."

After I parked my Jeep in front of the house I grew up in, I took a long inhale and even longer exhale. "Hey," I hollered in the hallway.

"Out here," my dad yelled through the screened back door.

"I'm starving," I said as I stepped out onto the back deck, where he was grilling a sizable number of steaks.

"Good thing," Dad said with a grin. "Hunnie's parents dropped off these steaks. They got them from a friend of theirs over in New Hampshire. They're excited I'm agreeing to this petting zoo venture and goat yoga, to say the least."

Shrugging, I said, "If it sells syrup, who cares?"

"There you are." My mom came bursting out the back door, her black hair threaded with gray swinging with the movement. Everyone said I resembled my mom, but I have my dad's height.

"Hi, Mom," I said, pulling her in for a hug.

"Want a beer?"

I shook my head. "Can't. I have an early morning tomorrow."

"Sit," she said.

Knowing Mom wouldn't let me help unless I had a reason, I said, "Let me wash my hands, and then I can help you bring stuff outside. I assume we're eating out here."

Back inside, I used the kitchen sink to scrub my hands and noticed a big bowl filled with my favorite pasta salad.

"I made your favorite," my mom said, walking to the fridge.

"I see. Buttering me up?"

Mom chuckled. "Never."

I grabbed the bowl of pasta in one hand and a stack of napkins in the other, and then headed back outside.

"Myra, I need a plate. These are done," my dad called out, and Mom came running with a platter. Together, they were a well-oiled machine.

"Sit," Mom said again, and when I obeyed, she went back into the kitchen and returned with corn on the cob and fresh green beans.

"Am I that predictable?" I asked. "You knew I wouldn't turn down a steak?"

"Don't be silly," my mom said, laughing as she sat down.

Once we'd all sat down and filled our plates, I said, "I bought some land and a house over by Mad River, close to skiing and biking paths. It's private and quiet."

Dad nodded approvingly. "Good for you, son. You deserve it."

After chewing a bite of steak, perfectly medium rare, just like I like it, I said, "Well, it's more for Branson. We can spend time there together. It'll be good for him."

Dad nodded and let it go, but he gave Mom a warning look as she squirmed in her seat. Obviously, she was waiting to pounce.

"This is good," I said, ending the uncomfortable silence that followed.

Dad reached for his glass to take a sip. "Yeah, I think Hunnie wants her folks to start carrying these steaks locally for sale. She's expanding their business in every direction. That girl has big plans."

"She does," I said, not knowing where this was going, but remembering Murphy asking me if Hunnie and I had ever had a thing. "I wonder why she didn't try to partner with Scott. You know, Brenna's friend from high school."

"Eh," my mom said, "he can be a jerk. He dropped Brenna."

"Darling," Dad said gently. "She was pregnant with someone else's baby. There's only so much rejection a man can take."

He turned to face me, and I noticed how gray he was going at the temples. "Speaking of Hunnie, sometimes I think she wants to not only combine ventures, but lives, if you get my drift."

"I do, and that's not going to happen." Before I could say any more, I stuffed my mouth full of pasta.

Mom pointed her fork at him. "Didn't you hear me say his Murphy is back, Bill?"

"Myra, you gotta get those silly fantasies outta your head. Ben is a big boy, all grown up. He's not having an affair with some girl from high school, a city girl yet. He may have gone off to that fancy school, but he's back home now."

"Actually, she lives in Vermont now and likes it," I said carefully. "She's doing some work for Hunnie too."

"Really?" My mom's eyes narrowed as she went in for the kill. She was a barracuda with only a tiny morsel of information.

"On social media. I would think she'll be helping with the animals too."

Mom put down her silverware, taking in every word I said. "This is so great. It's time you did something for you, Ben. Not just the house in Mad River, which we all know is a veiled attempt at pleasing Brenna, making up for what Branson is missing. Plus, Bill, remember—Ben may not be here forever. Maybe a city girl is good for him."

Ignoring her wink, I said, "It's not anything yet, Mom. Please don't run with this."

"Oh, Ben, I can't help it. You were crazy for the girl back then. I'm sure she's an even more fabulous woman."

"Let's hear about the house and land," my dad said, changing the subject.

And thank fuck for that.

Later that evening, I showered and slipped into bed. Inhaling, I was pleased that Murphy's scent still lingered on my sheets. I'd wanted her to stay the other night, but I could tell some sort of anxiety took hold of her and I didn't want to push.

As I laid my head back into the pillow, I couldn't help but compare this newer version of Murphy to the older one.

She was still skittish, but in a different way. She used to obsess over pleasing her parents, but now she seemed to be overly concerned with doing what she thought was the best or smartest move. She still seemed to need reassurances from some outside source and hadn't learned to just be happy with herself.

I didn't have a chance to think about it any further because my phone chimed. I wasn't on call, so I wasn't obligated to check it, but I did.

You up? the text read. Two words from the woman of my thoughts.

I am, was all I sent back, and then my phone rang.

I tried to hide the want and huskiness in my voice when I answered. "Hello, Murph. This is a nice surprise."

"I didn't want to bug you, but had to call and thank you."

"For what?" A smile took over my face as I swept my hair out of my eyes.

"You pushed me to tell Zara about my idea, and she loved it. We didn't even discuss the new kid. She was worried about me —*me*—afraid that I didn't want to work at the Bean anymore. Anyway, she loved my book club idea, and I'm going full steam ahead, no pun intended. Get it? The Bean? Full steam?"

Turning on my side, I liked this a little bit too much. Lying in bed, chatting with a woman. Only thing better would be if she were here.

"I get it. This is awesome," I told her. "You have great ideas. By the way, I ran into Hunnie earlier when I was on my way to have dinner with my parents."

"You did?"

"Yeah, no big deal." Secretly, I liked the hint of jealousy that sneaked past her confident exterior. "We drove past each other on the road and rolled down the windows. She's dying for you to get those straw samples."

"They're on their way. I was going to tell her tomorrow, as well as that Gigi came and found me and roped me into helping her too."

"Really? I pick up cupcakes there for my staff sometimes. And I know Brenna loves her cupcakes for a special occasion."

"Well, she found me at the Bean and accosted me. Ha." Murphy let out a little chuckle over the line, and I could feel her lightness in my chest. "Wants me to relieve her of some of the social media stuff. Of course, Hunnie put her up to it."

"Hunnie is Hunnie. She seems to get her way, no matter what. Just ask my dad."

"Oh yeah, how was your dinner?"

"My mom is like a dog with a bone after speaking with Marley."

"Uh-oh. I'm shaking in my boots."

"Like Nancy . . . Sinatra?"

"No, really. By the way," she asked, "what do I hear in the background?"

"'A Little Less Conversation' by the king himself."

"You didn't put music on the other night when I was there."

"I regret that," I said. "It was unlike me, but I was in a hurry. You sat on the bed, and I was done for."

Her voice lowered, probably out of embarrassment. "I feel cheated out of the whole Ben Rooney experience."

Deciding to tease her, I said, "You really have perfected this flirting thing, haven't you?"

She cleared her throat, I assumed trying to collect her composure. "Not exactly. Honestly, there's something about chatting with you. It comes easily, naturally. It feels fun, and I feel more free. Freer than I ever have."

Her transparency hit me in the gut. I wasn't sure why, because I'd never been the guy who women opened up to. In high school, I didn't have the right pedigree. In college, I was too distracted, busy, or self-centered. And since being back home, I'd been flat-out disinterested in making the effort until Murphy showed up in my life.

"I'm glad," I finally said. "We always had a good way between us."

"We did," she said softly.

A long silence stretched out between us, full of undeclared feelings and unanswered questions.

"I believe the experts call that a pregnant pause," I said, my brain getting in the way of my emotions.

"Apparently, they're very good when making a point. At least, my dad always said."

"We don't need to make a point. That's just how we are. We flow. Let's not allow all this underlying stuff to get in the way this time."

Before I could ask her to agree, she said, "Okay."

"See? No pregnant pause required. Maybe I know something your dad doesn't." Closing my eyes, I couldn't believe I said that.

"I just meant we probably have different perspectives. I wasn't putting anyone down. I'm sure your dad is a very smart man."

"It's okay. I think you may be on to something. It's like the social media stuff I work on. Honesty and transparency are the hallmarks of a good post. Maybe it's the same for relationships . . . I mean, friendships."

"Relationships," I said, correcting her indecisiveness.

"Anyway, I don't know how we got on this topic, but I just wanted to tell you about the book club. We're going to aim for an introductory meeting a week from Friday, chatting about a popular book that many people have probably already read. I haven't decided which book yet. I may ask a few coffee patrons, if Zara doesn't mind."

"Ha. Well, I can't help you with that, but I'm sure you'll figure it out."

"Okay, well, I'm going to go. I'm working the morning shift," she said, her voice groggy.

"I won't see you there then. I'm operating in the morning and then going to see Branson play in a summer basketball league. Do you work Friday?"

"Yeah. Only eight to twelve, a short shift."

"I'll be sure to pop in."

"Night," Murphy whispered.

"Sweet dreams, Murph."

As we hung up, I wished we could have stayed on for a lot longer. It was easy between us in a way I'd never had.

Murphy's mind and her body got me equally revved, and I couldn't help my hand sliding south, taking hold of my length, which was as hard as a rock. I needed to handle business before falling asleep. With memories of Murphy against her door, me sliding to my knees, and a flashback to her in my bed, it didn't take long.

BEN

I pulled into the Busy Bean's parking lot in a daze, having spent the entire drive there worrying about Branson. He didn't seem right the night before. The kids seemed to leave him out of the team huddle, and he appeared relieved to hang back on the bench. He didn't give the game any effort, and I didn't like what I was seeing.

I might not have appreciated the opportunities thrown at me—football, boarding school, Harvard—but I always gave everything I did my all. In a world full of rich kids who didn't care about underachieving because they had trust funds, I was the one who always strove for overachieving.

Branson seemed like he was getting complacent, and it ate away at my gut. My sister worked too hard and wasn't around enough, and I was too close to the situation.

Yanking open the side door to the Bean, the one closest to the coffee bar so I could catch a glimpse of Murphy, I considered sending Branson to Pressman. *Christ.* I shook my head to relieve myself of the idea.

"Hey, Zara. How are you?" I said at the register.

With a twinkle in her eye, she said, "Can't say I'm surprised to see you in here. Murphy's about done."

I nodded. "No getting anything by you."

Zara laughed. "Hey, Dave said if you stopped in for me to ask you if you have any contacts back in Boston. He has a friend who needs a hip replacement."

After thinking for a second, I said, "I wish. I know a great team in Brooklyn. I'll do some asking around."

"Thanks. The usual?" Zara asked.

"Yes, but I forgot my mug."

With a raised eyebrow, she looked me over. "That's unlike you."

"A lot on my mind, but I'll be okay."

"No worries. In fact, I'm going to gift you a Bean Yeti." She grabbed a dark green one off the shelves and rinsed it out. "Murph, an extra hot Americano on the house," she said, waving the mug in the air.

It was the first Murphy and I had made eye contact since I came in, and in an instant, a wave of calmness washed over me. Putting my worries of Branson behind me, I looked forward to spending the afternoon with Murphy.

Slipping a ten into the tip jar, I moved down toward the end of the coffee bar and waited for Murphy to finish making my drink.

"Here you go, hot and ready to go in your new mug." Murphy held the Yeti until I took it from her, our fingers brushing.

"How about you? Are you ready to go?"

"Where? We didn't make plans."

"Now we do. Thought we would take a hike. I even brought sandwiches and snacks."

With a wide grin, Murphy asked, "What kind of snacks?"

"Oh, that's a secret."

"Sweet or salty?"

"I wouldn't dream of salty when it came to you."

"Deal."

Murphy quickly untied her apron and washed her hands. The new kid slid under the counter to take her place, waiting for his turn at the sink.

"Hey, buddy, don't mess up," Murphy teased before yelling, "See you on Sunday, Zar."

Zara gave us a wave, and I waited for Murphy to grab her purse.

"Oh, shoot. Look at my shoes," she said when she reappeared from the back.

"Yeah, those aren't going to work," I said, taking in her fashion sneakers. "I was counting on you wearing your boots."

"I'm sure you were."

Taking her hand in mine, I led her toward the side door. "We'll swing by your place so you can grab something better."

"Hey, are you Murphy?" A young girl in her mid-twenties peeked out from behind her book and asked.

"I am," Murphy said, giving her all her attention.

"I heard about the book club. I can't wait. If you need any recs, I'd be happy to share. This is awesome." She held up a book with a sexy couple on the front, sitting on the kitchen counter, making out.

Whoa.

"Oh," Murphy said nonchalantly. "I have that one on my to-be-read list."

"It's really good so far."

"Terrific. What's your name?"

"Corrie."

"Fabulous. I'll see you at the first meeting, Corrie, and I can't wait to hear your recs."

"'Bye," Corrie yelled after us, but Murphy was on a mission to get to the car.

"Did you hear that?" she asked with a huge smile.

I nodded. "Told you it was a great idea."

Holding her hands together as if praying, she said, "Finally, something is going my way."

"It's only up from here," I told her, and she gave me a doubtful look. "Really."

"Fingers crossed and toes," she added.

After a sip of my Americano, we were off to grab her shoes.

"This way I can use the bathroom too," she said.

"But no makeup or any of that. We're going on a hike, and you look beautiful naturally."

"Deal, and thank you."

Once Murphy had her running shoes on, we got back into the Jeep.

"Hungry?" I asked her.

"For the snacks?"

"No. How about a sandwich? The snacks are for later."

"I'm actually not hungry. I had a scone at work."

With a quick nod, I pulled away from her place. "I picked a relatively easy trail, probably around moderate in difficulty."

"That's good since I have zero experience hiking other than walking on an incline on the treadmill." As she scraped her hair back into a ponytail, the long red strands cascading down her back, she laughed at her own joke.

"Well, you live in Vermont now. It's about time," I told her.

"Agreed. I see you've selected something from the king for the ride." She pointed at the stereo, where Elvis crooned "Love Me Tender" through the speakers. "You know, I think you may be a softie, Ben Rooney."

I wanted to open up to her, to tell her about the apps, the extra income, and other recent developments, but my phone rang.

"Shit," I said, glancing at the caller ID. "That's Branson. Do you mind if I pick it up?"

"Of course not," she said quickly, and I hit the TAKE CALL button.

"Hey," I said into the Bluetooth.

"Ben? It's me. I'm sorry to bother you, but . . . but I—"

"What's up, Brans? You okay?" We were only about ten

minutes outside of Colebury when he called. We still had twenty or thirty minutes to the trailhead, so I kept driving.

"Well, I . . . I sort of . . ."

My heart started to beat a frantic pace at his stammering. Couldn't be good news. "Are you okay? Your mom?"

"Yeah, yeah, Mom's fine. It's just, I got caught. *Caught doing something*."

Before I could pull over and pick up the phone to give Branson some privacy, he launched into it.

"Beau asked me to take his ATV out past Grandma and Grandpa's. Way out. He put it in the back of his dad's pickup, and we drove all the way out there. He has his license, so it's nothing like that. The police aren't involved. But Beau picked an area marked private and said it was fine."

I glanced over at Murphy. She was staring ahead, wringing her hands.

"No one is hurt?" That was my first thought about why he was calling me.

"No, we're fine. But Dan, who owns the land, caught us. I'm sorry. Really. I told Beau we shouldn't, but he said it was fine." His voice lowered to a whisper. "And then called me a pussy. I can't have people saying that because I take care of Mom. Ya know?"

"Following the rules doesn't make you a pussy."

"I know, but . . . Dan is here, and he made me call you. Well, he wanted me to call Mom, but she's working a double, and I didn't want to upset her. We didn't do any damage, but Dan said he could've let the horses out and that would have been really bad."

Branson finally take a long breath on the other end of the line, and I took one myself.

"Also, Beau left right after calling his dad, who was in the middle of ripping him a new one, so I'm stranded here."

Oh. "I'm in the car but was headed a little farther away in the other direction. Let me turn around and come and get you. Can you ping me your location?"

"I'm sorry, Ben. Please don't be mad. Please don't call Grandma and Grandpa. Dan said he's not going to tell them."

"I'm not mad, but I am disappointed. We can discuss it later. Send me your location, and I'll be on my way."

"Okay, thanks. 'Bye," he said and then disconnected the call.

"I'm sorry," I said to Murphy while looking for a place to turn around.

"No reason, seriously." She half turned in her seat.

"Do you mind coming with me? I'll get Branson settled at home, and then maybe we can rent a movie or something?"

"Can we eat the snacks then?"

Like a crack of thunder, the tension broke inside me, and it felt so good.

"Absolutely," I told her. "All the snacks, but I'm still not telling you what they are."

"Fine," she said, pretending to be mad as she crossed her arms in front of her for a few seconds. Then she fooled around with the stereo, finding some eighties station. "Maybe a little pop will make you feel better."

More tension drained from me, and I felt lighter already.

24

MURPHY

With Branson sulking in the back seat, we pulled out of Dan's property after Ben shook his hand and made promises of a stern lecture and punishment. Ben was laser focused on something in front of him, but it wasn't until I looked ahead that I saw what. A colossal black cloud was forming in the sky.

"Good thing we didn't go hiking," I said, trying to lighten the mood again.

"I don't know. The storm seems to be moving north rather than south. But it's right where we're heading to cross back over and down to Colebury." Bumping along the half-paved, half-gravel road, Ben eyed Branson in the back. "Dude, you're lucky your mom isn't the first to hear about this. She'd have a fit."

Tugging on his hair that he wore a little shaggy like his uncle, Branson said, "I know. She'd be having a hissy fit that I'm just like my no-good father."

"You know you're not," Ben said, his voice softening.

"She'd say everyone would be talking about how I'm like him. He's gone, so how could I be like him? Maybe Mom should worry more about letting me be me, and less about my being like him."

"I hear you on that," Ben said, gripping the steering wheel.

This was probably why he wasn't always so forthcoming

about Brenna and Branson. I could practically feel the guilt and responsibility radiating off of Ben, and he shouldn't feel either of those things.

"Whatever, let's talk about it when she's not here. You know, you look familiar to me?" Branson said, eyeing my back. I could feel his gaze drilling into me.

Ben had briefly introduced me as his friend Murphy when Branson got in the car. For a minute or two, I think he'd forgotten I was there, but now he was putting it all together.

"You sold me some syrup a few months ago," I said, turning back to look at him. "At the farmers' market."

Branson scowled. "What are you, a spy? You can't be his girlfriend. My mom hasn't said a thing about you, and she's all focused on Ben getting married someday and having his own family."

"Brans, it's not necessary. Let's just get you home."

Suddenly, the cloud broke and rain poured down in sheets.

"Shit," Ben said softly.

"Another thing you can blame on me," Branson muttered.

"You can't blame a storm on someone," I said, interjecting like an idiot.

"The road we have to cross floods when it's been dry for a while," Branson said matter-of-factly.

"Oh."

We puttered down the dirt road a little longer, and I was hoping we made it. All of a sudden, my stomach growled, and I reminded myself Ben had sandwiches.

On our left, we passed a large farm sign marked STEVENS' CATTLE. As soon as we passed it, we came to a crossroad that was in fact flooding.

With another round of cursing, Ben made a U-turn and turned left onto the Stevens's property. "Looks like I'm going to say hi to an old friend."

"Who?" I asked. "Here?"

"Here. Scott Stevens was a few years older than me, but he

was a mentor in the Pee Wee football league and a friend of Brenna's back in the day. I think they went to a homecoming or two, and then things went cold."

Having been quiet for a while, Branson piped up again. "Oh, great. Just what I need."

I nodded for lack of nothing better to do or say, all the while wondering if Scott was Branson's dad. But Scott sounded like a stand-up guy, which Branson's dad definitely didn't sound like.

"They have great cattle," Ben said, "and also do cheese on the side. Not in direct competition with my folks, but enough that we don't sell their steaks. We're working with a new steak supplier." He rambled on, probably due to nerves, I thought.

Pulling up in front of the farmhouse, Ben said, "Let's make a break for it."

Not giving either of us a chance to respond, he was out of the Jeep and running to open my door. With my hand in his and Branson trailing behind us, we dashed toward the door.

Ben didn't even need to knock when the door was opened by a tall guy, probably about six-foot-one with blond hair and blue eyes.

"Scott." Ben extended his hand in greeting while the rain pelted the covered porch.

"Ben Rooney, what are you doing here?" Scott shook Ben's hand, his blue eyes taking me in, absorbing every detail. Then he offering me his hand, ignoring a sullen Branson. "Hi, I'm Scott."

"Murphy," was all I could say before a huge bolt of lightning lit the sky, quickly followed by a loud roll of thunder.

Scott waved us inside. "Come in, and then you can tell me why you're here. Not that I'm not thrilled, but . . ."

"Road's flooded," Ben said when we were inside.

"You know that road floods."

"Yeah. Murphy and I were heading in the opposite direction when I got a call to pick up Branson near here." Ben cocked his head toward his nephew. "Do you know Branson? He's Brenna's—"

"Of course I know," Scott said, not letting Ben finish.

My head swung back and forth, taking all this in. The whole scene was feeling like something out of a soap opera.

"I got into trouble," Branson blurted.

"Well, you're Brenna's boy," Scott said with a laugh.

"Hey, that's my mom," Branson said sharply, coming to his mom's defense.

Ben stepped in to smooth things over. "Your mom and Scott were friends back in high school. She had a good time. Classes were easy for her, and she didn't get a chance at prep school like me."

"I know," Branson said, fidgeting from foot to foot. "I saw his picture in Mom's albums. You know when she gets sentimental and starts going through memories?"

More awkward silence filled the foyer.

"Listen," Ben said to Scott, "I'm sorry to barge in on you so unexpected. But like I said, the road's flooded, and I don't want to take any chances with these two. If we're not in your way, can we wait it out here?"

Scott waved a hand. "Of course. It's no bother. In fact, I just came in from checking the barns. I was going to do some paperwork, but it can wait."

Feeling uncomfortable, I said quickly, "You don't have to entertain us. Do people do this here, show up at other people's houses and wait out a flood? This wasn't how I was raised."

"Murphy's from New York," Ben said to explain.

Scott gave me a small smile. "Welcome to Vermont."

"You got anything to eat?" Branson asked abruptly, just as my stomach growled again, and Ben frowned at him.

"Looks like everyone is hungry. Go sit down," Scott said, pointing toward a comfy family room.

"Are you sure?" I whispered again, this time to Ben when we sat down. As my butt sank into a leather couch with a plaid blanket folded behind me, Ben sat next to me.

"It's fine, Murph. No one wants anyone to get hurt here. The

Jeep might be able to drive through the water, but it could get shorted out and we'd be stuck."

Branson plopped into the chair across from us. "So, you have a girlfriend and we don't know?" he said to Ben. "Mom's gonna shit."

"Brans, cut it out."

"She is . . . seriously. She kept saying you seemed busier than usual, maybe you were inventing something new."

"Branson, it's enough," Ben said sharply.

There was an edge to his voice that I didn't quite recognize. Maybe he was worried his sister wouldn't like me? I didn't know what he could be inventing, but I was hung up on him not telling his sister about me.

"Here." Scott reappeared with a charcuterie board filled with enough cheeses and meats for thirty people. After setting it on the coffee table in front of us, he took a seat in the chair opposite Branson.

"Wow," I said, unable to help myself.

Scott beamed at me. "We're making these in our tasting room now. People can come and taste a bunch of different cured meats and cheeses, and drink wine. We sample local varieties. It's popular with all the tourists."

"Interesting," Ben said.

"I do some work for Hunnie. From the apiary—"

"Have some." Scott interrupted me, and I helped myself to a cheese cube. "Yeah, I know Hunnie. She's something."

"She lives near Grandma and Grandpa. She wants to put in goat yoga," Branson said, reaching out to snag a piece of what looked like jerky.

"She is doing it. Goat yoga," Ben said, correcting him.

"She's putting together a petting zoo too," I told Scott. "I'm working with her on her honey infusions."

Scott nodded, understanding. "Gotta capitalize on these people wanting the whole Vermont experience."

I wondered if this was what Ben would be doing had he not gone to Pressman, and then on to college and med school.

Scott turned to Branson, ending any business talk. "How old are you, Branson? You at the high school?"

"Sixteen. My mom was only nineteen when she had me."

I wasn't sure why Branson chose to reveal this tidbit. Ben didn't look thrilled, and I guessed it was to piss him off.

Scott nodded but shrugged like he knew but it wasn't a big deal in his mind. "Your mom was so much fun in high school. One of the best. I don't see her much now . . . I miss her smile. She was always a bright spot in everyone's day. What's she up to lately?"

It felt like he was fishing for information, but what exactly, I didn't know.

"She still is the bright spot in everyone's day. Right, Branson?" Ben said, both defending his sister and joking with his nephew.

I wasn't sure how he did that, instinctually knowing how to lighten the mood. I'd been trained to control the room for most of my life, and I still struggled with it.

And just like that, the tension eased and we sat together comfortably, eating and chatting like we were all old friends.

The rain pounded on, thunder rumbling in the background every few minutes or so, and no one seemed to think this was the strangest moment ever. I tucked my hair behind my ear and caught Ben watching me. His eyes crinkled when he smiled at me, and a warmth spread through me.

"She works at the hospital," Branson told Scott. "My mom," he said to clarify.

"Oh? With you, Ben?"

He shook his head. "No, my offices are at the medical building over by the Wayside. I operate at the hospital two or three days per week, depending on emergencies. It makes for a little driving back and forth, but it's okay."

"She runs the information desk. Uncle Ben got her the job."

"I didn't, Branson. She got it all on her own."

Tension started to build again. Something was a little off with this Scott guy, but I couldn't put my finger on it. Either he was really nosy, or he genuinely cared for Brenna.

"Honestly," I said to Scott, "forgive me for saying this, but this is all so strange. You guys haven't seen each other in a long time, yet here we are at your house without an invitation, chatting and sharing food with no end in sight."

All of that just spewed out of me without my thinking it through first. My mom would have scolded me for being so blunt.

"It's just the way here. We're a tight community," Scott said to me. "You must be from New York City, not the Finger Lakes."

This made me giggle. "How did you guess?"

"Just a hunch," Scott said with a grin, and Ben put his hand on my knee.

I lifted a palm in surrender. "I didn't mean to be rude. I swear. I'm getting used to all of this Vermont niceness."

Scott pulled out his phone and swiped at his screen. "Something else for you to get used to, the water is going to keep rising. We've been so dry, and radar shows it's supposed to rain straight through the night. Looks like you're either going to spend the night here, or turn around and go back to where you came from."

"We can't do that," Branson said sheepishly.

"Speaking of which," Ben said to his nephew, "you have to call your mom and explain what happened. And now you'll have to explain why you won't be home on top of it all." He stood up and headed for the hallway, motioning for Branson to come with him. "Let me tell my answering service what's going on. I'm not on call. I'd have to call the fire chief if I were, so I guess that's a silver lining. I'm sure he'd rather not have to rescue me. I should let them know, though, just in case any of my patients call. Then it's all you, buddy."

Ben stepped into the hallway with his phone, and poor Branson followed with his head lowered like he was walking the plank.

"What about you?" Scott asked me. "Do you have to call Hunnie? Or you don't work on Friday?"

"I only work for Hunnie part-time. Actually, I often work Fridays. I'm a barista at the Bean. Luckily, I'm off tomorrow but I'm back on Sunday, opening shift."

"Over in Colebury? Zara and Audrey's place?"

I nodded.

"I know the Shipleys. Griffin's a good friend of mine," Scott said with a smirk. "Oh, I don't think you would know about that. He and Zara had a thing, but that's long over."

Defending my bosses, I said, "I don't even think I want to know."

"Ha." Scott was teasing me again, and I found myself missing the warmth of Ben's palm on my knee. Scott was obviously nice and successful, but way too much of a flirt for me. I wondered if he carried a torch for Brenna, since he kept asking about her. "Griff makes the best cider. We serve it sometimes with our platters if he has a new one he wants to share."

I leaned forward and plucked what felt like my hundredth piece of salami from the board. "I'm sorry, but I'm so hungry."

"That's what it's there for. Do you want something to drink? Water? Wine? Coffee? Cider? You've got me thinking about it now."

A blush crept up my cheeks. "I've never had cider."

"Well then, it's decided. We'll have a drink when they get back in here, since you have to spend the night."

Ben came back into the room, leaving Branson out in the hall on the phone.

"You trust him to tell the truth?" I blurted to Ben. "Oh my God, I'm sorry. I didn't mean that. It's just if it were me at his age, I'd lie through my teeth to my parents."

Ben shook his head. "I trust him. He's not going to lie. Branson wasn't raised that way. He wants to be cool for the girls," he said to me, then focused on Scott. "But he's also protective of Brenna."

"Hey, it wasn't me who knocked her up," Scott said quietly.

"I know that you weren't, but you were the one who dumped her as a friend when he went off to agriculture school."

"Man, I was eighteen. I didn't know my ass from my elbow."

"I get it," Ben said. "Never mind. What's done is done. Listen, thanks for doing this. I don't know why I didn't pay more attention to the weather and the road."

"No worries. Like I said, your sister meant a lot to me back in the day, and we're all neighbors here."

"I was distracted by this beauty," Ben said out of nowhere, taking my hand in his. "And Branson's behavior," he added, squeezing my hand. "I can't fail him. Or you. That's why this was a major error."

He'd taken his seat on the couch next to me as soon as he came back into the room, which was possessive enough, but now he was pulling out the big guns. Based on my racing heart, it was working.

"Well, you're here now," Scott said, "and your lady here said she's never had hard cider, so we were thinking of having a glass before dinner."

Ben shrugged. "Why not? If we're stuck here."

"Come on, let's go into the kitchen and I'll see what I have. Tell Branson to meet us there. I have some root beer too."

The rest of the evening passed easily with cider flowing, along with tales of Brenna over grilled steaks. Before I knew it, Scott was showing Ben and me to a guest room and setting Branson up in the basement with a movie.

25

BEN

"What should I sleep in?" Murphy slipped out from the bathroom, her cheeks ruddy from the cider.

"Nothing?" I raised an eyebrow, hoping for the best, and she frowned.

"I can't do that. I barely know Scott."

Her voice soft, Murphy walked toward me and rested her head on my shoulder. My lips grazed the top of her head. We slow-danced in place, moving to a silent song.

"Sorry about all this," I told her, lifting her chin and kissing her softly. "Getting stuck here, and not being prepared to take care of us."

I kissed her again and our lips moved in an easy rhythm, in sync like our bodies that still swayed to music only we could hear. "I wish we were at my place. We'd curl up under the covers, and I'd rock your world a few times. Your moans would be louder than the rain pounding on the roof."

Murphy leaned back and let out a tiny giggle. "You're pretty confident."

Our light banter and flirting was heavenly, fueled by traces of alcohol and a heavy dose of desire.

"Oh, I am," I murmured. "Maybe I'd even press you up

against the door again and slip down to my knees and do that thing you like so much? Or maybe I'd pour maple syrup all over you, and lick it off slowly."

"Oh my God. You're too much, but that does sound kind of fun if I can return the favor," she said before pressing her lips to mine again.

On a quiet moan, I slid my tongue into her mouth while backing her into the dresser, finally lifting her onto it and spreading her legs. As I stood between her thighs, we devoured each other hungrily, our fused mouths only breaking apart when Murphy yanked my shirt over my head.

Her lips grazed my stubble, traveled down my neck over my clavicle, and kissed all of my chest. My head lolled back, and goose bumps covered my skin. I'd never felt so turned inside out with pleasure, and stifled the moan that begged to be freed. There was no need to clue Scott into what was happening under his roof.

Running my hand under Murphy's shirt, I lifted it off, then unclipped her bra before I held her tight. We were skin to skin, our mouths fused, pressed so closely together that her heart beat against mine.

"I want you so badly," Murphy whispered, grinding herself into me.

"Even in the heat of passion, you still use your adverbs," I mumbled while unbuckling my belt, then shoved off my shoes and dropped my pants in one quick move.

Murphy called me out as I dropped to my knees, yanking off her pants and socks and shoes and tossing them into a big heap. "I see you don't mind."

Sliding back up her legs, I tasted every inch of her skin. I wanted to inhale all of Murphy, unable to get enough of her scent, her taste, her moans or sighs—all of it. Before I combusted, I gently moved her panties to the side and made good on my promise to rock her world.

"Shhh," I mumbled against her core, and the vibration of my

lips set her off. With tiny quakes, she came quietly, and I swallowed all of it.

Lifting her into my arms, I took her over to the bed and laid her down, then grabbed a condom from my pocket. As quickly as I could, I stepped out of my boxers, then rolled it on and entered her slowly. Sliding all the way in and pulling out even more slowly, I took my time with Murphy at the edge of the bed as she spread wide open for me, her luscious skin on display before me.

I wanted to hold on forever to the moment until she whispered, "Faster."

Picking up speed, we both started to reach a crescendo pretty quickly, and I leaned over her, sealing my mouth on hers to catch her screams and absorb every tiny bit of her pleasure.

Later, once we'd cleaned up and crawled back in bed, Murphy snagged my shirt from the floor and slid it over her head before she snuggled against me.

"Well, that's a good solution for what you're going to sleep in."

"I hope Branson doesn't come looking for us," she whispered into my chest.

"Look up, and let me see if you're blushing," I teased.

I couldn't believe that this amazing woman hadn't captured the heart of a man yet. Despite having a hard-shell exterior, groomed for a life she wasn't meant to live, she was golden on the inside.

Rather than show me her cheeks, Murphy pretended to shove me further into the mattress, and I fell easily for the woman. Literally and figuratively.

"I doubt he's looking to hang with me," I told her. "Even though he knows I don't judge and will always give him an objective opinion, he knows I worry about him. Constantly."

Shadows deepened as rain continued to pelt the window. I imagined us in my bed rather than in Scott's guest room, curled up on a stormy night. It felt as if that might be all I needed in this world.

Murphy. In my bed. Forever.

But as quickly as the idea flashed through my mind, Murphy brought me back to reality.

"Still, I'm not so sure Branson was so happy to know you had a girlfriend . . . or you were dating at all," she said, stopping herself from labeling us.

"He'll have to get used to it, especially in the new place." The words slipped from my mouth before I could stop them. Lying there with Murphy, our legs entwined and our hearts beating in unison, I felt too good and my guard fell down.

"What new place?" she asked.

I wasn't surprised to hear it. This was Murphy, and she didn't miss much.

"I bought a piece of land with a ski house on it over in Mad River. I thought it would be nice for Branson and me to get some guy time there. Now, of course, I can't wait for you to see it."

"Wow, you never said anything about it, which is okay, but that's amazing. Look at you, Mr. Successful with two houses, and me struggling to figure out what I want to do." A note of melancholy tinged her voice.

I didn't know why, but I felt as if what she described were what she should have had, rather than me. But I couldn't apologize or say a thing before she went on.

"Honestly, you should be proud. The guys from Pressman, none of them are doing the big-time doctor thing and killing it like you obviously are."

"That's the thing," I said, turning to face her now glistening green eyes and smoothing her out-of-control red hair behind her ear. "When I got hurt playing football and had to figure out a new position, I had a lot of time on my hands. I wasn't social to begin with."

My voice got raspier with every word. I knew this wasn't going to sit well, but I had to get it out—eventually.

"I started playing around with apps, and I was pretty good at it. I developed an app that helped run medical records a little easier, and instead of growing it—or the company—by myself, I licensed it. Medical school was still my priority, and I didn't want to get stuck with a failed venture."

"You what, licensed it? So, you got rich in college or what?"

Murphy looked like she wanted to run away. Her gaze was pinging all over the place, and her heart felt skittish. Then a tear formed in the corner of one eye.

"Why didn't you tell me?" Her expression anguished, she glared at me. "Even when I bared my soul, when I shared all of my darkest moments with you. Did you think I wouldn't be happy for you?"

As her gaze bore into me, I desperately wanted to go back in time and handle this all differently. So very, very differently.

"Wait," she shrieked, nearly choking. "Did you think I would want something from you? That I would use you? Is that how little you think of me and where I come from?"

"No. No, none of that. I believe you're a good person, Murph. When it comes to this, I don't really tell anyone. I feel like they'll only like me because I've got cash to burn, or maybe not like me at all since I don't fit in. The thing is . . . the app thing, it's sort of an ongoing side gig for me. I use the money it brings in help my parents and Branson, and to build a nest egg. And I make investments for later too." I closed my eyes for a second, wishing I could stop my rambling.

"What are you? A cross between Doogie Howser and Richie Rich?" Her tone had an edge of anger, but her face scrunched in pain as she tried to school her emotions. "It's great, really," she said, and if I didn't know her so well, I would have missed the faint quiver in her voice.

"Murphy, that's not fair. I wanted you to love—I mean *like*—me for me. Just for me. You didn't think enough of me back at Pressman to be friends openly with me, and that hurt. I wanted to make sure this thing we have isn't because I've got all this . . . money and stuff now."

I couldn't believe my bad fucking luck at having to reveal my secrets and feelings at Scott's house. What kind of man was I? My heart raced as Murphy dropped her head to sob against my chest.

"I can't breathe," she murmured, taking in deep breaths. "Why? Why would you think that? Did you carry this grudge all these years? Why would you punish me for my parents pushing me so hard? They controlled me, and it didn't go so well. Now I'm trying to spread my wings. Maybe a little late, but still . . . why would you think of me like that now? I thought you believed in me. I'm changing, Ben. Getting better."

"I do believe in you. I just had to know you believed in me."

"That's not fair," she choked out, rolling over to face the other way.

"Murph, look—"

"Don't *look* me. I'm exhausted from the day and the cider. Let's not talk anymore. Let's just go to sleep and get through tonight, and then go home in the morning."

"But, Murph . . ."

"No."

Her voice was hoarse with tears, and I was too much of a nice guy to push further. I didn't think I was wrong to protect myself, but Murphy obviously disagreed.

26

MURPHY

The morning after Ben and I had sex at Scott's was more awkward than the morning after prom.

We didn't talk as I'd promised we would. Instead, I'd dressed as fast as I could in the clothes I'd worked in the day before, smoothing out the wrinkles and hoping I didn't reek.

I'd looked more like a tired hag than someone doing the walk of shame while saying good-bye to Scott and thanking him for his hospitality. He made me promise to buy some of Griff's cider. I didn't have the heart to tell him I couldn't possibly ever drink it again after the night I had.

Branson had been quiet for the majority of the ride home, probably dreading seeing his mom. I'd made up some excuse as to why I needed Ben to drop me off first—laundry day—and jumped out of the Jeep as soon as he pulled to a stop in front of my place. I did tell Branson it was nice meeting him and gave him a warm smile, but he just responded like a teenager with an apathetic chin lift.

Now, a week later, I was still avoiding seeing Ben.

It's not like he tried very hard, texting me his partner had to travel out of town to care for an ailing parent and he was working overtime. He sent apologies and heartfelt expressions of his feelings, not to mention updates on Branson and helping him find some better activities, but Ben didn't push to see me. Granted, I'd only texted back with *Okay. No worries.*

"The book club was so much fun," Hunnie said as I sat on her couch, my head only half in the conversation. "Hey, what's got you in knots? I know it can't be working for me, because I love everything you do. Is Gigi giving you a hard time?" She leaned over and poked me in the shoulder. "I'm talking to you, babe. Where the heck are ya?"

"No, it's not you. You feed me sweet, sticky goodness, so it could never, ever be you." I brought a spoonful of honey to my mouth.

"Hey. That right there is top secret. I'm upping my game when it comes to the cinnamon honey. That little bite of nutmeg and clover really makes it pop, though, am I right? I'm warning you, though, don't mention it to Gigi. She and Holden . . . they're enough to handle without all the honey innuendo."

"I think that's you, Hunnie, with all the innuendo. Not Gigi."

"Whatever. To-may-to, to-mah-to. One woman's honey is another woman's aphrodisiac."

Laughing, I choked out, "Now, there's a caption for a picture."

"Maybe we could make stickers with that saying on it. *Here's your aphrodisiac . . . I mean honey.* I could send them out with orders."

"I was kidding, Hunnie."

Sitting up straighter, I pushed all thoughts of Ben out of my head. "In all seriousness, we should pour it over oatmeal. Add some fresh apple chunks, sprinkle some cinnamon on top. It's the perfect fall combination and will make a fab photo, and we'll think of something a little more PG to say."

"Yes."

At the sound of the kettle whistling, Hunnie popped out of her chair. She poured two mugs of tea and put them on a tray with bottles of various honey infusions, then was back in a hurry. Once I had my tea in hand, she stared me down.

"Now tell me what the hell is irking you. The book club was a success. Gigi is gushing something ridiculous over the navy-blue-colored cupcakes . . . people are coming in and requesting them. The women want color-coordinated icing for their kids' parties and sports teams and their own damn parties. Zara said at least five have already come in and asked when the next meeting is, and you gotta remember, this is Colebury. Five people means a hundred. Gossamer said they're selling navy lingerie to go with the book. You've turned Colebury topsy-turvy, and you're moping around."

I shook my head at Hunnie. "Are you ever going to be quiet so I can answer?"

"I'll shut up now," she said, rolling her eyes.

"Ben and I had an argument."

"Over what? I'm sure it was something silly. The guy's a sticky puddle of goo when it comes to you. Did you ask Gigi about when I told her to lather Holden's . . . you get my drift, right? I'm your boss, so I'm trying to be professional, but all she had to do was lick it off, and he was all *Weekend at Bernie's* for a few hours. Catatonic, if you get my drift. Have you tried that?"

Before I could answer, someone knocked on Hunnie's door, which never happened.

"Are you expecting someone?" I asked her. "Shoot, it's Saturday night. Do you have a date?" Here I was feeling sorry for myself, not realizing maybe Hunnie had plans.

Not bothering to answer me, Hunnie got up and looked out the side window before opening the door. "Ben," she said with surprise, like it was the Pope himself.

"Hunnie. Sorry to barge in, but I was heading over to my parents', and Zara told me Murphy was coming here. I need to talk with her."

"I'll bet you do. Got yourself in a sticky mess," Hunnie said through a cough.

With my feelings clogging my throat and my heart barely beating, I pushed to my feet. "Ben."

"Let's go outside," he said to me, then looked at Hunnie. "I'm sure you're busy in here, Hunnie." He gave her a look, letting me know her cough didn't hide any of what she'd said.

My feet walked toward the door while my head nodded, but my heart stayed on the floor of the she-shed.

"Thanks, Hunnie," Ben said, pulling me out of my mental fog.

"Is this okay?" I asked her.

Hunnie waved us off. "Go. We'll talk later. Want some honey?" she added with a wink, and I had to stifle a groan.

When we walked outside, Ben simply said, "I'm sorry."

"No, I was out of line. You were trying to be honest, and I disregarded it."

"Listen," he said, pulling me close and kissing the top of my head.

It felt heavenly to sink into his soft T-shirt, smelling all woodsy like Ben, and feel his lips pressed to my hair.

His words came out on a whisper. "You know I've never been very good with the social stuff. Maybe that's why I didn't argue about keeping us behind closed doors at Pressman. I didn't feel comfortable really being out there. Then college was hard too. I still wasn't the cool guy, part of the 'in' crowd, someone who was interesting because they traveled or was a foodie or whatever. I was the smart kid. The introvert."

"That's okay," I mumbled into his chest. The sun was starting to set, and I wanted to look up at Ben, but he held my head close to his chest for his confession.

"Then, when I moved back here and finally got what I wanted, I was the outsider. The kid who had seen the world—*ha, as if*—because I'd been to a fancy school and Boston and become a doctor. I'd see people and say hi, occasionally go for a beer, but I never was fully back, you know?"

I nodded against his chest.

"If I spread it around about the apps, I'd be even more of an outsider. Don't get me wrong—everyone is nice to me, and I'm nice back, but seeing Scott reminded me how some people stayed and made something of themselves right here. They furthered their family's business or whatever, made a good life for themselves by staying in Vermont."

Pulling back, I tilted my head to look up at him. "Ben, you're a doctor. You help people, fix people, save lives. Right here in Vermont."

He laughed a little, staring down at me. "I'm an orthopedic surgeon, Murph. I work on ski accidents and people who get hurt riding four-thousand-dollar bikes."

"Stop. Seriously, you help little kids who get hurt, and old people who fall. Ben, I think you're confusing acceptance with reverence. I'm pretty sure everyone here is impressed with you." I lightly tapped my fist against his chest. "Your heart is bigger than anyone's I know, and you put your whole self into helping the people who grew up all around you."

Ben shook his head. "Let's just agree to disagree. I'm not the local kid anymore, and sometimes it hurts. When you showed back up, I didn't want to be *poor Ben* to you anymore. I wanted to be someone who could take care of you, cherish you, spoil you like you deserved. I wanted to be someone you liked for himself. As a doctor, I could be all of that. You know, I'd always dreamed of being someone who could give you the life you had while growing up, but that's impossible. I left that dream back at Harvard. Then you showed up here, and I didn't know what to make of it. You were different, and I didn't want to be the solution to your problems. I wanted to be your partner. But I couldn't do that while telling you everything in the beginning."

I pressed my cheek to his chest again. "That's harsh. I get it, but it's harsh, nonetheless. I don't want the life I had growing up, and I don't want secrets between us. My parents ruined my entire childhood with secrets and empty promises."

Hugging me tight, it felt like Ben might never let me go, but we had to resolve this. I had to speak my feelings.

"I get it now," he said softly. "That's why I avoided you all week. I needed to think. Having my partner away was good.

Being by myself, I had to work so hard that I realized I don't want work to be the main focus of my life. I want you, and more time with you. For all these years, I've been a loner, focusing all my affection on Branson and Brenna and my parents. Now, I've fallen for you, and I want to give it all to you. Please forgive me?"

He stepped back, holding my arms as he looked at me, waiting.

"I've missed you," I said. "I wanted to call and tell you about the book club. Share a crappy pie or breakfast for dinner."

"Let's not fight again."

Ben pulled me in tight and kissed me in front of Hunnie's she-shed, even though she was probably peeking through the window. We stayed like that a long while until the wind picked up.

"I'd better get going," I said, looking at the sky.

"One more thing." Ben raised an eyebrow. "My mom wants you to come to dinner tomorrow."

"Okay. Yes. Now, let me drive out of here before I change my mind."

"Can I follow you home?" he asked. "Make sure you get there safely?"

As I gave him a quick nod, I wondered if we were going to make up properly. I'd never had make-up sex before, probably because I'd never cared enough about someone to make up.

BEN

My mouth skimmed Murphy's cheek, winding its way to her collarbone and down to her breast. She was naked before me in her bed. We'd ripped our clothes off as soon as we got inside her door.

I'd wanted to fall to my knees right there, back her up against the door and do what I'd done before, only better. But Murphy wouldn't have it. She yanked me up with surprising strength and bit my ear before telling me to take her quickly. I couldn't argue when I slipped my hand down to her core and found how ready for me she was.

Afterward, we'd cleaned up and climbed in her bed naked. I was kissing my way down her body when I decided it was time to make good on another promise.

Leaving a tiny love bite on her chest, I said, "Don't move."

I jumped up and ran into the kitchen where I'd seen Murphy had stashed the bottle of my family's maple syrup. She smirked when I walked back into the bedroom carrying the glass jug.

"Did Hunnie give you that idea?"

Stopping in my tracks, I stammered, "Um, pretty sure I don't rely on Hunnie for bedroom advice."

Murphy laughed. "It's just she mentioned telling Gigi once about some honey and Holden's—"

"Ugh, enough," I said, holding my free hand in the air. "Like I told you, I may not have an exciting social life, but I don't need to hear this stuff."

Murphy gave me the side-eye.

"Look, I know Holden keeps to himself, but I have seen him in my office, so I can't say anything more because of doctor-patient confidentiality. Either way, Holden's a good guy, and I don't want to hear about his . . . well, anything other than his knee or ankle."

"You mean his dick?" Murphy blurted with a sly grin.

"I meant cock, babe, but I was stumbling over using that word in the presence of a lady. A society lady, no less." I lay down next to her, running my palm over her smooth skin.

"What's the syrup for then? I don't think a society lady would be into getting all sticky and dirty," she teased, her voice husky.

"You know what? You're here now, which means you're not a society lady anymore. So I'm going to forget about any other man's cock and defile you with this syrup."

When she simply said, "Please," I started drizzling a path of Vermont's finest maple syrup over her torso, her core, and down the inside of her thigh.

Next came the best part. I got to lick it all off her . . . and then she did the same for me.

I couldn't get the taste of syrup combined with Murphy out of my mind or my mouth when I asked my mom to relax about Murphy coming for dinner. Mom had good intentions, but she could try the patience of a saint. I was smart enough to call her in advance and warn her off her usual heavy-handed antics.

I knew Brenna would be there—even needing to swap a shift at work wouldn't stop her from missing this dinner. Of course,

Branson had filled her in about me seeing Murphy, and then I might have mentioned things were strained. I wouldn't put it past my sister to give Murphy the third degree, but I knew better than to call her first.

Trying to calm my nerves, I went for classical music on my way to pick up Murphy. As I pulled up in front of her run-down place, I was listening to Vivaldi and thinking about how we needed to stay at my house more often.

Murphy stepped outside, her face glowing as she walked toward the Jeep holding a huge bakery box, and I felt a tug at my heart again. But I couldn't stay distracted for long because she was opening the back door and sliding the box in the back seat before I could put the Jeep in park.

"I should've driven myself," she said while getting her stuff organized in the back. "You had to come to Colebury just to drive back in the other direction."

"I was halfway already. Had a quick patient to see in the medical office, over by the Wayside. No big deal." Once she was settled into the passenger seat, I said, "Smells good. By the way, you didn't have to bring anything."

She turned to look at me. "First of all, there are a few things my mom drilled into me. You know, when I was a society lady? A few of them were worthwhile. One is you never go to someone's home for a meal emptyhanded."

Not wanting to argue after the mind-blowing sex we'd had last night, I switched gears. "What is it?"

"Oh, the best thing you'll ever eat. Gigi made them just for me. I called in a favor this morning on my way to the Bean, and since I have her booked for every book club, she owes me."

"So, spill. What's in the box?"

"Gigi calls them Vermont-y Cupcakes. Doesn't seem that original when you first hear it, but they have this apple glaze, almost like a fondant, over a maple frosting on top of a vanilla cupcake with flecks of cinnamon in it, and it's absolutely decadent. So sweet, yet not. I can't explain it. They're delicious, and may even be better than the Arnie Palmer. Wait—no, nothing is better than that one. But I thought this was perfect to bring tonight."

"Why? You have syrup on your mind?" I asked, unable to resist referring to the night before. When she side-eyed me, I raised a brow. "You didn't like it?"

Murphy gave me a mock stern look. "Don't make me break society-lady code and talk dirty when we're not in bed."

I loved this easiness in our teasing and joking. It was similar to what we had at Pressman, but now more R-rated. "I guess I'll just have to get you back in bed and do it all over again."

"Promises, promises," Murphy said with a smirk.

I made a mental note to snag a bottle of syrup or two from my parents' place tonight.

"You look amazing," I said, changing the subject again as I took a quick peek at Murphy in tight jeans and an untucked long-sleeve button-down white shirt. The buttons were open at the top and the sleeves were rolled up to her elbows. "I see you have your boots on."

"Quite perceptive, Doc," she said, grinning. "You look pretty good yourself."

"I had to run in and x-ray one of the kids from down the road today. Poor guy took a topple on his two-wheeler and banged up his ankle. Luckily, it was just a sprain, so I wrapped it and set him up with crutches."

I didn't mention that I'd slept with the kid's single mom a few times and she was a nice woman. In fact, she'd pawed all over me when I told her it was only a sprain, and I had to run home and take a quick shower. It was probably my imagination that I had her smell all over me, but I didn't like the way any of it felt.

Murphy shifted in her seat. "Neighbors must love having you on the street. Their own personal doc in a box."

Like I said, she was better off not knowing. Ryan's mom didn't mean much of anything to me. For a while, we'd just had a mutually good time.

"It has its perks, and I don't mind."

"Zara said you were amazing with Nicole. Dave said you have big-city training and a small-town bedside manner."

I burst out laughing. "Okay, enough. I just do my job."

"So, Vivaldi?" Murphy asked, glancing at the stereo.

"Yes, Four Seasons. Probably something no one around here listens to very much, but it calms my soul."

"I love the jumpiness of it. That's probably not the right word to describe it. It's just so peppy in parts that I can't help but feel good. But, why do you need calming?"

As I pushed my hand through my hair, I stole a quick look at Murphy, her bright red hair blowing in the wind, her cheeks and lips lifted in a smile. "You. Because of you. Sitting next to you, being intimate with you, chatting with you there in the seat next to me. All of it. I need to calm myself from letting my mind get carried away with what *could* be."

"Will you stop already?" She brushed off my admission with a wave of her hand, and I worried I shouldn't have been so transparent.

"Only when we get to my parents' house and you see how crazy my mom goes for you, and then you'll need calming too," I said, joking back as we turned onto my parents' long driveway.

"Murphy, come in," my mom practically shrieked as she opened the door and pulled Murphy in for a hug. Obviously, my earlier message had gone in one ear and out the other.

When I saw Mom had Murphy's face smushed into the shoulder of her flannel shirt, I started to panic. "Mom, let Murphy breathe, okay?"

"Oh, yes. Sorry, dear. I got so carried away." Mom loosened her grip on Murphy but still held on, observing her at arm's length. "We've heard so much about you over the years, and then Branson here . . ."

She finally let go of Murphy and moved toward Branson, pulling him to her side. Quickly deducing Mom needed to have something to do with her hands, I put my arm around Murphy, saving her from another bout of my mom's affection.

"Branson said he met you already," Mom said, "and you all spent the night at Scott's? You know he's always had a thing for Brenna."

"Nana, please." Branson wriggled out of her embrace.

Dad joined us, and I gave him a desperate look, silently pleading with him to take control of this already high-speed runaway train.

"Nice to meet you, Murphy." My dad extended a hand to Murphy, and of course, my society girl knew what to do with that.

"Nice to meet you too," she said, politely shaking my father's hand. "Oh, I brought dessert. We left it in the car."

Turning, Murphy looked toward me. I was trying to figure out if she meant for me to go get it, or was silently begging me not to leave her, when my mom spoke.

"You didn't have to bring a thing, sweetie." My mom clasped her hands delightedly in front of her like an evil gangster planning his next move, except that move was probably my wedding.

Deciding to escape, I said, "I'll go get it. Branson, where's your mom? Maybe she can get Murphy something to drink while I run out to the car."

Just then, the front door banged open, and a frazzled Brenna hurried in.

"Sorry I'm late." Barely out of her coat, Brenna looked up and got the same half-crazed, far-off, dreamy look as my mom. "So, you're Murphy?"

Oh no. I could practically see her wheels turning as she took up where Mom left off, planning my wedding in her mind.

Although Murphy was used to nonstop cocktail parties and blue-blood fundraisers, now she looked like she'd swallowed a fly when faced with my overbearing family.

Deciding we'd gotten the introductions out of the way, I took charge. "I'll be right back. Bren, can you take Murphy to the kitchen and get her something to drink?"

As I made a beeline for the door, I heard my sister saying to Murphy, "Oh, sure. Do you like wine?"

When the fresh air hit my face, I wasn't so certain I should even go back inside.

28

MURPHY

Ben found me after delivering the cupcakes in the kitchen amongst a rainfall of hushed whispers.

Glass of wine in hand, I tried to look comfortable perusing the photos lining the wall of the staircase. Little Ben climbing a tree, medium-sized Ben eating a stack of pancakes drizzled with syrup, Brenna with her arm around Ben in his Pee Wee football uniform, and a distinguished Ben at his Harvard graduation.

"I see you found the wall of memories." Ben came up behind me, pulling back my hair to place his lips on my neck, sending chills down to my toes.

"And I see you were always a fan of breakfast food," I said, pointing at a framed photo of him eating pancakes.

"Always, but especially now that you had your first breakfast for dinner with me."

Silence fell between us as we took in the photos on the wall, snapshots of Ben's life before and after Pressman.

"There's none of you while you were at Pressman," I said.

Ben shook his head, pressing it closer to mine. "My parents never came up to visit."

"Why? That seems . . . out of character." I turned to look into

Ben's blue eyes. "You know, now that I remember, they never did come up for any games or parents' weekends."

Ben swallowed, a lump of something undetermined passing by his Adam's apple. "I asked them not to. I barely fit in as it was, and my mom . . . Well, she's just my mom and was never interested in being something she's not. They didn't have the right clothes or anything."

"I'm sure they would have loved to see it." I ran my palm down Ben's arm and wove my fingers through his.

"They did from their car when they dropped me off. Just picturing me there was enough for my dad, and he cautioned my mom, making sure I paved my own way there."

"And Brenna?"

"She got pregnant my freshman year, and then she wasn't exactly in a position to visit."

"I'll bet she regrets that. You can tell she loves you."

"Yeah, when she's not trying to run my life. I swear if she had a man, she'd be less concerned with me."

That made me laugh. "Somehow I think she'd find room in her life to boss both of you around. By the way, what's the deal with her and Scott? Your mom seemed to think there was something more."

"Who knows. They dated in high school. Brenna's a long way from there now, raising a kid by herself and trying to make ends meet. Who knows what my mom is angling at." Changing the subject, he said, "Since you saw the wall of shame, want to see my room?"

"Of course. Are we allowed to go upstairs?" I teased.

Ben tossed me over his shoulder and ran up the stairs to his room. The floorboards creaked under us and I punched his back, hoping he'd put me down. This was hardly how I wanted to get to know his parents, slung over his shoulder caveman-style.

Inside his room, he set me down, and I spun around taking it all in—blue plaid wallpaper, bunkbeds, and a huge lineup of trophies on the bureau. "I see it's pretty much untouched."

"Branson used to think it was fun to sleep in here, in Uncle Ben's room, so my mom left it. Now she can change it, if she wants, considering how Branson thinks I'm the enemy most of the time these days."

Moving closer to Ben, I ran my fingers through his hair and placed a quick kiss on his lips.

"What was that for?" he asked before kissing me again, making it impossible for me to answer.

We stayed like that for a while until we needed to catch our breath.

I rested my head on Ben's chest. "Hey, don't be so hard on yourself about Branson. He's just a confused teen who's lucky to have a great family to support him."

Ben brushed his lips over the top of my head before tipping my chin up so he could meet my eyes. "Thanks."

After spending a few more minutes exploring, picking up trinkets and taking it all in, I looked out the window from his bedroom. "Can we walk around the property?"

"The tasting house is still open for tourists. Marley is doing my parents a favor and helping out with the stragglers. Let's go later? It's beautiful at night."

"Sure."

Truthfully, I was itchy to get out of the house. This was nothing like my experience growing up, or like any of the families we had Sunday dinner with. There were always butlers and formalities and not a single bit of this type of down-home feel. This was all too real for me.

"Hey," Ben said softly. "Stay here with me."

He tipped my chin up again to bring my gaze back to his, and I felt a moment's respite from the anxiety. I was falling for Ben and he was falling back, but this house—a paragon of normalcy—was starting to feel like a foreign country to me.

"I am. I'm trying."

"See all those trees?" Ben distracted me by nodding toward the window and pulling me in front of him.

With my back to his front and his arms holding me firmly against him, I could feel his breath on my neck. "They're beautiful. How long have they been here?"

"You can't tap a tree until it's forty years old, so a long time. Soon, my dad will start walking the rows of them and marking the ones to be tapped. When it dips below freezing, the sap starts to run during the day," he said, and I swore I could feel him smiling against the back of my head.

"Those trees are like extended family. I can tell."

"They are. Many of them came with the property when my parents bought it. A few years before Brenna was born, they planted a lot more. It was an expensive process, and they're now only starting to realize any profits on them. That's why they were always so strapped for cash back then."

Ben pulled my hair aside and kissed my neck.

"Hey," I mumbled. "We don't want to get caught making out in your bedroom."

He rumbled out a laugh. "My mom would be thrilled, I'm sure. Let's go eat, and then we'll take a walk around the trees. In the meantime, I promise to protect you from my family. They're a bit much," he said while squeezing my hand as we headed back downstairs.

I wasn't sure whether I should be happy or nervous when Brenna plopped down next to me at dinner. With Ben seated across from me, I felt like I'd surrendered my security blanket. Branson sat across from his mom, eyeing me, and Mr. and Mrs. Rooney were at either end of the table.

Although I'd never been nervous in social situations, I wasn't prepared for this one. I was surrounded.

Taking a deep breath, I pulled on past lessons in social graces from my mom and glued a smile to my face. Complimenting the house got me some extra credit, and then there was a small lull in the inquisition when Brenna poured me a second glass of wine and then went to help her mom bring in the rest of the food.

Now, I wasn't so sure about Ben's promise to protect me as his mom told stories about his childhood. Soon, she'd ask about mine.

How could I compete with the time Ben helped deliver a calf when he was ten years old, or when he was the MVP of his eighth-grade Pee Wee football league? I'd have to tell a tale of nannies and housekeepers caring for me, combing the tangles out of my hair and making sure I was quiet.

"And Brenna used to dress him like a little girl and make him act in her shows," Mrs. Rooney was saying when Brenna finally said, "Okay, Mom."

"Yeah, that's probably enough walking down memory lane for one night," Ben's dad said kindly.

"Branson said you came from New York," Brenna said to me. "He said he ran into you at the farmers' market."

"Yes. I remembered how good the syrup was from our time at Pressman. Ben would bring it back to school when he went home, and honestly, I think I dipped everything into it for weeks. The market was one of my first stops when I got here."

"Do you like the area?" Ben's dad asked. He seemed genuinely curious, probably trying to gauge why I was really here.

I felt confident Ben hadn't mentioned my recent sordid history to his parents, and I didn't take them for the googling type.

"You know, at first I wasn't sure," I said carefully. "It's growing on me, though. I love the people I work with at the Bean, and I'm doing some marketing on the side."

I took a much-needed break from talking and ate a bite of my lasagna, chewing it slowly, then followed it up with a sip of red wine to put off any more talking.

Brenna gave me a curious look. "Marketing?"

"Oh," Mr. Murphy said. "She's helping Hunnie with her potions and goats—"

"It's social media," Ben said quickly. "Tell Brenna about the book club too." He looked at me while he spoke, all smiles.

"I'm also helping Gigi a bit with her cupcakes," I said, "although she doesn't need very much help. Anyway, I combined all my passions and set up a book club at the Bean. We color-coordinate cupcakes and nail polish to the book cover. I know . . . it sounds ridiculous, but it's a lot of fun and makes for an exciting GNO."

"GNO?" Mrs. Murphy asked.

"Girls' night out."

"Oh, that's so whimsical. I'm sure everyone loves it," Brenna said with a wistful look in her eyes. "Who doesn't need something fun and light like that?"

"You should come," I told her.

"It's when?" Ben asked. "Next Friday?"

"Girls only," I said with a teasing warning look.

"Really? Me?" Brenna asked, sounding surprised.

"Of course, you. But fair warning, we really dive deep into the books. Mostly romance."

Ben glanced at his nephew before nodding at Brenna. "I was going to say Brans and I could hang Friday night, so you should go."

"Really? That would be so much fun," Brenna said to me. "But I need to know which book."

Ben's parents' heads swung between Brenna and me, and I could see their mental wheels turning. They were probably thinking I'd settle here in Vermont, run book clubs and maybe peddle syrup, and be besties with Brenna after marrying Ben. What they didn't know was this was a step in my plan. I was establishing myself as an out-of-the-box marketer.

"How does this help Zara?" Brenna asked. "I'm not looking to steal secrets. I have a job with benefits, which is exactly what I needed, and thanks to Ben—"

"Don't," Ben said firmly.

"Okay, fine. Forget the part about me. Strike that from the conversation," she said to me. "Now, about Zara, I'm curious."

Brenna looked older than I knew her to be. Tired, but tried to cover it up with concealer and lip gloss. Her white T-shirt was loose and askew, revealing her nude bra strap slipping off her bony shoulder. I wished she had a different life, one with a partner so she could achieve her dreams in front of Branson's eyes. I could tell she was holding a lot back—especially her own wishes. After all, I knew the type.

"Well," I said, "I've been combining the marketing of several small businesses to increase revenue at all of them. If not revenue then awareness, word of mouth, new interest . . . which all lead to revenue if the marketing is done correctly."

"Murph went to Columbia," Ben said, unabashedly bragging.

"You went to Harvard, and you're happy here, right?" his mom asked, silently letting me know I'd better not have any more big-city ambition.

But I did.

"You should go grab one of those cupcakes," Ben said, rescuing me. "They're a new recipe of Gigi's, and part of this whole thing Murph has going on."

Brenna went into the kitchen and came back with a platter of the cupcakes. "Do you eat these at book club? If so, I'm in. I love Gigi's place. It's such a special treat."

As I thought back on my New York days when a stop into Magnolia Bakery was nothing, Brenna's words gave new meaning to *special treat*. This was a woman who worked hard as hell to support her son and herself. Stopping at a bakery for a two-dollar cupcake was an extravagance for her.

"We do, and Gigi sells them for a dollar that night. Coffees are also a dollar, specialty drinks two. And I just heard from Colleen over at Cosette's salon they'll be doing half-price mini-manicures for book club attendees."

"I didn't even know they did manicures," Mrs. Rooney said.

Smiling at her, I said, "They do now. Roxanne from the salon over in Montpelier is working at Cosette's on Thursday, and seeing how it goes."

"I get my hair cut there," Brenna said, then nodded decisively. "I'm going to try it. I went last time to the place in Montpelier, but Cosette's is so cute. I love its old-fashioned vibe with its white walls and barebone chairs, and combs in blue Barbicide. But more than that, I feel like Colleen really takes pride in everyone's hair she does." Focusing again on me, she said, "Bet you're not used to salons that are cute or old-fashioned?"

Her question was innocent, but it started my gut churning. I wasn't used to those things. Even though this was a fun passion project, could I be happy doing this long term?

After a stroll through the trees, where Ben pointed out sap lines, we popped into the tasting room. It was dark, and he flicked the lights on dim. It was a beautiful room with pine paneling and floorboards, light bulbs inside empty syrup jars hanging down from the ceiling, and leather stools lining a tasting bar made of the same pine. The whole vibe was rustic, homey, and romantic in equal measure.

"Sit," Ben told me, and I did, my butt sinking into soft leather.

He went behind the counter and opened a bottle of syrup, sticking his finger inside before leaning across the table and tracing my lips with it. When he was done painting my mouth, he leaned closer and kissed me, taking his time, running his tongue along my lower lip and then my upper, finally swirling his tongue with mine.

"Mmm," he murmured while making love to my mouth.

A warm sensation flooded my veins. Need, ecstasy, love, or lust—I wasn't sure, but a flurry of emotions I'd never felt before took over my body. I wanted to stop this, but I couldn't.

Worry bombarded my brain, but my heart was a goner. I'd be leaving Vermont eventually, right? My parents would never let this charade go on forever. And would I want this forever? It certainly felt comfortable, but I had something to prove to everyone. I needed to show the world I could make it on my own.

It was impossible to focus on my goals as Ben continued to tease my mouth, his forearms on the bar, straining to stay close to me. I had no clue what inspired me to crawl on the bar, resting on my knees, barely breaking the kiss with Ben.

Our moans rang out in the quiet room, and I swore I could hear my heart pounding inside my chest. In the battle of my better judgment versus my insatiable need, my desire to be with Ben won out as he hopped up on the bar with me.

We were front to front on our knees on the bar top, my hair a tangled mess and sticky on the ends that brushed along my lips. We ground into each other, trying to create greater friction with our clothes on, and then Ben leaned over to grab the syrup.

When he took my hand in his and dipped it in the syrup, guiding me to paint his lips like he'd done mine, I decided to enjoy the moment. It was so decadent, a memory I would have for a lifetime. Stars twinkled in the dark sky outside the windows as the dim lighting in the room brought out the sparkle in Ben's eyes. Blue for days, a sky I'd like to fly into, maybe forever.

But even as my lips moved in sync with his, I needed to face reality. Eventually, I was leaving for Miami or Boston or maybe San Francisco. Somewhere big and bold, where I could make a name for myself. A city away from New York where my parents reigned and I'd been disgraced, yet somewhere impressive enough that they would be proud of me.

I told myself until that time, I could savor these luscious maple-flavored lips.

In the city, out in the real world, things worked differently. There would be fix-ups and dates because of convenience or connections. Nothing would be real like what I was experiencing with Ben, grinding into each other on a hardwood bar, sticky with pale syrup.

Of course, somewhere deep inside, I knew I wasn't being fair, but I was selfish. I wanted to have this now, and to deal with making something of my life later. Somewhere deep in the recesses of my mind, I knew I'd been stunted, but I'd deal with that later too.

"God, you taste fucking delicious," Ben mumbled against my

mouth. "I want to lay you on this bar and strip you down and devour you."

Pulling back, I hopped off the bar as if a glass of cold water had been dumped over my sticky hair. "We can't. I've already been part of one scandal and painted a harlot."

Ben laughed as he hopped down too. "No way you're a harlot, Murph. You have to know that." He came up behind me and held me close, his mouth making its way around to my ear for a quick nibble.

I nodded, turning in his arms to look up at him. "I know, but I like your parents. I hardly think it will win me any extra credit if they find me spread eagle on their tasting bar with you tasting *me*."

This got me a bigger laugh. "Fair enough, but we're going to recreate this on my kitchen counter soon."

Reluctantly, I moved back, immediately missing his closeness. "Deal."

Straightening my shirt and self-consciously running the back of my hand along my mouth, I winced as guilt swept over me. It wasn't fair to Ben to keep moving along with this relationship, but I couldn't stop if I tried.

"Let's get you home," he said, knowing I had to work the next day, or maybe sensing my internal conflict.

"Okay," I agreed reluctantly.

Ben gave me a naughty smirk. "I need to get home and deal with this," he said, glancing down at the tightness in his jeans. "You have me all kinds of wound up. For a minute, I thought I was a gangly teen in your dorm room and not a board-certified physician."

"Now I feel bad," I said, and I did. Not only for leaving him with blue balls, but for thinking he would understand the personal war I was having.

"Don't. Just be prepared for a good time later this week," he said as he opened the door, the chilly air rushing in a welcome slap to the face, bringing me back to reality.

29

BEN

"Hey, Gigi," I said as I walked into Oh, For Heaven's Cakes on Tuesday morning.

With a touch of flour on her nose, Gigi looked up and smiled. "Ben, you're the best boss I know. Your office staff must love you with all the cupcakes you take them. Not to mention, I'm pretty darn happy about it too."

Clearing my throat, I bent over to stare into the pastry case, surveying what was in there. As I suspected, they were out of the autumn cupcake Murphy liked—no, loved. It was kind of amazing.

"Here's the thing, I'm not here for my staff. It's just . . . I remembered Murphy's birthday is this Thursday," I rambled, "and she hasn't said a single word."

It occurred to me the other night when I dropped her off. Although the dinner with my family had been a little tense and overwhelming, I thought we ended it on positive note in the tasting room. Especially when we'd been able to sneak out without another encounter with my parents, and promises of a continuation of the good time.

But then something in Murphy changed. She seemed distracted, and it hit me on my way home.

Her birthday is coming up.

"I've always known it's this week. I don't know how I forgot the date until now, but it was in the back in my mind and I need to put together some sort of celebration fast."

Gigi walked out from behind the counter, clapping her hands. "This sounds like a job for me. And should we call Hunnie?"

This was turning out exactly how I didn't want it to go, so I thought quickly on my feet. "If Holden were surprising you, do you think he'd want all your friends involved?"

Gigi thought for a moment. "No, he likes my girl gang to be my girl gang, and my time with him to be with him."

"Exactly. A man who does things like I would. This is me, doing this for Murphy. Anyway, I was thinking of taking her to dinner at the High Hill Inn in Woodstock. We could even make a night of it and stay there."

"That sounds like a perfect idea," Gigi said with delight, practically jumping in place. "What do you need from me then?"

"Calm down. This is where I need your help. I wanted to do some sort of special dessert, and Murphy seems to be wild for your autumn cupcakes."

"She loves those. That girl of yours has a wicked sweet tooth. Wait." Gigi disappeared in the back and reappeared with a magazine. "See, look at this."

She showed me a picture of a cake decorated with leaves and some sort of glitter, whipping the magazine through the air and back again.

Frustrated, I sighed. "I don't think you heard me, Gigi. Murphy likes the cupcakes you make. I don't want a cake."

Starting to sweat along my brow, I shoved my hair back with my hand. I had patients to see before I took a few days off, and I needed to finish this negotiation.

Coming closer, Gigi said, "Ben, Ben, Ben. That's a cupcake cake. Inside that cake are a whole bunch of small cupcakes. I've been wanting to try one out, and why not make you and Murphy my guinea pigs?"

"Gigi, I'm looking to impress Murphy, you know? Make her happy?"

She waved a hand, dismissing my concerns. "It'll be fine. I'll make a double batch of cupcakes so we can have a backup. Now go, go, go. It will be ready on Thursday." She shooed me out of the shop before I could even ask how much the cupcake cake was going to cost.

Jumping into my Jeep, I thought about calling Holden and asking him to come over for a beer and some dating advice, which was kind of funny. The guy gave new meaning to keeping to himself, but he was making this whole thing work with Gigi.

Gigi called out to me as I got to the door.

"Wait a minute," she said, filling a box with random cupcakes. "For your staff. A little advance thank-you for letting me experiment with the cupcake cake. It's going to be great."

Handing me the box, she shooed me off again, and I didn't object.

Murphy wasn't working this morning at the Bean, so I passed on stopping in. We'd gone over our schedules when I dropped her off on Sunday. I'd only heard bits and pieces of what she had going on because I'd been so worried about what was bothering her.

And then out of nowhere it had hit me. Murphy's birthday was always the date of the back-to-campus bonfire at Pressman. Every year, she would parade around with a crown on her head that her friends insisted she wear. They'd sing and hug and act like fools, and I always swung by her room later to wish her a happy birthday in private.

But this year, I didn't have to do anything in private.

Heading the Jeep back toward Montpelier, I called the High Hill Inn. Once I had dinner reservations and a room secured, I decided to not tell Murphy until Thursday morning. It wouldn't be hard to keep the secret from her since I was operating tomorrow, and she was working at the market this evening with Hunnie, another tidbit I knew from our domestic conversation.

"Hey, Ben," Zara said cheerfully, greeting me on Thursday morning when I reached the register at the Bean.

"Hey." I smiled, trying to look calm, even though my nerves were in overdrive when it came to surprising Murphy.

"Haven't seen you in a few days," she said. "Been hiding?"

"Nope. Was at the hospital late yesterday, making some extra notes in charts and prepping a few things. I'm off for the next couple of days. It's my partner's turn to work a little extra after taking off this summer."

"Nice. Must explain the jeans and flannel . . . and lack of scrubs."

As she said this, Murphy looked up from the bar and gave me the once-over. Raising an eyebrow her way, I wondered if she liked my look. Or just me?

With her hair pulled back into a low bun and hardly any makeup, she looked natural and fresh, ready for me to mess it all up in bed. I imagined her hair a mess, strands falling out of her bun as we rolled between the sheets.

"Americano?" Zara asked, bringing me out of my dirty thoughts.

I nodded, swallowing the lump of desire in my throat.

After I handed over my Bean Yeti and paid, I made my way down the counter toward the end and watched Murphy finish making a to-go drink. I was admiring her natural beauty and how far she'd come behind the bar when she finally took my mug and added a shot of espresso. As she filled it with hot water, the door to the Bean banged open.

In unison, every person inside the café looked up.

This was quiet little Colebury. No one banged doors or made grand entrances here. Yet, here we were witnessing something like that, as an older woman with perfectly styled hair, decked out in a Burberry trench coat and a pair of sky-high heels, waved her hand in the air while calling out, "Murphy! Look who's here."

A tall, elegantly dressed man trailed behind her, recognizable from his photos splashed all over the news during his scandal. This was Marshall Landon, the disgraced politician and Murphy's father, which meant the woman was Murphy's mother, Lyssa Landon, the society matron.

Shocked, I turned toward Murphy, who had a look of horror on her face. For a second, I was pissed because my surprise was getting ruined, but then all my caveman tendencies to protect and care for her kicked in. Tendencies I didn't even know I had, by the way.

"Murphy!" The decked-out woman screeched her name again while waving her hand like Miss America.

Zara made her way down the bar and spoke softly to Murphy, probably encouraging her to take a break. Smelling drama, Roderick appeared from the back, his apron smeared with streaks of whatever he was baking, and assumed a position by the register like he belonged there. All we were missing were Audrey and Hunnie to waltz in here with their outspoken selves, and this would be like one of those ridiculous reality shows.

Murphy blindly handed me my Americano as she made her way out from behind the bar, not making eye contact with me or anyone else, so I didn't know if that meant she wanted me to go or stay.

"Mom," she choked out.

"Darling," the woman said, all crocodile smiles. "Isn't this a cute little place you found to work in? It's a perfect hideout for you to reinvent your image, don't you think?"

I wasn't sure if Mrs. Landon was addressing the last part to her husband or to Murphy.

Ignoring her mom, Murphy addressed the man. "Hi, Dad."

"Hello," he said, his response curt.

"We flew in to surprise you for your birthday," Mrs. Landon said, "and to talk about when you're coming back. Dad is being awarded a lifetime achievement award from the cultural trust."

"I'm sorry," Roderick said, moving closer to insert himself in the conversation. "It's only ten o'clock in the morning. How did you fly in so early? We're hours from the airport, and it's always a connecting flight."

"Roddy, not now," Murphy said, waving him off.

"We flew private, darling," Murphy's mom whisper-shouted as Roderick walked away, disgruntled but continuing to eavesdrop like the rest of us.

Murphy's hands fluttered uselessly as she tried to compose herself. "Mom, Dad, this is a surprise. Truly. And not necessary."

I'd never met her parents because Murphy always traveled to school by private town car. If she saw her parents, it was when she went home to fill out their family's pictures at an event they had to attend. In fact, I recalled Murphy's parents not attending her graduation because they were on a grand tour of Europe.

"Of course it is. It's your birthday," Mrs. Landon said, "and it's been over six months since you've gone. Time's up, darling. It's time to come home."

Blinking wildly, Murphy stammered, "I—I'm not sure."

"And you are?" Her mom abruptly turned to me, her lip curled in distaste as she took in my jeans, hiking boots, and flannel shirt, along with the scruff on my face and my hair in desperate need of a cut.

Although it was obvious she'd decided I was nothing but a country bumpkin, I offered my hand and said politely, "Ben Rooney. Nice to meet you, ma'am."

"Very nice to meet you too, but we're trying to talk with our daughter. Honey," she said to Murphy, "I thought you said you were doing marketing. Then why are you wearing an apron and back behind that counter?" She waved her hand toward a scowling Zara.

"Ben and I are seeing each other," Murphy said, not bothering to explain her employment status.

"I came to wish your daughter a happy birthday in person and surprise her with dinner at the High Hill Inn." I spoke as if they knew the place and would be impressed. In a flash, I was once again the scholarship kid at Pressman, desperately trying to impress everyone around me in the hope I'd make it big one day.

"Oh, that's where we're staying. I heard it's lovely," Mrs. Murphy said, disregarding the rest of what I'd said. "We plan to dine there with Murphy tonight. Marshall's assistant made the arrangements."

"You know what?" Murphy said quickly. "I'm working now. Maybe we can discuss this all later?"

Murphy's mom looked her up and down again with a sniff. "You will need to clean up."

"Yes, Mom, I know what I need to wear. And we'll be four, so can you handle changing the reservation? Or should I text Betty or maybe Dad can? Ben will come since he planned to take me there." Murphy let out a short breath and turned to me. "I'm sorry. Rain check on just the two of us?"

"Um, yeah." I stumbled over my words, not sure why she was agreeing to go with her parents so easily. But family was family.

"Zara, is my break over?" Murphy called over her shoulder toward her boss. "Doesn't Nicole have that show at school you wanted to see?"

I didn't know if Murphy was lying, but Zara went along with it and nodded.

Turning back to her parents, Murphy said firmly, "Mom and Dad, I'll see you later."

"Seven. Don't be late, darling," her mom said, failing to register the tension building inside the café. "I'm going to the spa this afternoon and your dad is golfing, so we'll be busy. Thanks for texting Betty to make a change in the reservation."

With one more quick once-over of me, the couple glided out of the Bean as though they hadn't just turned Murphy's world upside down.

30

BEN

I didn't hear from Murphy for the rest of the day.

After leaving the Bean, I downed my Americano in one gulp and headed over to Brenna's to do a little handiwork. I was off and had nothing to do other than obsess over how today was going completely wrong. This was supposed to be my day to spoil Murphy.

And then I remembered. I had to pick up the cupcake cake.

How could a dumb cupcake cake ever be enough for Murphy with family resources like hers?

Not entirely sure Murphy really wanted me to join her with her parents, I decided to give her space. Of course, I wanted to text or call, reach out, run over and hold her while she told me I was enough, but I fought the urge.

My phone finally dinged as I was changing a light bulb at Brenna's.

I'm sorry I ruined the day. Do you want to drive? I don't need my parents to see my car.

That was it. No mention of her really wanting me there or needing me to be with her, but I chalked it up to her being stressed. Imagine being embarrassed about your car when it came to your own parents? The excuses I made for her might have been more for my benefit, but I needed to tell myself something.

I texted back, trying to sound as businesslike as she did.

No worries. Pick you up at 6.

Then I called the inn to cancel my own dinner and room reservations. Normally, they'd be sticklers about me canceling so late, but I mentioned being a doctor and needing to sleep at home tonight. It wasn't a nice trick, but I wasn't in a nice mood.

My despondent mood only grew worse when I knocked on Murphy's door and a way-too-made-up version of her opened it, wearing a pressed blouse and sleek pants and mega-high heels. Her hair was blown out so straight it looked hard and brittle, and an inch of makeup she didn't need was layered on her face.

Seeing how she'd changed herself to suit her parents, I felt my blood boil.

"Hi," she said with a small smile.

"Happy birthday," I said softly, trying to ignore Society Murphy as I leaned in for a kiss. Thinking about the cake, I decided we could salvage the day later—in bed. Just Murphy and me, and icing, and all the makeup long gone.

But then Murphy surprised me by saying, "Lipstick. Can't kiss." Waving me off, she didn't even offer me a cheek to kiss. Instead, she secured her purse over her shoulder and stepped outside to shut the door behind her.

Even though I was physically outside her place here in Vermont, I was mentally transported back in time to our days at Pressman, where our relationship wasn't meant to be public. When I was just the kid Murphy sometimes talked to. A shudder ran through me.

No, this is now. Murphy invited me to dinner. She wants me there. She said so in front of her parents.

Yet, we walked toward the Jeep in silence. Chatty Murphy was long gone—no sign of the retro combat boots or her freckled nose anywhere.

She let me open the door for her before she slipped in and checked her reflection in the mirror, not noticing the giant cake box in the back seat or whether I walked in front or back of the car. Sneaking a peek at Murphy after I closed her door, I found she was entirely consumed with herself, wiping some invisible smudge off her cheek.

"Christ, what did I get myself into?" I whispered to myself as I rounded the back of the SUV.

As I slid into the driver's seat, Murphy finally acknowledged me and gave me an apologetic look.

"If you don't want to come, you don't have to. I know . . . it's my fault. I volunteered you for dinner, but please don't think for a second that this will be anything but work. It won't be a fun and relaxing evening. This isn't a fun social date. But this is my life, working for my parents. I can't seem to escape it, even here in Vermont."

"Of course I'm going," I said against my better judgment, accepting that this wasn't going to be an evening where I'd leave feeling good about myself or successful in my own right. "I'm your guy," I added, not knowing if it was for my benefit or hers.

Murphy sighed. "Again, I'm sorry. I know you were trying to surprise me for my birthday, but my parents swooped in and now it's ruined. I just can't discuss it, though. I have too much on my plate. They're going to try to convince me to leave, and you don't get it. They *always* get what they want."

It was an added benefit that I had to keep my eyes on the road, because it kept me from staring at Murphy's lips painted with an expensive red lipstick that didn't even suit her as she talked like this.

"It'll be okay," I said. "We'll celebrate your birthday on our own another time."

Murphy gave me a slight nod, and we endured the rest of the

ride in uncomfortable silence. The damned cupcake cake taunted me from the back seat, and even Mozart couldn't calm my nerves.

Pulling up in front of the inn, I swallowed my pride. I could have paid to bring Murphy here all by myself for a month or longer, but allowing her parents to bring me (us) here was a bitter pill to swallow. I didn't like feeling like the scholarship kid again. I'd played that role for too long, and now I was my own man.

The valet opened the door for Murphy, and I wanted to deck him. That was the kind of mood I was in. It only worsened when he asked me, "Does the box go inside?" He nodded toward the giant box from Gigi's bakery that Murphy had yet to notice.

Blowing out a long breath, I said, "I'm not sure."

Turning on her heel, Murphy saw the label for Oh, For Heaven's Cakes and quickly whirled back to me. "What's that?" she demanded, venom lacing her words rather than the excitement I'd expected.

"It's nothing. A cake. Someone once told me never to show up emptyhanded." We spoke in hushed tones next to the car with the valet waiting patiently nearby, pretending not to listen.

"Please don't bring that." She flung her arm toward the car. "Whatever it is, I can't eat it in front of my mother. This isn't Vermont. Well, physically we're in Vermont, but my parents never leave their little bubble. Unless it's an aged bottle of Scotch or a vintage red wine, they don't care, okay? Just drop it. It's time for me to eat a salad with the dressing on the side and salmon for dinner. Is breakfast for dinner better? Yes. But you have to understand, that isn't my parents' scene. That's not even in their world. It. Does. Not. Exist."

She paused between each of her final words, for effect I assumed, but I wasn't a stranger to the curiosities of her world. It's just that I'd thought she wanted out of it.

Refusing to make eye contact with me after her choppy monologue, Murphy wrung her hands until she'd transformed her entire demeanor—fake smile, perfect posture, ready for a photo opportunity.

"I didn't get it for your parents," I said. "I got it for you. For you, Murph. I don't care what world they live in. I live here, and so do you. In the real world."

Rather than argue with me, Murphy just gave me a short nod and made a beeline for the entrance. With no further discussion on the cake, I followed behind her, trying for small talk. I couldn't stand the mountain of silence between us. I was a hiker, but this was an incline I couldn't seem to climb.

"It's cool, right?" I asked her, taking her elbow in my palm, trying to touch her any way I could. The inn was an old Victorian that had been restored, and was well known in the area as the nicest place to stay.

"I didn't even notice. I'm sorry," she said, stopping suddenly to give me an anguished look. "Shoot, I'm sorry . . . I seem to be saying that a lot today. Of course it's nice. My parents wouldn't be staying here if it weren't the best."

This time it was my turn to clam up. I simply took her elbow again and led us to the bar area, where we would walk the plank. I mean . . . meet Murphy's parents.

I'd been here once before for a pharmaceutical gig, but had hoped that this time would be more memorable. And it probably would be, but for all the wrong reasons. When Murphy's mom caught sight of us and gave her combo shriek-yell, "Murphy, over here," with her Miss America wave gone wrong, I knew so.

"Hi, Mom." Murphy greeted her mother with a practiced air-kiss to the cheek.

"Mr. Landon," I said, and shook hands with her father.

"Hi, Dad," Murphy said, not bothering to give him an air-kiss.

I didn't get to greet Mrs. Landon because she looked at me and said, "You clean up nice." After that backhanded compliment, I had no idea what to say to the woman.

At least I'd gone home after working at Brenna's to pick up the cake, and showered, dressing in slacks and a button-down. I didn't bother with a tie. I gave those up years ago.

"Mom, Ben is an old friend of mine from Pressman."

We still stood around their lounge table awkwardly, and I wasn't sure what to do. *Should I ask the ladies to take a seat?*

"Why don't you sit, son?" Murphy's dad suggested at the mention of Pressman. Just like always, the mere mention of the elite school opened up doors.

"Is that so?" Murphy's mom seemed surprised, but it was hard to tell. Her eyes widened but her forehead didn't move. Botox, I'd guess.

"Yes. Murphy and I were in the same class," I said and left it at that.

"Does your family have a long history at the school?" her dad asked, obviously wanting to peg me right away.

"No, sir. I attended on a scholarship."

Luckily, we were interrupted by a peppy server. "Hi, can I get you something to drink?"

"My wife will have a gin and tonic, and I will have an old fashioned," Murphy's dad said before turning to his daughter. "Murphy?"

"Red wine," she said, as meek as a mouse.

"House cabernet?" the server asked.

"That would be nice," Murphy said before noticing her father's disapproving frown.

"We could get a bottle of something better," he said, raising a brow.

"It's fine, Dad."

"And for you, sir?" The server stood waiting for me, pen in hand.

"Soda water with lime."

"Great. I'll be right back."

"That's all?" Murphy's dad asked, questioning my beverage choice.

I couldn't help but think how differently the night would have gone had they not shown up. I'd be having a nice Scotch, with Murphy snuggled in next to me. We'd be in no rush because we'd only be going upstairs after dinner.

Giving him a tight smile, I said, "I have to drive home later."

"It's a few hours away," he said. "We'll be eating a big meal between now and then. A man never likes to drink alone."

Here I thought being prepared to take his daughter home safely would impress the man. Instead, it was more important to him that we clink glasses.

"There must be some sort of car service the hotel can arrange for," Mrs. Landon said, twirling her wrist, admiring her diamond-studded watch catch the light.

"Mom, there's no car service." Murphy chimed in but didn't say a word defending my choice.

I held my tongue, unable to get a word in during the bombardment.

"Oh well," Mrs. Landon said. "Let's hear a little bit more about what you're doing. You know, our annual holiday card and letter is just around the corner, and we want to make sure we get it right."

"I'm mainly working at the Busy Bean, serving coffee, Mom. It's fun and easy, and I work with good people."

Murphy sat up in her seat, her ankles crossed. She looked more like she was on a job interview than seeing her parents after several months. I couldn't help but notice her hair. Not a single strand moved or curled against her face. It was poker straight and practically shellacked over her shoulder.

As Murphy began to talk, the server appeared, placing our drinks in front of us.

"Bring the gentleman a Scotch," Mr. Landon barked at the server.

He turned to me and asked, "Neat?"

I wasn't going to get out of this drink, so I decided to take the easy road. "Johnny Walker Black on the rocks," I told the server while filled with self-loathing. I couldn't understand why I was giving in after years of being who I was and acting the way I wanted.

"Nice choice," Murphy's dad said smugly.

A small smile spread across Murphy's face, and I couldn't believe she found some sense of satisfaction in the exchange.

"I mean, other than that coffee business," Murphy's mom said, picking back up on the conversation about what Murphy was doing, presumably for their holiday card.

Murphy stiffened. "Most of my hours are spent working at the Bean. Zara is very good to all of us, the employees—"

"Oh," her mother said quickly, interrupting. "I forgot to mention that guy flitting around, the one who asked me about the flights. Is everyone so simple here in Vermont?" She punctuated her slight with a sip of her drink.

I waited for Murphy to defend Roderick. He was one of the best, a good friend to Murphy and everyone at the Bean.

Instead, Murphy talked about herself. "Actually, I'm working on a marketing project involving the Bean too. I started a book club, and we've had one successful meeting."

"That's hardly marketing, Murphy," her mom said.

After taking a big sip of wine, Murphy placed her glass down before she spoke. "I've been incorporating several small businesses into the theme of the book club. Pastries, manicures, and such. Several local small businesses all get a good bit of exposure."

Her mother sniffed. "Sounds like a hobby to me."

I waited for Murphy to explain more, like how Cosette's had someone doing nails for the first time because of her. I didn't even know what that truly meant, but it was something, and it meant something to the town. What about Gigi's business, and how it was growing thanks to Murphy? She neglected to mention that, or Hunnie and all the work Murphy was doing for her.

"We could spin it, though. How you're breathing big-city life into this sleepy town," Murphy's dad said. "Take a picture of you holding a biography of one of my fellow supporters. It'll be fine. Lyssa, why don't you tell Murphy about the cultural trust?"

Just like that, the talk about Murphy's marketing was over,

and my Scotch was sitting in front of me, the ice melting into the whiskey.

"I have some wonderful news." Murphy's mom's face lit up like one of the billboards in Times Square.

Sadly, Murphy didn't move a muscle. She sat stock still, obviously waiting for the next bomb to drop.

"The trust's marketing person is getting married and moving to Ohio. Really, who would leave the city for Ohio?" she said, referring to *the city* as if New York City were the only city. "They heard you were available. I couldn't help but mention it. Honestly, Murphy, the whole Columbia thing is long forgotten. Preston Parker went back to whatever small town he was from with his tail between his legs. I'm sure even Columbia would have you back, but this is better, don't you think? A huge opportunity with lots of exposure."

Murphy nodded dutifully. "I'll think about it."

Pulling my phone from of my pocket, I pretended to get an urgent text. "Excuse me." I pushed back from my chair and retired to a private corner, feigning taking an important call, but the truth was I really needed a moment to myself to regroup.

I didn't know who this version of Murphy was, but it wasn't the girl who picked car locks or poured maple syrup on everything. This wasn't the woman who set Hunnie straight or fumbled behind the coffee bar, refusing to give up. I had no idea who this woman was, but she wasn't the person I was falling for—after all, she was giving in to everything her parents said.

Where was the headstrong version of Murphy I'd come to know and love?

I had to get out of here. Walking back to the table with purpose, I simply said, "I'm really sorry, but my partner has an emergency he can't deal with alone. I need to go."

I waited for Murphy to say she was coming with me, or to plead with me to stay or to take my hand and squeeze it. But none of that happened.

"You know what?" she said. "I'll stay here with my parents, and they can take me to the Bean in the morning."

And that's all she said. Nothing at all about the emergency or me.

"Good thing you let your whiskey sit there, getting watered down," her father said.

"Good luck," her mom said with a huge smile, obviously happy to see me go. They didn't even know me, or want to know me, because Murphy didn't belong here in Vermont.

Or with me.

31

MURPHY

Crawling into bed Friday afternoon, I didn't even bother getting out of my smelly clothes.

It was three o'clock in the afternoon, and I hadn't been home since the night before. My parents had dropped me off at the Bean this morning, where I worked my shift in a borrowed T-shirt, dress pants, and expensive heels.

Poor Roderick had gaped at me as I made my grand entrance, thinking I was doing the walk of shame. "Rough night?" he'd asked, raising an eyebrow.

"I'm sure you're hoping for something salacious," I said while finger-combing the hairspray out of my hair, "and I wish it were something like that. But I spent my birthday feeling like I was sixteen all over again, being told what to do and how to act. Ben walked out, stranding me at the inn. My mom couldn't believe there wasn't a car service to take me home, and paid for me to get a room."

"Wow." His eyes wide, Roderick opened the pastry case and pulled out a scone, plating it before handing it to me. "For you."

I didn't bother to refuse or explain I'd already had a three-course breakfast at the inn. Taking the plate with me behind the bar, I set it next to the sink and washed my hands.

"You sure you're okay?" Zara asked from behind me.

When I nodded and turned around, she handed me a Bean T-shirt and told me to change in the back. It was the first shift I'd worked without wearing one of my out-of-place expensive aprons.

Roderick and Zara let me be for my shift, giving me the space I needed to work mindlessly with my hands. Every so often I caught a weird glance from a customer or a pitying look from Zara, but I ignored it all.

Until now, when I walked in the door of my place after Roderick came to the rescue and dropped me off at home.

Moving automatically, I made sure to shut all the blinds and leave the lights off, wanting to sob in peace. I couldn't even look at myself. Smelling like coffee grinds and Chanel No. 5, I burrowed into my pillow, allowing hot tears to flow for the first time since Ben stoically walked out of the inn the night before.

Of course there wasn't an emergency. Even I knew that. He left because he despised my parents and me. Why wouldn't he? We were a selfish, self-centered bunch, and he was the most selfless person I knew.

I'd texted him this morning as soon as I woke up. With one eye open and before having any coffee after a mostly sleepless night, I sent two words.

I'm sorry.

Not that I expected a response from him, but my heart ached at the lack of one. No text, no call, no pop-in at the Bean, nothing. Not that I expected any of it.

My tears drenched the pillow beneath my head, and I let them continue to fall. I didn't even care what I looked like, sure that my eye makeup was smeared all over my face, and my skin was probably blotchy.

I wasn't sure how long I lay there like that, but when my phone rang, I jolted up, hoping it was Ben, but wasn't surprised to see it was my mom. I considered screening the call, but she'd only call back.

"Mom?" I said tentatively.

"Murphy, I only have a minute," she said, and I breathed out a sigh of relief. "Dad and I have to leave now. We thought we'd be able to stay one more night, but it looks like he needs to meet with a donor in the morning, back in the city. Well, we didn't mention we were coming here. We thought it would make bringing you home even sweeter."

What she didn't say was it would be the ultimate feel-good story for the press.

"It's okay," I murmured, my voice hoarse and strained.

"You should be coming back with us," she said.

I'd told them over breakfast I wasn't interested in the trust position or coming back to New York. Not now, or ever. "I'm paving my own way," I'd said.

This announcement was met with a series of objections, followed by, of course, pronouncements about Ben being a bad choice for me. In fact, his being a doctor was a negative in their eyes because he'd constantly be called away for emergencies. "You need someone who's available to you," they'd said.

"I can't, Mom. Like I told you, I have commitments here. I like it here." It was the first time I'd said it aloud, and it was true. I liked Vermont and all its small-town hippie-dippyness.

"What? Making coffee? Running book clubs? That's what you like?"

Breathing a sigh of relief that there wasn't a book club until next Friday, I said, "Safe travels," to my mom and disconnected the call. I was a disappointment to them, and now I'd lost Ben.

Curled into a ball on my bed, I continued to cry, feeling like the worst kind of failure.

The phrase *too little, too late* kept running through my head. I'd made fun of Vermont and then put Ben in the back corner when it came to my parents. After all, I was well-practiced at putting Ben in his place after Pressman.

Still clutching my phone, I typed another text to Ben, feeling awkward because I'd never begged someone for forgiveness before.

I'm sorry. I was wrong. You planned something special for my birthday, and I acted like a small child. Please, Ben, call me.

Ben's absence hurt so much, it felt like my heart was stuck in the coffee-bean grinder at work. I needed him to call me, but somehow I knew he wouldn't. Pride would keep him from coming to me.

A while later, I fell asleep with my palm massaging my chest where my heart lived, and my head pounding over Ben's silence.

Monday, I pulled up to Hunnie's shed, a constant punishing pain in my gut. I'd worked Saturday and Sunday, hoping for a glimpse of Ben, but he never showed his face.

Roderick bombarded me with questions about where I came from, what my parents did, and what life in New York City was like . . . until he noticed I wasn't up for small talk. It might have been the death glare I gave him while slicing a piece of pound cake for a customer.

"You're here bright and early," Hunnie said, greeting me from her tiny porch. Funny how her she-shed was small in size but big on personality, just like she was.

I was wondering if there was anything notable about me when Hunnie shouted, "Wait until you taste this honey with rose petals. It's going to go perfect with the pale pink cupcakes. That book cover was so much fun to work with."

Approaching, I tried to smile. "It was a great book. Layton worked so hard to get Charli to like him just for himself, but then he realized he couldn't force it." I recounted part of the story *To*

See You, leaving out how the characters finally got their happily ever after.

I crossed the threshold into Hunnie's and collapsed in my favorite velvet chair.

"Here," she said, spinning around from the counter. With a spoon of honey in hand, she walked toward me. "What do you think?"

Taking the spoon, I tasted it with a lump in my throat and tears threatening to fall. Thankfully, Hunnie was as talkative as ever.

"Colleen said Cosette's is booked solid for Thursday. I ran into her at the Kwikshop yesterday. Everyone wants watercolor nails like Bubble Bath from Essie, and some shade of pale blue and mint green, specifically."

I smiled, but it didn't feel as natural as it normally would. I'd ordered some nail polish samples for Colleen of pale watercolor shades but never imagined it would explode like it had. I didn't think Colebury had ever seen a manicure revolution like this.

"Hey." Hunnie stood directly in front of my chair, hovering over me.

"What?" I looked up, swallowing the tidal wave of emotion about to pour from me.

"What's wrong?" she asked, still towering over me.

I waved her off. "Sit down. You're making me nervous."

Clearing my throat, I tried to channel the emotional stifling my mom had drilled into me, but there was nothing there. Even in my reserves.

"Ben . . . it's over," I managed to choke out.

"What?"

"Stop saying *what*. We were bound to end. It wasn't going to work."

"Murphy, don't say that," Hunnie said, pulling her legs underneath her and throwing her braid to one side.

"We were—*are*—too different. I'm from a world so different from this one, a world I don't even understand. There are spoken and unspoken rules, and no matter how hard I try to let them go, I can't. Keep in mind, they're stupid and ridiculous rules, yet I still feel like I need to follow them." I paused to sniff back tears. "And Ben, he's too real. Too good, too . . . too . . . too better for it," I said, rambling. "I'm not even making sense, but you get what I'm saying. I'm part of one world, and Ben is too special for that world."

"Zara mentioned your folks coming in," Hunnie said with a frown. "I should have assumed it meant disaster. You didn't say they were coming, and Zara said it felt like a surprise, even though she stressed she was trying to mind her own business. I thought maybe when I texted you a happy birthday, you would have mentioned their visit or what happened, or the cake Gigi made for Ben. She's been waiting like a pig in heat to hear."

"It was awful." I proceeded to explain the whole debacle to Hunnie, ending with, "Now you see why I didn't mention anything over text? It was better for me to say I was busy with work or whatever, because opening my mouth is a land mine of awfulness. Oh, and we never had the cake."

I pulled the blanket out from underneath the coffee table and wrapped myself against the emotional chill.

Hunnie patted the blanket over my arm. "Oh, sweetie. That's horrible, but your mom and dad, they're something otherworldly. You're nothing like them, and I'm sorry you need to deal with that. You shouldn't. My advice is to break away. It sounds harsh, but my grandma, the one who called me Hunnie, was a wise woman."

She gave me a wink, trying to make me laugh.

"Grandma used to say you need to evaluate what's sweet in your life and hold on to it extra hard, even if it's slippery. And when something is bitter, you toss it away like a spoiled lemon. I know they're your parents but they're bitter for you. As for you and Ben, I've never been in love, so I've got nothing for you other than he's sweet, so you need to hold on to him."

This actually made me laugh out loud. "Oh God." I grabbed

my temples, trying to massage away the tension. "I can't believe you're my boss."

"Boss-ish," Hunnie said. "After all, you're only an intern."

"Either way, this discussion is silly because we're not in love. Ben likes me and I like him, but it's just a thing. A fling for old times' sake."

"Huh-uh. You're in love, honey. Like golden honey infused with lemon basil, you two go perfectly together. Absolutely perfect."

I shook my head, but maybe . . . could we be? "Maybe that's why this hurts so much?"

"That's likely, honey bear," she said, moving to the arm of the chair where I was sitting so she could run her hand down my back. "Look, it's not your parents' actions Ben's blaming you for. That much I know about him. He doesn't judge people about where they come from."

"I know that all too well," I said.

"Sounds to me like it's your problem to solve. Ben believes in the good in all people, especially you. Maybe he doesn't get why you can't see all the best parts of you and break away? I know I can't understand it. You're amazing, Murphy—giving, caring, warm, and real. You need to see the good in yourself and stand up to your parents, which it sounds like you did."

Fresh tears broke out at her words. "All my life . . . my family, the other kids at Pressman, college friends and coworkers at Columbia, nobody made me feel like I was filled with *good.* Thank you, Hunnie."

She pulled me in for a giant hug—something else no one ever did for me—and held me tight.

"Now, you need to strategize how you're going to get your guy back. Maybe some honey and a paint brush and no clothes?" She winked again, adding, "Gigi can give you some tips."

I smacked Hunnie playfully on the shoulder and stood. "Let's get through book club before you dive into all your sexual suggestions. I need some time to think about this. Obviously, it's my responsibility to make things right." I sniffed back snot and salty tears, trying to compose myself. There was no question my skin was blotchy as hell.

"Attagirl. Now, something came to mind when I mentioned lemon-basil honey. You know what that is?"

With Hunnie, I had zero ideas. "Should I be afraid?"

"No way, girl, you should be happy. I was thinking hot toddies made with lemon-basil honey." She stood and was whipping up a batch of her creation within moments of mentioning it. "By the way, what did you think of the rose-petal honey?"

And that was Hunnie, right back to business as if I hadn't just had an emotional meltdown. I needed to catch a dose of her *joie de vivre*.

"It's perfect," I said, "and you know it."

This made her laugh and give me a bow.

"Keep mixing," I barked at her from the velvet chair. "I'm going to need several hot toddies for the liquid courage to even think about getting Ben back."

MURPHY

With the next book club on the horizon and opening at the Bean with Roderick all week, the days passed in a haze of busyness while I constantly thought about Ben.

He hadn't stopped into the Bean for an Americano, or texted or called. There had been nothing from him. His face, his palm running down my arm sending shivers up my spine, his breath hot on my neck—so many memories of him were on repeat in my mind.

My pulse beat at a frantic pace as I worried if he was okay with all of this. I assumed he was done with me, which hurt more than being cast out from my social circles in New York, or my parents turning their noses up at me.

By Friday, I was so upset, I decided not to go home between my shift and the book club. I sat in the back of the Bean, moping and going over last-minute details. My hand shook so much while I was applying pale pink eyeshadow in the back room of the Bean, Roderick told me, "Snap out of it, Murph. Go get your guy. Period. Stop drowning in your own misery."

This made me laugh. At the very least, opening with Roderick granted me some much-needed laughter and a lot of home-baked sweets. I had a little extra curviness to my hips.

"I have to get through this first. Apparently, reps from Essie and one of the big publishing houses checked out our posts on the blog from the last time, and they want to sponsor a book club."

Plopping into a chair, Roderick sighed. Wow, that's big-time. You're really doing it. You may not fly private, but you're still making it big," he teased.

I shook my hairbrush in his face. "Quit it."

Looking down at my hands, I was pleased that my pale pink and blue nail polish had survived my coffee shift. I was ready to tackle book club.

But stopping thinking about Ben, not so much.

Walking out into the Bean, I spotted a crowd gathering in the corner. Everyone was dressed in watercolor shades of pink, blue, and lavender with copies of the book *To See You* tucked in their arms.

Gigi had arranged the special cupcakes on one of the tables, and even Zara had gotten in on the fun, making pink-foamed lattes behind the bar. It was hard not to absorb the positive vibes filling the Bean, but then I saw Brenna, and my mood dropped like an elevator in a shaft.

It had been over a week since I'd seen or heard from Ben, and almost two weeks since I had dinner with the Rooneys. Seeing Brenna hurt like losing a toenail right before wearing high heels. I know, because I lost one once before attending a fundraiser.

"Hi, Murphy." Brenna bopped over to me, smiling like nothing was wrong.

"Hi," I managed to choke out.

She beamed at me. "This is so cool. Just like you said, but better. Way better. I'm so glad I came."

"Thanks. It's something. A little twist on the mundane. A break from reality."

"This might be the most fun Colebury has ever seen," Brenna said, swinging her arm out around her. "Usually on Fridays, I lay on the couch, exhausted from the week, mentally preparing myself for working on the weekends. But Branson deserves it. I need to work for him, you know?"

I nodded, not sure what she was driving at. "He's a good kid, and you're a good mom. Seriously, one of the best I know." I felt uncomfortable, not knowing what good could come of this conversation, but I needed to get back to the book club.

"He gets into some trouble. It's expected, but he's a good kid. But I don't want to talk about Branson. I really did come here to check this out, but I also wanted to chat about Ben."

Lowering her voice, she stepped closer. "I need him to let go of this obsession he has about taking care of Branson. It makes me feel like I can't do it, and I'm his mom. Plus, Ben's done enough. For the last month, since he started seeing you, he's been happier and seemed to be finally living his own life, giving me some space. The last week, though, I've seen and heard from him too much. All his opinions on Branson and what he should do, where he should be aiming to go to college, what he shouldn't do. Ugh, I can't take it."

Brenna grabbed her forehead and met my gaze. "I'm sorry. You don't need me to dump this on you while you've got an event going on. But know this—you need to call Ben and try. He needs you. And honestly, without you, he's going to run himself ragged trying to run my life. So, *please,* from the bottom of my heart, please go talk with him."

The words clogged in my throat. "I've tried, but he won't talk with me. Ben is such a good guy, one of the best, but he doesn't want me."

I knew she believed in her brother, but she was right. Ben needed his own life, so she could have hers. But there wasn't much I could do about it.

Brenna gave me a fierce look. "You need to fight for him. This is Ben we're talking about. He's always been a bit unsure of where he stood with people, at prep school and Harvard and then back here. He's always been an outsider, and when he feels that way, he makes himself more of an outsider by stepping back."

I nodded. "Surprisingly, I understand this because . . . well, never mind. We have history, Ben and me. Also, you should know that I've been nearly squeezed to death by family before, and not for all the right reasons like Ben is doing to you. But either way, it hurts like a bitch. Pardon my French. Ben means well," I said, defending the guy who hadn't talked to me in over a week.

"It does, though. Being squeezed hurts like a bitch. And I know Ben has a good heart, but sometimes it's too good. Now, come on. Let's go eat cupcakes and talk about romance books. That's way better than this, but promise you'll go see him."

I didn't promise anything, but I felt my head nod.

Then Brenna looped her arm through mine, and I noticed how skinny she was, her bony arms hidden under a silky lavender blouse. She needed to take care of herself. I imagined life was hard for a single mom to a teenage boy in rural Vermont, but Brenna didn't strike me as the type who complained. I took all of her in with her chocolate-brown leggings, tan ankle boots that were scuffed and worn yet stylish, and her hair in soft waves.

"Do you know Scott?" I couldn't help but ask on our way toward the cupcakes.

"Scott Stevens? Of course," she said with a twinkle in her eye. "We went to school together."

"Oh?" Yep, there was something more there. "I was at his farm with Ben and Branson, and he seemed to have fond memories of you."

"Not now," she said before grabbing a cupcake.

I made a mental note to explore the matter later and went about leading the book club, eating cupcakes, and admiring everyone's nail polish while smelling phantom Americanos and Ben's woodsy scent.

I decided after a good night's sleep, I would do what Brenna (and I) wanted and make amends.

33

BEN

Saturday morning, I moped around my house, hoping my dad would call with a chore he needed help with, or maybe Branson would text me, wanting to hang. I could take him to see the new house, and he could pick out a room to use when he was there.

Or I could make some notes of work I needed to have done on the new house. It would take less time than I'd originally thought, but I didn't dwell on that either.

Frustrated, I glared at my phone, lying there all quiet on the counter.

Idle time wasn't my friend. Rather than pace or head into the hospital to check on patients who didn't need checking on, I opened my laptop and reviewed an app contract. It was perhaps my biggest one yet, and I had no one to share the good news with, no one to toast with, not a fucking soul to even congratulate me.

Rather than wallow in self-pity, I went over some of the details in the contract. I was lost in the provision where it explained my medical license was accepted through endorsement of the state of New York when there was a knock on my door.

For a second, I thought I was imagining it, and then I heard it again. It was soft and timid, but someone was rapping on the wood.

I opened the door to reveal a disheveled Murphy with windblown hair framing her tear-streaked face and ruddy cheeks. Mentally, I reprimanded myself for wanting to grab her and hold her. Her car was at the bottom of my driveway, and for a moment, I thought it was running. I guessed she was here to say good-bye. She must be heading off to somewhere with her parents, a place where she could be a well-known Landon.

"Murphy." I blew out her name with a sigh of relief. I was unbelievably happy to see her, yet still angry about what had happened with her parents, contradictory emotions that swirled into a cocktail of confusion.

"Ben, I'm . . . I'm sorry . . . to just show up like this." Her eyes glistening, she sniffed back tears. "But I didn't know whether you would see me or not."

"Murph, I would always see you," I said, knowing it was true. My heart lashed at my mind over how I'd ignored all her messages, giving her the impression I wouldn't see her. "Come in."

She walked slowly over the threshold. "Ben," she said, her voice hoarse and strained. "I'm sorry."

I noticed she was wearing those boots I loved, and couldn't help the small jolt of lust running through my body.

"It's not your fault," I said, leading her toward the family room that had no family to enjoy it. Speaking to her as we traversed the hall was the coward's way. "Your family is your family, and I can't change that."

"Ben, look at me," she said, taking control of the conversation, and I did as she asked, turning and leaning my hip into the wall. "It was a shock seeing my parents like that. It took me totally by surprise. For all my life, they said jump, and I did exactly that. I didn't know any better. When they walked through the door of the Bean, I couldn't reconcile this life here with the life I've lived for the majority of my life."

She approached and hesitated before placing her palm on my

chest. I wasn't sure what she wanted to do, but I nodded. Her hand landed over my heart, her gaze still locked on mine.

"I left New York because of the terrible way they treated me, and you were the one person who didn't judge me about what happened. Your heart has always been larger than life. Even back at Pressman, you never judged me. I took all of that for granted years ago, and then again when we went to the inn."

Her gaze fell to the floor, and mine dropped to watch her chest rising and falling. She was trying to catch her breath.

"You didn't deserve what I did," she said. "I can't apologize for my parents' actions, but I can apologize for mine."

Her hand slid down my chest before she turned and walked away, and I followed her every move. My head thought it was a good thing she was leaving, but my heart started to crack at the idea of her going, despite what I was about to do myself.

But then she stopped in front of the sectional sofa and slid to the floor, her back to the front of the sofa, her legs stretched out in front of her.

Dropping her head back, she blew out a long breath. "I can't stand it anymore," she said matter-of-factly.

"Can I get you some water?" I asked.

When she shook her head, I joined her on the floor, plopping my ass down next to her. Unable to resist this woman anymore, I wove my fingers through hers and squeezed her hand.

"Murphy, here's the thing," I said, turning to look at her. Her eyes met mine for a second before her gaze dropped to the carpet. "Look at me," I told her, and when her red-rimmed eyes locked onto mine, I said, "The thing is . . . I love you."

The weight that had been sitting on my chest was back in earnest. Pressure rang in my ears. *Does she love me too?*

"I don't deserve your love," she said, squeezing my hand back. "Ben, what I did was awful. I should have stood up to my parents in the Bean, told them we had plans. Then I dragged you to the inn with them, when it should have been just us. They were terrible to you and me, and I let it go on. The thing is . . ."

I thought she was going to say she loved me back, but she continued to ramble.

"I like Vermont. It's growing on me. The syrup, the honey, and all the trees. The weather. My boots," she said, looking at her feet, and then her gorgeous green eyes met mine again. "And you."

The weight fell away from my chest, and my heart soared with hope.

"I don't belong in my parents' world," she said firmly. "I never want to go back there, and I told them so the next morning. I like serving coffee and helping Hunnie. I want to be here for Gigi's wedding, and strangely, I think your sister and I could be friends. Apparently, these boots are made for staying."

Her words seeped into places I didn't know existed. Tiny crevices where I held my feelings tight.

"Murphy," I said quickly. "There are some things I should tell you—"

"No, let me finish. I need to apologize and make this right. You see, I went to see Hunnie and she told me this story, actually it was a lesson from her grandmother, about the sweet in your life and holding on to it. Ben, I want to hold on to you because you're my sweet."

I needed to tell Murphy what I'd just signed, but my mouth had a mind of its own and found its way over to her lips. We kissed with all the pent-up emotions we'd been struggling with, and I had no idea how long we stayed like that.

Minutes melted into each other as I made love to Murphy's mouth. At first, we were tender and then we weren't, punishing each other's mouths with the tension of this past week.

Finally, when we needed to breathe and I was certain her lips were bruised, I broke away, panting. Still on the floor, my ass full of pins and needles, I blurted, "I don't know the right way to say this, but I've been hired to work on a full exercise and nutrition line, complete with an app and training program."

"Ben, that's amazing," she said, her palm cupping my cheek.

"The thing is . . . it's going to take me away from here. From my family, and now, I guess, from you."

"Where are you going?" Her eyes wide, she swallowed hard.

Feeling like the worst kind of jerk, since she'd only confessed to liking Vermont moments before, I sighed. "New York."

"What?" Her question was quiet, but the pain in it was clear. "The one place I thought I'd never have to see again."

"Brooklyn, actually," I said to clarify, and this got me a reaction I didn't expect.

Murphy tipped her head back and let out the loudest laugh I'd ever heard from her. "Brooklyn?"

I nodded. "Yeah, I've already rented a place there. I'm going to mostly work on the app and nutrition stuff, but I'll also see patients two or three days a week and operate one day a week. It's a heavy schedule, but I'm young and up for it. Then I can decide which is the better match for my life, because I can't keep up with both forever. But . . . I don't get why you're laughing."

Her reaction had totally confused me. I didn't know if she thought the idea of a country bumpkin like me living in New York wasn't plausible or what.

Smiling at me as she pushed her hair behind her ear, she then ran her hand down my cheek again. "Because this is the cherry on top. My parents already find you below their standards, you know, being a doctor and all that, and the only thing worse to them than Brooklyn is Queens."

I swallowed hard and took a deep breath. "Are you saying you'd come with me? I'm sorry, that's too much to hope for," I said, more for myself than her. I'd take her with me in a heartbeat. "Would you at least visit me? I guess that's a more appropriate suggestion, right? Is that what you meant?"

Murphy shook her head, giving me a small smile. "Well, I meant I would visit, but if you're offering for me to come, um, I wanted to tell you that I was just offered a social media job for a nail polish company. I negotiated the job to be remote, to help build my portfolio, and since it's freelance, I can do it anywhere. I was going to do it from here. Which is why I was prepared to tell you I'd move here, permanently, but now you're off to Brooklyn."

Unable to find the right words, I kissed her again, telling her what I wanted to say with my mouth and tongue, running my hand up and down her back as she leaned into me.

"I don't want you to visit, Murph," I murmured against her lips.

"You don't?"

"Selfishly, I want you with me all the time. You could do marketing there, make a name for yourself on your own. Remember your Brooklyn romance book and how you thought you'd never have your own love story? You can—I mean, you are. You're having it, and it could be in Brooklyn." My words came out so jumbled, I clarified. "You won't have any expenses because you can live with me."

This made her pull away, and I cursed myself mentally. I'd come on too strong, suggesting too much, too soon.

"This is coming at me quick," Murphy said, "and there's no denying I love you back, Ben. But . . ."

The love of my life had finally said the words to me, and then they were followed with a *but*. Everyone knows nothing good comes after a *but*.

"But we have to be equals.," she said. "I can't mooch off you. I've mooched off my parents all my life. My plan was to make it on my own, and I still plan to do that, but with you by my side. And you have to get over this hang-up with where I came from. I'm leaving all that in my past, like Hunnie told me to." Then Murphy gasped. "Oh! Hunnie."

"Hunnie what?"

Murphy's brow scrunched, and I could practically see the wheels turning inside her head. "She's going to miss me. And Gigi. They've become my friends, my first real friends. And her wedding."

"They'll visit," I told her. "And we'll be back."

"Ugh, I never wanted to go to New York again, but I'm going," she said. "And this time I'm going on my own terms. For you. Plus, I've never lived in Brooklyn."

Smart enough not to argue, I only nodded and smiled. I wanted to pinch myself at what was happening. If that made me a softie, I didn't care. When it came to Murphy, all my caveman tendencies came out.

Finally, I stood and scooped Murphy in my arms, then kissed her all the way to my bedroom, where I laid her down on the bed and stripped off her clothes. Within a minute, she was on the edge of the bed and I was on my knees, my mouth on her most intimate spot.

"I want you," she murmured, wanting for me to be inside her, but I had different plans.

"You have me," I said into her core, the vibrations of my words setting off tiny waves inside her that I could feel all the way to my spine. I rode each one and continued to tease and bring her to the brink before slowing down and revving back up.

Only when she muttered, "Please, Ben, I can't," did I give in and let her climax. I wasn't sure who liked it more, her or me.

Needless to say, we spent the rest of Saturday in bed, only stopping to order some Asian takeout. On our way to pick it up, Branson called. He said his mom told him about Brooklyn, and he was happy for me. I promised him we would spend holidays at the ski house, which I'd planned to keep, but would sell my current house in Montpelier.

"Brenna knew about Brooklyn?" Murphy asked over the Beethoven when I hung up.

"Of course. I wouldn't keep that from her. My parents, on the other hand, I just told them. I think they're genuinely happy and want me out of their hair. To be honest, these negotiations have been going on for a long time. And then when you walked back into my life, I wasn't sure if I wanted to follow through with the deal. Last week, when I took some time off, it was to consider it . . . because my licensure came through, and they presented a final offer I couldn't refuse. It's a collaboration between the university's medical school, and the hospital, and a wealthy triathlete who had the idea but didn't know how to execute it. That's where I come in."

I glanced at Murphy and noticed that her eyes looked a little glazed over as I rambled on. "I know. This is boring."

Another throaty laugh came from her. "No, I was just thinking. Brenna came to see me and told me she needed you to back off and let her be a parent to Branson. She encouraged me to get you back because you needed to have your own life and let her live hers. She never mentioned New York, but she forced me right back into your arms."

"My sister might not have graduated from college, but no one ever said she wasn't smart," I said with a chuckle.

"You can say that again," Murphy said, stealing a glance at me. "I need to finish up with Hunnie, though. I can't leave her stranded."

"You can still help her. Don't worry—we'll come back to visit. We'll need a break from all the New York craziness. I don't want you to give up anything you want."

"Are you ready for all of that?" she asked, and I reached over to squeeze her knee.

"With you, I'm ready for anything, Murph."

"And Zara, I guess she knew the Bean was never a permanent thing for me, but I'm going to miss her. Roddy will have a bunch of shifts to cover until they find someone."

"Speaking of, we're going to have to get a real espresso machine for our place so you can make me an Americano occasionally."

"And I'll have to get a tip jar," she said with a giggle.

When we got to the restaurant, I ran inside and picked up the food. By the time I got back into the car, Murphy was playing Ed Sheeran.

"My turn to pick the music," she said, and I just grinned.

As I turned back onto the road, Andrea Bocelli joined in with

Sheeran, and I couldn't help but give her a huge smile. "You found a mix combining something for both of us."

"That's life, Ben," she said while tickling my arm. "You're from one place and I'm from another, and together we make a new mash-up."

I nodded. "Speaking of where I'm from and Brenna, I do want to talk to her about taking on an ownership role at our parents' farm. They're getting old, and she knows the sap business better than anyone. I don't plan to inherit the farm, but it should be there for Branson if he ever wants it. And with Hunnie running all these joint ventures, it's a good way for Brenna to get reconnected and be a part of something new and exciting. Branson can help her and stay out of trouble." I glanced over at Murphy. "Maybe you'll back me up now that you two are so close?"

"Oh yeah," Murphy said, grinning. "With her little manipulation, we're real close." Then she added, "By the way, did you know there's something going on with her and Scott?"

"Stevens?" I asked.

"The one and only. So, yeah, I'm going to insert myself in this whole maple-syrup business discussion, but with a side of Scott talk."

"Oh boy."

We laughed all the way home about the scare tactics Murphy planned to use on Brenna.

When we got back, we set the food on the kitchen counter and made it as far as the hallway before letting the food get cold.

34

EPILOGUE

Murphy

"Close your eyes," Ben called out as he opened the door, and I smiled. He was always up to something.

"Don't let all the leaves in," I shouted back. It was early October, and I swore every day, a few hundred new leaves collected in our tiny foyer, blowing in from the yard.

"A few won't hurt," Ben called back, and I chuckled. He was always teasing it was Vermont's revenge on Brooklyn . . . the endless foliage with nowhere to go but inside.

I was sitting at the dining table, finding it hard to concentrate on my latest social media client. A family-run chain of counter-service hummus-based restaurants had hired me after checking out my portfolio of work for Hunnie and Gigi. They liked how I'd infused a family-type feeling to all of the posts I'd done for Hunnie and Gigi, a feeling they felt was essential to community building.

Instead of making notes on my future client, I was staring at my wedding band, so I did what Ben had asked and closed my eyes.

A year ago, Ben and I got married at city hall, just the two of us, and then had dinner in an all-night diner. For old times' sake, we had breakfast for dinner and brought our own bottle of Vermont maple syrup like real Vermonters. We also used another bottle of syrup at home to commemorate the day . . . and then we woke up and dealt with the wrath of Brenna, Hunnie, Gigi, and Zara.

Of course, we gave in to their demands to celebrate our wedding with us, so a month and a half later, we came home and threw a big private party at the Bean. Zara closed down for us and Roderick manned a makeshift bar—with some recipes from friends of his up at Vinos & Veritas in Burlington. Gigi made me a cupcake cake, and this time I actually got to eat it. Hunnie made straws of a special-edition rose-petal honey. The straws had been the last project we'd finished before I left Vermont. We'd found a manufacturer for the straws, and now they were sold all over Vermont in little gift shops and boutiques, not to mention a few places outside the state that had started carrying them.

It had been a magical night. To be honest, returning to New York had been hard, but with Ben by my side, I was fine. We'd enjoyed the last year—being married, working hard, and exploring dive restaurants around Brooklyn. It was a New York I didn't know growing up, and it was all ours.

I was still waiting for Ben to appear, so I opened my eyes and focused again on the hummus-filled photos in front of me, trying to funnel my creative thoughts. They would be a fun client to work with when I got my mojo centered.

Yes, the big dogs had come calling a few times too. Just the week before, I'd met with the Tao group, but I didn't have the time to dedicate to a client of their status. If I did, I'd have to drop all my small-business clients and be prepared to travel all the time. Neither would work with our upcoming move back to Vermont, spending time with Branson on his college breaks, or anything else we planned.

A high-profile marketing career wasn't what I wanted from life anymore. Brooklyn had been fun, but two years was long enough.

I was looking forward to celebrating the holidays back in Vermont and not having to rush back to the city.

"Are they closed?" Ben called again.

"Uh-huh," I mumbled, squeezing my eyes shut and wondering what he was up to, thinking he'd brought champagne or something.

"Don't say a thing. Shhh," I heard him say from across the room.

Our brownstone wasn't that big—it was mostly an open floor plan on the first floor and two small bedrooms and a bathroom on the second. One good thing about moving back to the Mad River house was it had space . . . and lots of it.

"I thought we were celebrating later?" I asked with my eyes sealed shut. I knew better than to ruin one of Ben's surprises.

"We are. I'm officially done at the office here," he whispered.

My nerves tingled as I sensed him moving closer.

"Put your hands in your lap," he said. "Palms up."

"Ben, seriously, don't play a prank with my laptop out."

When we first moved to Brooklyn, he'd constantly joke that my parents were at the front door. I fell for it every time, running to look out the window and simultaneously finger-combing my hair. Then there was the time he fed me calf's liver and onions after telling me to close my eyes, assuring me it was Chinese take-out. Yuck, I almost threw up in my mouth at the memory of it.

I sensed Ben very close to me. He still smelled like Vermont, what I thought of as a mixture of pinecones and rushing water. Lost in Ben's scent, I nearly jolted when I felt something soft like mink in my hand.

"Open up."

Sitting in the palm of my hand was the tiniest puppy I'd ever seen. Midnight black and white and tan, and probably only a couple of pounds. Maybe four. Or three.

"Ben, what did you do?" I whispered, not wanting to wake the sleeping puppy. Truthfully, I was in a bit of shock myself.

"We talked about getting a puppy in Vermont, and well, I decided to go ahead and get us one."

"He's so sweet, but . . ." I lifted the pup and checked to be sure I'd gotten the gender right, and when he barely opened his eyes, I giggled. "He looks drunk."

"A while back, I put us on a waiting list. Someone else backed out of taking home this little guy," Ben said, smiling down at the puppy, "so now he's ours. He traveled a long way to get here today. I couldn't wait to surprise you, but you don't seem so happy. I thought we talked about it," he said, his voice wavering slightly.

"No, we did talk about it. And he's absolutely precious. It's just, I took on this new client . . ."

"Well, let me take him and you can finish up. You also have to think of a name. The breeder called him Red Beagle, but I'm sure you can come up with something more creative."

"I don't have to finish anything now. I was going to wait until tonight to tell you—"

The tiny beagle rolled over in my hands, revealing his pink belly and those big brown eyes staring at me, waiting for me to love. Of course I melted.

"He looks like a toy," I said, smiling. "He's pretty cute. Such a little peanut."

Ben knelt on the floor at my feet and rubbed the puppy's belly while staring at me.

My cheeks heated. "That's a cute name, right? Peanut? Isn't Snoopy a beagle?"

Ben nodded. "That's it then. Mr. Peanut."

Despite being a bit overwhelmed, I blurted, "I'm in love already." It couldn't be helped.

"You said you were going to tell me something tonight. Is everything okay?" Ben asked, interrupting my moment of happiness.

Pulling Peanut up to my face, I inhaled his sweet puppy breath before cuddling him back on my lap. I'd had a show-quality miniature poodle growing up. Penelope was her name. Peanut was better already because he was shedding all over my lap. He wasn't meant to be looked at and admired but not played with. "This is a Vermont type of dog, right? I don't want to have some froufrou pup."

"Ha, yes, he's not a froufrou pup. Short hair, musky, a little sneaky and adventurous is what the breeder told me."

"How did he get here?" I asked.

"Actually, he's from North Carolina. He flew here today and landed at JFK a few hours ago. I met him at baggage claim and took him to the vet, and here we are."

"You gave this a lot of thought."

Leaning in to kiss me, Ben murmured, "First, I asked you to move back to New York with me, and you did, and now I'm dragging you back to Vermont. I wanted to make it special, and like you were taking a new friend with you." He knelt in front of me, eye level with the puppy but gazing up at me, his hand on its soft fur.

I'd reconnected with a couple of old friends in New York, but mostly I'd kept in touch with Hunnie and Gigi over the last two years, scheduling visits back and forth. I'd joined a women-only workshare space and sometimes got together with a friend from there. I'd loved living in Brooklyn, and I'd miss it, but Vermont was my home in my heart. Especially since it was where Ben and I had reconnected.

"Well, we're taking two friends now, kind of," I whispered.

Ben stilled and met my eyes. "What?"

Goose bumps broke out all over my body. "Yes," was all I said.

"We're taking who, exactly?" he asked, glancing at my belly.

I'd thought he'd forgotten. We hadn't used protection for about six months, deciding to let things happen when they happened. And now they'd happened . . . a few weeks before we moved.

"I'm actually around nine weeks already. I saw the doctor today. When I first missed my period, I thought it was stress and the move. I waited about ten days and then still didn't get it, so I used a home test. Yep, positive. But I wanted to make sure-sure."

"Peanut, you're going to be a big brother." Ben's hand still rested on the puppy before his lips landed on mine and his tongue quickly entered my mouth. We didn't let go of each other for a long time.

Pulling back, Ben stood. "What did the doctor say? Does he . . . or she . . . know I'm a doctor? Did they give you any information? Did you hear the heartbeat?"

"She said you'd be upset about not being there, and told me to come back on Friday with you so you could hear the heartbeat too."

"Smart doc."

"She's very well regarded, and is going to ask around for a referral in Vermont for me."

"You know what? You're making me the wealthiest man alive, Murphy. Damn straight, the richest."

He moved close, being careful of the puppy as he kissed me, then pulled back. "We should probably add on to the house, in the back."

Deciding to distract him, I asked, "Does Peanut have a crate?"

"In the front hallway," he said, raising an eyebrow.

"Let's go, Baby Daddy," I said playfully.

Ben placed Peanut in his crate before lifting me gingerly and carrying me off to the bedroom.

I snuggled close, whispering, "Funny how I never wanted our friendship to leave my dorm room at Pressman, and now you never want me to leave the bedroom, period."

All I got was a huge laugh.

Later that week, we were spread out in bed, naked and our limbs twisted in the sheets as Ben ran his palm up and down my thigh, deep in thought.

That morning, he'd heard the baby's heartbeat for the first time and had immediately cried. "I'm sorry, I know I should be tough or maybe not so affected by this because I'm a doctor, but I can't help it," he'd said in front of the obstetrician. With his finger, he'd traced the alien form on the screen like a small boy in wonderment over a new toy.

"That's our baby," he'd whispered, and we shared a quick kiss.

Now I asked, "What's up?"

I looked over and caught a glimpse of his bedhead and scruffy chin. Always the same Ben, no matter how many zeroes were in his bank account.

"I just want you to be happy. I want you to have the life you always dreamed about."

Emotion clogged my throat. In all the years I'd known Ben, he'd never been able to shake this odd insecurity. It wasn't an overt part of his personality, but it was there, an undercurrent that showed up in some conversations.

"I'm beyond happy," I told him. "Honestly, I never dreamed of any kind of life in particular, but if I had, this would've been it."

His hand found mine, and our fingers wove together.

With Ben's latest bonus, we were very comfortable. Not as wealthy as my parents, but who needed all the pressure that came with that kind of money?

"Ben," I said, making sure he saw me. "I love you, and I would love you with money or no money. Here, there, or anywhere."

"Dr. Seuss?" he asked with an eyebrow raised.

"Yep. I've been brushing up on my reading for when the baby comes. I can't read her or him romance novels."

This got me a huge laugh, and his tension disappeared.

"Speaking of, I got these today." He slid out of bed and walked toward the closet, his ass on display.

Smiling, I had no idea what to expect because this was Ben.

"Look," he said, coming out of the closet totally naked and holding something in his hands.

I looked more closely and realized he held a pair of Timberland boots in each hand—one in my size and one much smaller. "What are those?"

He beamed with pride. "Real boots for you, and bite-sized ones for the baby. We're not raising a city slicker, Murph."

"Hunnie put you up to this, didn't she?"

"You'll never know."

"Oh, I know. Don't you remember? She's the Vermont fashion police."

In seconds, Ben set aside the boots and was next to me, sliding his hand up my thigh when he whispered, "I could talk to Hunnie about some honey, though. For drizzling here . . ." He traced my leg and the dip between my thigh and my core, up to my belly button and back toward my most sensitive areas.

"You know what would be even better?" I said low. "A cupcake from Gigi, and I could smear the sugary-sweet icing all up and down." Surprising him, I flipped him over and used my mouth to show him everywhere I would put icing.

Groaning, Ben said, "You always did have a sweet tooth."

THE
END

ACKNOWLEDGMENTS

If I thought a lot went into writing a book, much, much more goes into being part of a story world! Although it's way more fun creating something with other author friends.

Special thanks to Sarina for including me in this universe and guiding all of us with a very gentle hand. Hope to see you soonish in Vermont for coffee and pastries at Umpleby's (yes, that's a real place).

To Jane, Natasha, and Jenn, thanks for the emails, reminders, marketing, and overall mojo throughout the process.

Huge thanks to Pam Berehulke, who stepped into a new story world and made my words look pretty. I say it every time we finish a book, but you make what I do work on the page, and I can't thank you enough.

Virginia Carey was the first person I met in the book world, and she's been a part of every book I've written. Thank you for your support, proofreading, and story advice.

A shining light during this process was meeting and getting to know Claire Hastings. Thanks for lending an ear and reading my original draft (giving gentle feedback), and also dealing with my son's college applications! LOL. P.S. Thank you for loving Hunnie and insisting I keep her.

Thanks to Michele Rodriguez for her excellent beta-reading skills and pushing me to make my epilogue longer. There's nothing like a juicy epilogue!

And as always, thanks to my family for their patience and doughnut/coffee deliveries.

www.ingramcontent.com/pod-product-compliance
Lightning Source LLC
LaVergne TN
LVHW020042110826
845155LV00029B/596

* 9 7 8 1 9 5 4 5 0 0 1 6 7 *